WHAT SHE SAW

WENDY CLARKE

Bookouture

Published by Bookouture in 2019

An imprint of StoryFire Ltd.

Carmelite House
50 Victoria Embankment
London EC4Y 0DZ

www.bookouture.com

ISBN: 978-1-78681-818-8
eBook ISBN: 978-1-78681-817-1

For my husband, Ian

CHAPTER ONE

Leona

I have no warning that anything bad is going to happen to me today. No premonition. No sense of something shifting in the shadows of my mind. As far as I'm concerned, this day is the same as the one before except for the swathes of purple bluebells that have appeared, as if by magic, beneath the trees that line the roadside.

The village shop is a mere ten minutes from my terraced cottage in the shadow of Langdon Fell and I'm enjoying the walk, pleased to have a break from soldering clasps onto the ends of silver bracelets in my workshop. Sometimes, on days when the rain sets in, dragging the sky down to meet the Cumbrian peaks, it's easy to believe that it will never stop. It's not like that today, though. Today is beautiful, a whisper of spring on its breath. The unfurling of the leaves, and the return of the birds to the hedgerow, a reminder that I've emerged safely from another winter.

Deep down inside, I still feel like me. Nothing has changed. I'm still Leona, mother of Beth. Leona, wife of Scott. *Wife*. Although it's in name only, as we've never signed a marriage contract, I like to call myself that. A piece of paper won't make me love him any more than I already do.

As I walk, I trail my hand along the swags of blackthorn blossom at the side of the road. Seen from a distance, the hedgerow looks as if it's been covered in a light dusting of snow – *the blackthorn winter*, the locals call it. Scott tells me it's because the white blossom often appears at the same time as the bitterly cold weather that turns the mountains of the Lake District white. It's not cold today though and, if I choose to turn and look back the way I've just come, I know the snow that's been clinging to the peaks all winter will have all but disappeared.

There's no one else walking this way and only one solitary car has passed me. It's how I like it and I savour the feeling of contentment. Hugging it to me as though it were a newborn. Contentment. The word conjures up images of sleeping dogs or grandmothers nodding over their knitting, but it will do for me. I'll take contentment over the alternative any day.

High above me, in the light blue sky, a bird of prey hovers, wings spread. It's seen its prey, somewhere in the scrubby grass and is waiting for its moment. I watch it until it gives up and soars away.

Unzipping my red walking jacket, I free myself from its water-proof prison, pulling my arms out of the sleeves and stuffing the coat into my shopping bag. I carry on, past the row of seventies houses high on the grassy slope to my left, their small glass porches overlooking the valley, and past the entrance to the campsite at Blackstone Farm. Last week there were only a few tents in the field up by the wash block. Today, I notice, more have sprung up like multicoloured mushrooms.

There are few people about. It's Friday afternoon and most of the locals are at work. Not that many people actually live in the village now: most of the properties that cluster around the church are holiday rentals. I pass a cottage with a blue plaque on the wall telling anyone who happens to stop and read it that it's owned by *Love the Lakes Holidays*. If I look through its window, I know I'll see a cold slate floor with maybe a rag rug beneath a stripped pine dining table. And it's a safe bet its stark white walls will be hung with pictures of Coniston Water or the fells in their splendid autumn colours.

It's what the visitors expect, but we locals prefer a warm carpet to step onto when we come downstairs in the morning to make our tea. Not that I'm really a local. I guess it takes more than nine years to be classed as that.

A strand of blonde hair blows across my face and I tuck it behind my ear. I should probably have it cut, but Scott likes it like this. My 'Rapunzel look' he calls it and, in a way, I think it suits me. My life is, after all, like a fairy tale – one made famous by the Brothers Grimm, not Disney.

As I walk, I'm humming. I'm not aware of the tune to start with – it's not the type of thing you'd hear on the radio and Beth would probably never even have heard of it. It's only as the words start to form in my head that I realise what the song is. The melody is haunting, dragging me back to a time I've tried to forget so, before that can happen, I force myself to hum something else.

In a field beyond the drystone wall that follows the edge of the village, a group of lambs stand with their mothers. I stop and watch them, my elbows resting on the hard, grey slate, fascinated by their spindly legs and bottle-brush tails. A little one with a black face races its sibling to an outcrop of rock, where it stands for a moment before running back to its mother and searching for her teat.

It's that picture I have in my mind as I push open the door of the small village shop and nod a hello to Graham Hargreaves who's leaning against the counter, a copy of the Westmorland Gazette spread out in front of him. The top of his bent head shows a round bald patch that shines in the sunlight that's coming through the window.

'Want a basket?'

Without taking his eyes off the page, he leans over and lifts one from its metal cradle. I take it from him.

'Thanks.'

Still there's nothing to make me concerned. No warning sign. No aura. In fact, as I move between the narrow aisles of tinned peas and boxes of cat food, the random assortment of goods you find in a local village shop such as this, I have a smile on my lips, the lamb's cute black face still in my mind.

'Need help to find anything?' He always asks me this, even though he's seen me shop here nearly every day since he took over three years ago.

'No. I'm fine.'

Pulling a scrap of paper out of the back pocket of my jeans, I run my finger down the short list to see what it is I need to buy. There's no order to the shop, or not one that I've ever worked out. Kitchen rolls are wedged up against boxes of Rice Krispies and bottles of anti-dandruff shampoo, and I have to step around the economy-sized packets of loo roll and bottled water that have been placed on the floor, being careful not to dislodge things as I pass. I put a carton of orange juice into my basket and let my mind drift to the afternoon ahead. There's a silver bracelet that still needs finishing and the last of an earring and necklace set in a silver leaf design, ready for the craft fair in Ambleside.

The eggs are on a shelf next to me. Lifting a box down, I open the lid to check them. One by one, I take each egg out of its cardboard nest, making sure none are cracked. But, as I lift the last one out, it slips through my fingers, falling to the floor with a soft crack that makes me wince. I don't move – just stare at the yellow yolk as it spreads across the tiles, mingling with the glutinous albumen. Bile rises and I cover my mouth with my hand. I look over at Graham, scared he'll be annoyed.

'No need to worry. I'll sort it.' With a scrape of metal on stone, he gets up from his stool and comes over, clutching a wodge of blue kitchen paper and a plastic bag to his chest. With a grunt, he kneels and, with a sweep of his hand, cleans up what he can. I turn away, unable to watch.

'Here.' He hands me another box of eggs. 'Take this one instead.'

Trying to empty my mind, I follow Graham to the till and lift my basket into its cradle, relieved that the nausea has passed. There's a basket of overpriced, cellophane-covered fudge on the counter, each bag tied with a curl of red ribbon. The fudge, along with the postcards that hang from a rack by the door and the boxes of shortbread biscuits with their pictures of Windermere and Colwith Force on the front, is meant for the tourists. Visitors who have already started to arrive in Church Langdon in cars and camper vans full of walking boots and gaiters. Visitors my husband Scott needs if he's to make a living.

'Want to try a piece?' Graham pushes a plate of misshapen brown pieces towards me. Samples to entice people to buy.

'No, thank you, but I'll get some for Beth.'

I add the fudge, in its crinkly wrapping, to my basket before remembering that, in the last few weeks, my daughter has been on some sort of health kick. I presume it's just a phase she's going through, but recently I've been worried about her, noticing how the ridges of her collar bones are as sharp as those on Causey Pike. I've seen how she folds her arms across her chest, as though ashamed of its fullness, and when she walks, her body is hunched as if to make herself appear shorter.

I know I should talk to her, but the closeness we once shared seems to be slipping away from us. I consider taking the fudge out again, then change my mind, deciding Scott might like it.

'Beautiful day, isn't it?'

Graham leans his back against the shelves of cigarettes and nods across the small parking area towards the distant peaks. I hear the soft click-click of the window vent as it turns and notice the way the sun streams through the window, picking out the cracks in the wooden counter.

'It is lovely, yes.'

'Scott out today?' He scratches the side of his cheek, his fingers rasping on the whiskers that grow there. His weekend stubble he calls it, even though the weekend is yet to begin.

'He's taking a party of four out to Castle Crag this afternoon. The nearer it gets to summer, the busier he'll be.'

'Well, it's certainly the perfect day for walking.'

I wonder if Graham Hargreaves ever walks. I doubt it. Like many of the people who have lived in the Lakes all their lives, a walk to him is a Sunday afternoon stroll along the flat path beside the River Brathay. The people Scott takes out are tourists seduced by pictures in the cottage brochures of majestic peaks and sky-blue tarns, the clouds reflected in their mirrored surface. I don't say any of this to Graham, just check my list.

'Hold on a sec. I've forgotten the frozen sweetcorn.'

Leaving the basket, I walk to the tall freezer cabinet and as I do, the bell above the door tinkles, making me turn. A young woman backs into the shop, struggling to drag a pushchair over the threshold but, as the wheels get stuck on the step, Graham lifts the flap of the counter and comes to her rescue. Shouldering the door to keep it open, he grasps the front wheels of the buggy with his free hand and lifts it over. I hear the woman thank him. She's not from round here – I can tell by her accent. Her back is to me but I can't stop staring at her long dark hair. It's like a magnet to me.

Dragging my eyes away, I reach out a hand to pull open the freezer door. I hear the woman's footsteps in the aisle and that's when it happens. In one heart-stopping moment, Ria's face is reflected in the glass – just as I remember it. She's standing behind me, her dark hair falling to her shoulders, her eyes wide in terror. The shock is like a fist to my stomach.

Instinctively, I turn, but the young woman has moved away and all I can see is Graham Hargreaves rooting around in a basket of discount DVDs. When I look back at the glass door, Ria's face has gone, but the feeling I had when I saw her hasn't. My hand is still raised to the door and I see it's shaking. I stare at it as though it belongs to someone else. With a great effort, I try to still my racing heart, but instead of lessening, the feelings become stronger.

'Are you all right, Leona?'

Graham is by my side, but it's as if his voice is coming to me through a fog. I want to answer him, but I can't. I feel light-headed and disembodied, as if at any moment I might float away. My fingers close around the handle of the freezer cabinet and I'm scared to let go.

'Is something wrong?'

The sense of terror I feel is debilitating. I'm unable to move, the nerves and muscles of my body unable to respond to the messages my brain is sending to them. Graham Hargreaves has his arm around me. He's saying something else, but I can't hear his words.

The young woman is there too now, standing beside Graham, unsure what to do. Now she's closer, I see she's nothing like Ria. How could she be?

'Do you know where she lives?' she says. 'Should we call someone?'

Like a dramatic scene on a stage, I'm watching it all unfold as if from a great height. I'm pressed against the freezer cabinet, the others hovering like extras, and their outlines are blurred as though viewed through dry ice. What's wrong with me?

Graham is asking me something, his face too close to mine, his breath smelling of the salami I saw half-open on the counter when I came in. He reaches into his pocket and, through the tears that make my eyes swim, I see he's holding out his mobile. He says the word *Scott*. He must be asking if he should call him.

I picture my husband on some windswept fell and I know how his forehead will crease with worry when Graham tells him he should come. He'll turn to the party he's leading and say he'll have to go back – that his wife's ill. And, when he gets here, I will have to explain all of this to him.

Every part of my body is screaming to run out of the shop, to get back to the safety of my cottage, but I make myself turn and look at Graham Hargreaves' worried face. 'Please. I'm fine now. You don't need to ring him.'

'You don't look fine, Leona. Can I get you a glass of water?'

'Yes, yes thanks. Just give me a moment. I expect I'm coming down with something, that's all.'

The girl has come back, her baby in her arms, and I close my eyes for a moment to stop the images that keep forming. Opening them again, I force a smile and she looks relieved. How could I think she looked like Ria? She's too tall, her face too round.

'And you're certain you don't want me to call Scott for you?' Graham has come back with the water. He hands it to me, but he looks uncertain. Probably nothing like this has ever happened in his shop before.

'Yes, honestly, I'm fine,' I say again. If I repeat it enough times, he might believe it. We all might.

'Well, if you're sure.'

Taking my arm, he guides me back to the counter. He takes my purchases out of the basket and places them into my shopping bag, ringing them up as he goes along. My hands are still shaking and, as I open my purse, I drop a couple of pound coins as I take them out. The sight of them rolling under the counter makes me want to cry again.

'Don't worry,' Graham says quickly. 'I'll fish them out later. Look, I can lock up and give you a lift down the road if you like?'

'Thanks, but it's not necessary.' I'm embarrassed enough as it is. I just want to forget today ever happened.

Picking up the plastic bag with my few things in, I turn and walk to the door, feeling the dark-haired woman's eyes on me. When I get outside, I breathe in deeply. A cloud has passed over the sun and the pikes that were a vivid green earlier are now darkened by shadow. I try to bring back the feeling of calm I had when I walked here only fifteen minutes earlier, but it won't come. Something is stopping it.

And I know that the something is Ria.

CHAPTER TWO

Beth

The house was in darkness when Beth let herself in. Reaching her hand behind the curtain that hung just inside the front door to stop the cold air from coming in, she switched on the light. With any luck, her mum wouldn't realise how late it was.

'Mum?'

On the settee, their cat, Wainwright, stretched, his claws catching in the tassels of the cushion he'd been asleep on. Beth bent to stroke his head.

'Where is she, Wain?'

Going through to the kitchen, there were signs that her mum had been in there: a plate and knife in the sink and the bread bin standing open. When she placed her hand on the kettle, it was slightly warm. Flicking the switch to make herself some tea, Beth went to the back door and opened it.

The fell that rose steeply behind the house was just a dark shape in the gloom. The terrace of slate cottages had been built up against it, leaving no room for a garden, just a small paved area big enough for the shed that her mother called her workshop. Her dad had put it up the previous year after Beth had complained that her mother's tools throughout the house gave her no space to do her homework. The silver, wires, cutters and soldering iron that had once taken up most of the table by the window were now spread out on the shed's workbench.

Expecting to see a light on in the workroom window, Beth was surprised to find it in darkness. Where *was* her mum?

Part of her was pleased that she wasn't home. For the last couple of days, as she'd turned the key in the lock, she'd found herself holding her breath. Wondering if anything would be said – if her mum had found out she'd been bunking school. It was, she knew, only a matter of time. She thought of the bag of clothes and walking boots pushed under the hedge at the bottom of the drive. On days when she couldn't face the thought of the classroom, days when escaping onto the fells was her only way to avoid going mad, she'd change back into her uniform before coming into the house, shoving her boots and jeans into the bag. She'd have to go out and get them before anyone came across them. Soon, the day would come when she'd have to explain herself and, when she did, her mum would make a scene. The thought made her go cold. She hated arguments, had done for as long as she could remember, and if there was ever any danger of one developing, she'd take herself off to her room at the back of the house. Not that her mum and dad argued much. Unless they did it when she was well out of earshot.

Her dad wasn't home either, but then she hadn't expected him to be. Sometimes, when he was taking out a group of walkers, he'd stop with them for a drink in the pub afterwards to get some feedback and wouldn't get back until late. She didn't blame him. Who'd want to come back to this pokey little place? So what if it was full of history, that slate miners used to live there? The slate miners were welcome to have it back.

Pulling off her maroon blazer, she hung it on one of the pegs in the little lobby by the front door. There was an assortment of coats and jackets already in there, pushing out into the small porch area and, as she bent down to take off her shoes, two of them ended up on the floor. She cursed under her breath. If her mum and dad could afford to send her to a snotty school like Lady Edburton, why couldn't they afford a place big enough to swing a cat?

As she straightened, she caught sight of the school badge on her blazer. Picking up the fallen coats, she hung them on top of it. Just the sight of the shield with its prancing lion and interlocking L and E made her feel sick.

After making herself some tea, Beth stretched out on the settee. Reaching behind her, she threw one of the many cushions onto the floor, then felt for her school bag. Unzipping it, she pulled out the A4 spiral-bound book that was in there, its pages full of her sketches. Drawing up her legs, she rested the book on them, noticing there was a hole in the knee of her opaque black tights. It must have happened when she was changing out of her jeans. It was her last pair and if any of the girls saw it, she knew what they'd say. Sometimes it was to her face, but other times it was saved for a Facebook or WhatsApp conversation. Her skirt wasn't the right length, her bag hadn't come from the right shop, her hair hung loose on her shoulders when everyone else had theirs tied back. Anything and everything. Didn't they realise that their so-called fashion statements made them all look the same? Just like the Herdwick sheep that grazed the fells behind their house. Her mum didn't seem to think there was anything wrong with looking like everyone else, but Beth couldn't see the point.

Her mum's views on conformity didn't stretch as far as social media. She wasn't keen on her going on it and, if she was honest, Beth didn't like it either. She couldn't help herself though – surely it was better to know what was being said about you. The WhatsApp group had been set up by Carina when she'd joined the school in Year 9, a year when Beth had been happy, when people had still liked her. It hadn't taken long for things to change.

A while back, Beth had stopped leaving comments on the group and now she was pretty sure everyone had forgotten she was even on there. Or she hoped so, for she couldn't bear the thought that they knew but said those things anyway. This way she could be like a ghost. There but not there.

The hole in her tights was making her anxious. Maybe she could mend it? Or stick it with some of her mum's jewellery glue. The thought made her weary. Every day was spent worrying about what they'd think.

Suddenly, it was all too much. Shoving her fingers inside the hole, she pulled them sideways, ripping it wider. Who cared anyway?

'Beth?'

Her mum's voice was coming from the top of the stairs. She'd been home all along. Beth shoved the book back into the bag just as her mum came down the stairs, rubbing her eyes. Her blouse was creased and her blonde hair awry. In the half light, she looked barely older than some of the girls in Beth's school.

'Mum, what are you doing?'

Her mum pinched the bridge of her nose and frowned. 'I must have fallen asleep.'

'What, at half past six?' As soon as she said it, she regretted it. She didn't want to bring attention to the time. It didn't look as though her mum had processed it, though.

'I haven't been sleeping too well recently,' was all she said.

It was true she looked tired. Dark circles under her eyes. And she'd been acting weirdly recently – forgetting where she'd put things and not answering straight away if she was asked a question. Since yesterday, it had been as though her mind was somewhere else.

'What's happened to your tights?'

Beth shrugged. Surprised she'd even noticed. 'I caught them on something.'

Even a week ago, her mum would have nagged her about looking after her clothes. Now she just drifted down the stairs and into the kitchen, stopping in the doorway as though wondering why she'd gone in there.

'Mum, are you all right?'

'Of course I am.'

Beth could see the effort it took to produce the smile her mum gave her. There were no questions about school and no mention of the fact that she was late home. Knowing she ought to be relieved, she was surprised to find she wasn't. Something wasn't right.

'I'm going to my room. I've got some revision to do.'

Her mum ran her fingers through her hair. 'Can't you do it down here?'

'No. I need the computer.' Picking up her bag, Beth went up the stairs. As she climbed, her bag caught on one of the photographs on the wall. She straightened it and then sighed. It was like a rogue's gallery up there. Some of the photographs were just of her, while others were of her and her mum or of the three of them together. The one she liked best was the picture of her standing on the slopes of Castle Crag, her hand shielding her eyes from the sun. They'd gone to the north-west of the Lakes for the day a few years ago, and the photograph had been taken while she'd been watching the falcons. She straightened the frame she'd knocked. Despite the smiling faces, the collection of photographs made her sad. Things had been different then. Easier, somehow. She could still remember that day. The way she and her mum had teased her dad about his sunburnt nose, giggling like silly schoolchildren when he stepped in a beck and got his walking boot full of water. It was a while since she'd seen her mum laugh like that. A while since they'd shared a joke of any kind.

When she got to her room, instead of switching on the overhead light, Beth turned on the small bedside lamp, then closed the door and the curtains. Her computer was on a desk under the window. She didn't turn it on but, instead, felt in her pocket for her phone. The colourful icons shone brightly in the dim lighting and she stared at them for a moment. If she looked, she knew it would make her unhappy – yet she couldn't help herself.

Pressing the green WhatsApp icon, she clicked onto the group Carina had made and scrolled down. She had altered the setting of her phone so that it wouldn't alert her to new messages on the lock screen. Had that been a good idea? With relief, she saw there was nothing to worry about; the talk was all about homework and what everyone was revising. She breathed a sigh of relief and was about to close the app when another message appeared below the last.

She closed her eyes, unsure whether to read it or not. Some sixth sense made her think she shouldn't. Her breathing had become shorter. What would she gain? But then curiosity got the better of her and she opened her eyes.

'Who enjoyed Jessica Rabbit's day off then? I certainly did.'

Beth folded her arms across her chest at the sight of the usual nickname, her eyes swimming. The comments began to appear straight away. *'Stupid bitch… fat cow…'* She threw the phone across the room, not needing to read any more to know the answers the girls would give.

CHAPTER THREE

Leona

'Can you do me a bacon sarnie?'

Scott's voice drifts through from the living room, which isn't difficult as there's only a few feet between it and the kitchen. I know he'd like us to move to somewhere bigger but, whenever he suggests it, I resist. It's been Beth's home for the last nine years and stability is important for her. Anyway, we've always loved it, or rather I have, as half the time I have no idea what Beth is thinking.

I look at the cramped space between the wooden units, the washing machine sticking out from beneath the Formica worktop. Just recently, since the episode in the shop, I've started to find the small rooms claustrophobic. Not just the rooms… the house and the village too.

'You don't want muesli then?'

Scott's large head appears around the door frame. 'Muesli? I'd be grateful if you'd kindly not swear.' He picks up the box and puts it back into the cupboard. 'You know the saying out of sight, out of mind…'

As he reaches around me to shut the cupboard door, his T-shirt rises up a little and I take the opportunity to pinch the soft flesh at his sides. 'For someone who spends most of his time up mountains, you're not exactly Bear Grylls. In fact, you look like you've just eaten him for breakfast.'

Resting his hands on the closed cupboard doors, either side of my face, he ducks his head and nuzzles my neck. The bulk of his body is comforting, his dark beard tickles.

'Are you complaining, wife?'

'Not at all. Why would I, when there's more to cuddle up to at night?' Reaching around him, I pull him closer, feeling the warmth of his body as it pushes against mine.

He laughs into my hair. 'Steady on. We've a teenager in the house. I don't think I can take any more of her "yuck, get a room" type of comments. Speaking of which, has she emerged at all this morning?'

'I haven't seen her yet, but you know what fifteen-year-olds are like. Their beds are their second homes.'

Scott plants a kiss on my lips, then pushes himself away. Walking over to the fridge, he pulls out a packet of bacon. 'Want some?'

I shake my head, the thought of the fat dripping onto the grill pan making me nauseous. 'No thanks. You're the only carnivore in the house at breakfast time.'

'Good job too. Somebody's got to be strong enough to fight off the mountain lions. Talking of which, were you wrestling a few last night? When I woke up, there was no duvet on my side of the bed.'

I think of the restless night I've just had, waking at two and only falling back to sleep again when a sliver of light showed through the crack in the curtains. I know it's connected to the incident in the village shop and am thankful that I don't have a full-time job to hold down.

I haven't told Scott what happened and it seems that Graham Hargreaves hasn't either, as I'm sure he would have said something about it to me. And if he had, what could I have said? That I thought I'd seen the face of someone I despise? That, for just a few moments, I'd thought it was all happening again?

Every day since then, I've wracked my brains to think what might have caused me to react like that. For twelve years, I've managed to push Ria to the back of my mind, to try to forget her and, until now, I've succeeded. I know something must have triggered it. Something more than just a girl with long dark hair and a pushchair. I watch Scott pull the plastic wrapping off the packet of bacon. All this time, I've managed to pretend that I can live a normal life. That Ria hasn't ruined it. She has though, and I have a horrid feeling she's not going to let me forget it.

'Well?'

Scott is looking at me expectantly and, for a moment, I can't remember what he asked me. 'Oh, sorry, no, I slept a bit better, actually.'

I've no intention of worrying him. If I tell him how I laid awake, watching the luminous digits of the clock slowly count down the hours, he'll ask me questions I might not be able to answer.

'You think she's okay?' Scott pulls a slice of bacon from the packet and drapes it across the rungs of the metal grid inside the grill pan.

'Who?' Instantly, my mind turns to Ria and my blood chills. Then I realise my stupidity – Scott doesn't know Ria.

'Beth, of course. She's been awfully quiet this last week.'

I pour milk onto my muesli, feeling guilty that I haven't noticed. 'She's got her exams in a couple of months. I expect they're playing on her mind. I remember when I was doing my GCSEs, I wouldn't speak to my mum, except in grunts.'

'I thought it was boys who were supposed to do that.'

'Well, I did too.'

The mention of my mum brings tears to my eyes, ones I have no control over. Scott's face creases in concern. 'Oh, babe. Don't cry.' He comes over to me and puts his big arm around my shoulders, hugging me to him. 'You still miss her, don't you?'

His sweatshirt is damp against my cheek. My tears have soaked into the material.

'Every day.'

'It must be hard to lose your parents so young, especially when you're close to them. I wish I'd met them.'

It's like a knife twisting in my heart. 'I do too.'

Scott cups my face in his hands. 'Are you okay?'

I nod, pulling a tissue from my sleeve and blowing my nose. 'Look, your bacon's burning.'

The bacon hisses and spits under the grill. Scott kisses my cheek, then goes over to it and turns each rasher over. Then he takes some bread out of its wrapper and starts to butter it.

'You don't think we made a mistake, do you?' When I don't answer, he carries on and I realise he's talking about Beth again. 'It might not have been the best idea sending her to Lady Edburton.'

I stare at him. 'What makes you say that?'

'I was just thinking the other day. She doesn't seem to have many friends. Well, none she's ever invited here anyway.'

'She doesn't need friends. She's got us.'

'What do you mean? Everybody needs friends. What an odd thing to say.'

'I just mean that she's not needy. She's happy with her own company. Always has been. Anyway, she's got Carina.'

By Scott's expression, I can tell that he doesn't necessarily think this is a good thing. Squeezing blood red ketchup onto the bread, he smears it with his knife before laying the bacon strips on top.

'You don't think she's finding it too difficult – the work, I mean. I wonder if she's struggling a bit.'

'If she found the work difficult, she would never have passed the entrance exam… or got the art scholarship.' His comment has hit a nerve. 'She's more than capable of doing Year 11 work.'

'I only meant that they push the kids in that school. It's a lot harder than if she'd gone to Lakeside Comprehensive.'

'That's exactly why I wanted her to go, Scott. I don't know why you're bringing it up now; we talked about it at the time.

You agreed that she would find it too easy there and that Lady Edburton would give her better opportunities.'

He looks at me. 'It didn't do me any harm going to the comprehensive. I just don't like to think of her unhappy. Besides, everything costs such a lot at Lady E. How many school trips do they need to go on, for goodness sake?'

I feel my hackles rise. 'I don't know why you're worried. It's me who's paying for these things with my jewellery sales. Are you saying you begrudge the money?'

'Of course I'm not saying that.'

'Then what are you saying, Scott?'

Before he can say anything else, Beth appears in the doorway. She's wearing a pair of tartan pyjama bottoms and a grey hooded sweatshirt. She doesn't speak to us but goes over to the fridge and takes out a carton of orange juice.

'Okay, Beth?'

She doesn't answer, just shrugs and pours the orange liquid into a glass.

'Revising today?' Scott leans his elbows on the table and takes a bite of his sandwich. 'Did they give you a revision timetable?'

Beth's face is pale; she hasn't inherited my warm colouring. Two spots of colour appear on the apples of her cheeks. 'No.'

'That's a surprise. Would have thought Sergeant Major Thompson would have had it planned out in military precision, hour by hour.'

'Don't call her that, Scott. Mrs Thompson runs the school very well. Anyway, it doesn't matter, you can make your own, can't you, Beth?'

The sound of the glass banging on the worktop makes me jump. 'Why can't you both just butt out of it!'

There's no chance for us to react as she's already gone, leaving behind the sound of her footsteps as she runs up the stairs and slams her bedroom door.

Scott looks at me. 'What was that all about?'

'I've no idea.'

'Do you want me to speak to her?'

I run my hand down his arm, registering the feel of the thick dark hairs under my fingertips. 'Do you mind? You're so much better at dealing with her at the moment. I can't seem to say anything right.' I close my eyes, remembering how close Beth and I once were. Recently, it's as if I've been living with a stranger.

'I'll tell her that we're worried about her.'

'No, don't do that.'

'Well, what do you want me to say?'

'I don't know… anything. Make something up.'

Scott rubs his chin. 'You know I don't like doing that.'

'For God's sake. Just say you want to look at her drawings or something. A little white lie isn't going to kill you!' Sometimes I wonder where his obsession with honesty comes from.

Ignoring my outburst, he puts his knife and fork together and pushes his plate away. 'I'll go and see if Beth wants a hand with her revision. Once the exams are over, she'll be back to normal, I'll bet.'

'You think so?'

'I know so. How about we have a day out – all of us, like we used to? Beth could do with a break from revising and you could do with a change of scene too, I'm sure. We can walk over to Slater's Bridge and have lunch in the Three Shires.'

I smile, unable to be mad at him for long. 'Won't it be a bit of a busman's holiday for you?'

Scott shrugs. 'I may spend half my life out there on the fells, but there's nothing I like better than sharing it with my family.'

Taking his plate, I plant a kiss on his thick dark hair. 'I love you, Scott Newman.'

'Of course you do,' he says with a smile. 'Who wouldn't?'

It's then that my phone rings. Picking it up, I see it's a number I don't recognise. It's probably a customer chasing an order.

'I'll leave you to it,' Scott says, getting up. 'If you don't hear anything from upstairs in ten minutes, send for reinforcements.'

Smiling, I press the accept button, then, tucking the phone under my chin, I start to stack the plates. 'Hello?'

They answer and I freeze, the smile dropping from my face. I turn to the door, terrified that Scott might have seen my reaction, but he's already upstairs. As I hear the voice from my past, I know that the vision I saw in Graham's shop wasn't a figment of my imagination. It was a premonition.

CHAPTER FOUR

Beth

'Want to talk about it?'

Beth walked with her hands deep in her pockets, her head down. Her dad's presence beside her was both a comfort and an irritation to her. She was only here because she'd known the fuss it would cause if she'd said she'd rather stay behind.

'There's nothing to talk about.'

'Sure?'

'I told you, didn't I?'

Her mum was some way ahead of them, her head bent to her phone, looking like she was on a mission rather than enjoying the beauty of the place. Instead of worrying about it, Beth turned her attention to the spiky leaves of the bluebells that had turned the fells into a blue sea.

She could feel her dad's eyes on her. It was clear he didn't believe her and a part of her was glad. Her mum was so bound up in whatever it was that was bothering her that she didn't seem to care whether Beth was unhappy or not. Her dad was different. He was a man of few words, but she liked that. When others around him were busy yacking, only interested in hearing their own voices, he would just listen and take things in. She longed to confide in him, but it would only make things worse. He'd tell Mum and then she'd be straight up to the school. Even the thought of it made her palms sweaty.

'Worried about the exams?'

He'd thrown her a lifeline and she caught hold of it. There was no need to mention Carina. 'A bit.'

'And that's all?'

'What else do I need? Exams suck.'

'Exams are what you need to get on in the world.'

'Like *you* did.'

Her dad frowned. 'That was a bit below the belt, Beth. So I don't make huge amounts of money and I never moved away from the place I grew up in, but I love what I do.'

'Then you can hardly lecture me, can you?'

She watched the shadows of the clouds move across the peaks, hating herself for what she was saying; knowing he was only trying to be kind.

'I just want you to take the opportunities your mum has opened up for you by sending you to Lady Edburton. Get your qualifications, go to university… Then the world's your oyster. It's about choice, Beth, and whatever you may think, I *chose* to stay here. Your mum and I just want the best for you.'

The rough path they'd been following had petered out and they'd joined a grassy track. Her mum was now just a small shape in the distance. So much for a family day out.

Her dad stopped and took her arm, turning her to the view. 'Just look at that.'

Ahead of them lay Little Langdale Tarn, navy blue beneath a cloud-swollen sky. Cradled by the heather and moss-coloured slopes of Swirl How and Great Carrs.

'You always say it like it's the first time you've been here when I know you could walk this route in your sleep.'

'Well, I wouldn't go so far as to say that.' He screwed up his face. 'I'd probably break a leg or two.'

They stood lost in their own thoughts, their previous conversation forgotten. It was something they had in common, this ability to be silent… That and their love of this place. Her mum liked it too – just not in the same way. She would sometimes talk about London, about the townhouses of Kensington and the chrome and glass buildings of the city and when she did, her voice would turn wistful. Beth had never been to London. Maybe in the holidays, she could persuade her mum to take her.

Not that she imagined she'd like it. The thought of all those people made her shudder. That's why she loved it here. The peace and the beauty of the place made her feel alive. Made her feel she could be herself without someone judging her.

Unzipping his rucksack, her dad took out a coil of rope and put it on the ground, then fished around for his water bottle. He took a glug, then held it out to her. Beth shook her head, wondering what he'd think if he knew she had been up on the fells alone only two days before. Not to this exact place, but to the disused slate quarry with its cave of midnight blue water. It was somewhere she liked to go when things got too much. Would he understand?

'Why have you got that in there?' She pointed to the rope. 'We're not exactly climbing the high peaks.'

Her dad shrugged. 'Wherever I go, it goes. You never know when you might need it.'

'You should be a boy scout.' She laughed.

Up ahead, her mum had reached a gate in the drystone wall and was leaning against it, waiting for them. When she waved to them, Beth felt unexpected tears spring to her eyes. She wanted to be held by her mum; for her to make everything go away. She was fed up with putting on a brave face and making out everything was okay when it wasn't. Instead, she turned back to the tarn again and imagined what it would feel like to walk across its stony shore and into the icy water.

Her dad's voice broke into her thoughts. 'Let's go. I'm ravenous.'

Dragging her eyes away from the water, she turned her back on it and followed him along the track to where her mum was waiting. When they reached her, she unlatched the gate and looked at her watch. 'The pub stops serving food at two. We'd better get a move on.'

Beth walked in silence, letting her parents go on ahead. As they always did, the fells had started to work their magic on her, lifting her spirits. Helping her forget. In no time at all, they had reached the final leg of their walk. It was marked by a wall, *Slater's Bridge* carved into the sign next to it. Squeezing through the narrow gap, Beth jumped down the other side. The small bridge was ahead of her, its slate arch jagged as teeth. It crossed the river in three spans and, in days gone by, had been the meeting point of several packhorse routes.

She stepped onto it, being careful not to catch her feet in the cracks between the uneven stones. When she came to the middle, she stopped and looked down at the rushing water. In the middle of the stream was a flat boulder, easily reached from the mossy bank. When she was younger, her mum would bring her here for picnics in the long summer holidays and they'd lay out their food on the boulder, pretending they were on a boat. She'd been happy in those days. Able to tell her mum anything.

'This has always been my favourite place, Beth.'

Her mum was beside her now, her elbow touching Beth's own. Beth knew she was trying to reach out to her, but however much she wanted to, she couldn't let herself be drawn.

Instead, she watched the water froth around the rocks. 'Why didn't we ever bring any of my friends here? We always came alone.' It was a thought that had only just occurred to her.

Her mum looked up at her. 'What a funny question to ask.'

'I just don't ever remember doing anything with anyone else in the holidays, that's all.'

'That's because I was always here to do things with you.' Beth saw the way her mum's face had tightened. Her lips forming into a narrow line. 'You're lucky you didn't have a mother that worked long hours and packed you off to a childminder.'

'I know but…'

'Didn't you enjoy the things we did?'

'Of course I did.' She couldn't be bothered to explain. 'Forget I said anything.'

What did it matter anyway? It wasn't as though she'd had that many friends: not at the little primary in Church Langdon or the one before it when they'd been living in Carlisle. Was it something about her that put other kids off or was it that her mum had never encouraged the friendships? She tried to think of a single girl who had been invited to their house for tea, and failed.

Sunlight glinted off the river, making her squint. The air was getting warmer. It would have been a perfect day to stop and have a picnic like they used to, but her dad had been promised a Sunday roast at the Three Shires. He was waiting for them now, his head on one side, his unruly dark hair mussed by the wind.

'What are we waiting for?' he said, his smile wide. 'I hear there's some roast beef with my name on it.'

'Yes,' her mum said, and Beth thought she saw relief in her eyes. 'We ought to be going.'

A short stroll across the field ahead took them to the entrance of the pub. There were a few cars in the car park but not so many that it meant they wouldn't get a table. They found one by the window and Beth and her mum hung their coats on the back of the chairs while her dad went to the bar for some drinks. Stretching her legs out in front of her, Beth looked around the room. Most of the other tables were taken and there was a hum of conversation in the bar. It was warm as, even though it was spring, the fire had been lit. She began to feel herself relax.

Her dad came back with a tray of drinks and three menus. 'What do you fancy? I was right about the beef – it's on the specials board.'

'Sounds good to me.' Her mum pushed a menu towards her. 'What about you, Beth?'

Beth glanced at it. The walk had made her ravenous, but Carina's words were in her head. *Fat cow.* 'I'm not that hungry. I'll just have the soup.'

Her dad raised his eyebrows. 'What? Since when have you not wanted the roast here? You've always said it's even better than your mum's.'

He winked at her mum and Beth was surprised when she didn't respond.

She closed the menu. 'I told you. I'm not hungry.'

'That's not like you.'

She started to speak, but her mum got there first. 'Stop it, Scott.' Her voice had an edge to it. 'Don't say things like that to her.'

'Woah!' He raised his hands in capitulation. 'I was only saying. Sorry Beth. I only meant that after a two-hour walk, we're usually all starving.'

Her mum hadn't finished. She closed the menu with a snap. 'Well, Beth's said that she isn't today, so don't pressure her.'

'Mum, leave it.' Beth shifted uncomfortably in her seat. It had been a nice afternoon and now her mum was going to spoil it. What was up with her? One minute she was normal and the next she was snapping at her dad over nothing. She wished she hadn't said anything. 'It's okay, Dad. I'll have the same as you.'

'Sure? You don't have to.'

'I've changed my mind. I'm sure.'

He left with the menus, but her mum was still looking at her, her forehead creased into a frown. Reaching across the table, she covered her hand with her own. 'You know you don't need to diet, Beth. You're lovely as you are.'

Although she knew she was probably imagining it, it felt as though the eyes of everyone around her had turned her way. Humiliation rose inside her.

'I'm not dieting,' she hissed. 'I told you, Mum, I'm just not hungry. Can't you leave it?'

Beth felt her mum's hand pull away from hers and they fell into silence. She took a sip of her coke, trying not to cry. The room that had felt warm and comforting earlier now felt stifling, the wood smoke from the fire beginning to sting her eyes.

When the pub door opened, letting in a welcome breath of fresh air, she was relieved. Looking up, she saw a couple with a small dog on a lead. It must have started raining as their hoods were up. They made their way between the tables, the dog snuffling beneath them for crumbs, and it wasn't until they passed their table, and the woman had pulled down her hood, that Beth realised who she was. It was her art teacher, Mrs Snowdon. Quickly, she bent her head so her brown hair fell around her face. Maybe, if she was lucky, her teacher wouldn't recognise her.

She hadn't been quick enough.

'Beth… Mrs Travis. I wondered if we'd meet anyone we knew today.'

Beth's heart sank. Dragging her fingers through her hair and pulling it away from her face, she gave a half-hearted smile. 'Hi.'

Her mum looked up, but her face was still troubled. 'Oh, hello, Mrs Snowdon.'

The little dog was straining at the leash, trying to reach a crisp that had found its way onto the floor. Mrs Snowdon pulled at his lead. 'I knew we shouldn't have brought him. He's such a scavenger.'

Beth was starting to feel sick. Willing her teacher not to say anything, she reached down and stroked the dog's head. 'What's his name?'

'Sherlock.'

'That's a good name.'

'He's never been able to keep his nose out of things, so I suppose it is.'

There was a pause and Beth felt her teacher's eyes on her. She knew she daren't look up in case her face gave her away. She was saved by Mrs Snowdon's husband, who had joined them.

'All the tables are taken in here, but the girl says there'll be one free soon in the other bar.'

'That's good.' Mrs Snowdon wound the dog's lead around her hand and pulled him away from the table. 'It was nice to see you.'

She started to walk away and Beth felt her shoulders relax. It seemed that things were going to be all right after all. Mrs Snowdon hadn't gone far though, when she turned back.

'I forgot to ask, Beth. Are you feeling better?'

She felt her face redden as she met her teacher's eyes. 'I am, yes… Thanks.'

Mrs Snowdon's eyes remained on hers a fraction longer than was necessary, then she smiled. 'That's good. Look, here's your dad. I'll leave you to your meal.'

With a parting smile, she and her husband moved off into the next room, leaving Beth with a heart that seemed to be beating unnaturally loudly.

'You all right, Beth? You look like someone's killed the cat,' her dad said, sitting down. 'Which teacher was that?'

'Mrs Snowdon. My art teacher.' How much had he heard? Or her mum, come to that? If her mum knew that the absence note Beth had sent to the form teacher had been from her email address, she'd kill her.

Her dad nodded at the teacher's disappearing back. 'Wasn't she the one we met at the open morning, Leona?'

Her mum didn't answer. Her forehead was pressed to the window and she looked miles away.

'Leona?'

'What? Oh yes, she was.'

She said no more and Beth took a gulp of her drink, relief washing over her. She'd got away with it. The crisis had been avoided. One thing was clear, though. She wasn't going to be able to get away with any more days off. She'd have to go back to school on Monday and take whatever Carina and the others threw at her.

CHAPTER FIVE
Leona

I sit bolt upright, my chest tight and my heart racing. What woke me? My senses are on high alert as I try to control my ragged breathing, I wonder whether I've had a nightmare, but, if I have, I can't remember it. There's a fear I can't get rid of, a feeling that something awful is going to happen, but I've no idea what. Reaching a hand to my neck, I feel it slick with sweat and my nightdress is soaking. I want to take it off, but my arms won't respond. My legs feel trapped too, pinned down by the heavy duvet.

Scott is asleep beside me. I hear rather than see him, wondering why I don't find the sound of his breathing comforting. With no street lights to give relief, the room is in complete darkness. It hasn't bothered me before, but now the velvety blackness is claustrophobic.

In a panic, I throw out my arm to turn on the bedside light, but, instead of the switch, my hand makes contact with the glass of water that I left on there last night. As it topples over, the sound of the glass hitting the bedside table causes Scott to stir. With a grunt, he reaches for his own light switch, then turns and looks at me.

He rubs his eyes with the heels of his hands. 'Jesus, Leona. What happened?'

The bedside table is awash with water. There's a river of it running over the edge and onto the carpet, and I know I should do something about it before it soaks in. With relief, I realise the panic that gripped me when I first awoke is beginning to abate, the dread I'd felt giving way to a milder anxiety. Looking at the clock, I see it's just after three. Maybe it's the heavy lunch I ate at the pub yesterday that's to blame. Even as I think it, I know I'm just fooling myself. The phone call I received yesterday is the cause of my dreadful fear. The call I'm trying to forget because to remember it means I've accepted that Ria will be part of my life again.

'I knocked over my water glass.' It's hard to get control of the tremor in my voice.

'Are you okay?' Scott pinches a piece of my nightdress between finger and thumb, then wrinkles his nose. 'This is drenched.'

'It was a bad dream, that's all, and the duvet made me hot. It's still the winter one.'

'It's certainly been warmer recently,' he says, shoving it down to his waist. 'We should probably change it to the lighter one.'

I push the duvet aside and get up, rescuing my mobile from the lake and putting it on the floor. Then I go to the bathroom for a towel to wipe the water. I'm just passing Beth's room when I stop. There's a thin strip of light under her bedroom door. What's she doing awake at this hour?

Putting my ear to the door, I listen, but there's no sound from her room. As quietly as I can, I press down on the handle and push the door open a crack. Putting my head round the door, I'm relieved to see that Beth is asleep, the duvet bunched up around her. Wainwright is curled up at the foot of her bed, fast asleep. He isn't allowed in the bedrooms, but I haven't the heart to move him.

Stepping inside, I walk over to the lamp to turn it off, then stop myself. Maybe Beth meant to leave it on. Maybe I'm not the only one to fear the darkness tonight. Sitting down on the bed, I gently stroke my daughter's dark hair away from her forehead. In the orange light of the bedside lamp, I see her eyes move beneath her translucent lids and wonder what she's dreaming about. I doubt she'd tell me – with every day that passes I feel she's moving further away from me.

As I pull the duvet up around her, I see a scrap of black wool poking out from beneath it. I recognise it as the mane of the stuffed horse Beth used to take to bed when she was younger, and I see she has it clutched to her chest. I hadn't realised she still had it. As I watch the rise and fall of her breathing, I feel a rush of love so fierce that tears spring to my eyes. Inside her teenage body, she's still my little girl.

With a last stroke of her hair, I get up and walk back onto the landing, closing the door behind me. I go to the bathroom, get the towel from the airing cupboard and mop up what's left of the water. By the time I've finished, Scott is fast asleep and I climb into bed beside him, curling up against his back, matching his shape.

I'm hoping sleep will come, but it doesn't. Instead, I lie and wait for daylight to filter through the curtains, unable to get rid of the feeling that things are about to change.

CHAPTER SIX

Beth

Beth pushed open the classroom door, hoping she'd timed it right. She'd waited until the last minute to go in: not so late that she'd miss registration, but late enough that she'd not have to endure the hateful time before proper lessons began. It was this time that was the worst. This and break time.

'Ah, Beth.' Her form tutor looked up from a pile of books she was marking. 'Better now?'

This was exactly what she didn't need. She'd been hoping to come in without anyone noticing. Now, through her teacher's unwanted concern, the attention she'd been hoping to avoid was drawn to her. Heads turned and the hum of conversation stopped. She felt herself colour.

'Yes, thanks.'

Carina and three other girls were sitting in a huddle by the window. Their form room was a twentieth century addition to the original Victorian building and, through the wide panes of glass, a large sweep of lawn, with tennis courts to one side, could be seen. Beyond that was Lake Windermere, its flat blue surface broken only by the white sails of yachts. It would have been a beautiful sight, if only it were viewed from somewhere else.

As Beth walked over to her table, she felt the girls' eyes on her, but she refused to look at them. She knew what it would be like. Carina would smile sweetly and pretend that nothing was wrong.

She'd ask Beth how she was and what she'd been doing, include her in their gossip about clothes and make-up. For a while, Beth would buy into it, thinking that today would be different, that they liked her after all. The sense of relief would be all-consuming. Then, just as suddenly, it would all change. She'd ask a question and it would be ignored, or she'd say something that would make Carina look at her with arched eyebrows. *What a bloody idiotic thing to say.*

Mouths that had, up until then, been curved into smiles of friendship, would harden into sneers, and shoulders would turn inwards so that she was no longer standing within the group, but outside of it. And then, as she heard their sniggers, it would dawn on her that, once again, she had fallen for it. Once again, she'd been made a fool of.

She'd realised she was different on her very first day at Lady Edburton. The others lived in large houses in Windermere and Ambleside, and their parents were solicitors and doctors. Nobody lived in small miners' cottages in villages that time had forgotten with a mum who made jewellery in her backyard and a dad who got paid for hiking the fells. If that hadn't been enough, Beth had also been taller than the other girls and one of the few who wore a bra because she needed to. And when the others talked about their periods, she was too embarrassed to say that she'd started in primary school. That would have only added more fuel to the fire.

She'd hoped it would get easier as they got older, and it had for a while. No one had invited her to their house, or suggested she go to the cinema with them at the weekend, but at least they were civil to her. Then it had all changed again. A new girl joined the school. One who was pretty and confident and unlike Beth in every way. That girl was Carina and she drew the other girls to her like a magnet.

Walking over to her table now, Beth sat down and took her English homework out of her bag. She started to read it through, bending her head over it so that her hair fell across her face. If she didn't say anything to anyone, they might ignore her.

She might have known it was never going to happen. The scrape of a chair next to her made her look up. For one horrible moment, she thought it was Carina who had sat down beside her, but it wasn't, it was Keira. She was part of the group, but had always seemed a little nicer than the others. Although she had never defended Beth, she had never directly attacked her either.

'Difficult homework, wasn't it?'

Beth looked across at her, searching the words for any trace of sarcasm, but she couldn't find any. Picking up the pages from the table, she flicked through them.

'It wasn't too bad.' In fact, she'd quite enjoyed it. They'd had to study a poem by Owen Sheers called 'Winter Swans' and then write their own using a variety of figurative devices. She'd loved the use of personification in Sheers' poem and had tried to emulate it in her own. Poetry was something she enjoyed nearly as much as drawing, and was the only other subject in which she applied herself. She knew her parents thought that she struggled because the work was too hard, but this couldn't have been further from the truth. Even subjects like Maths and Science she found easy, but in lessons, all she could concentrate on was whether the other girls were talking about her or how she might answer a question without them sniggering.

'Do you mind if I have a look? I struggled with my poem.'

Beth hesitated. She was so used to people ridiculing her work that she wasn't sure she wanted Keira to see it.

'Don't worry if you don't want me to. I'm like that as well. I always think my work isn't good enough to be seen.'

'Oh, I'm sure it is.' Beth started to relax. Carina and her cronies seemed to have forgotten her and were arguing about some programme they'd seen on television the previous evening. It was nice having a normal conversation. One where she didn't have to be careful what she said and analyse each word in case it was misconstrued and used against her. She pushed her poem across the table to Keira. 'I don't mind. Have a look.'

Keira took the page and read it, nodding now and again as she did, her forehead creased in concentration. Beth watched her anxiously, waiting for the snort of derision she was expecting. It didn't come.

'It's really good.' Keira smiled and placed the poem on the table. 'Really, really good.'

A warm feeling started to creep through Beth's body. 'Do you mean that?'

'Why would I say it if I didn't mean it? I like the way you compare yourself to a bird of prey. This part especially... *my heart soars like an eagle when you smile.* It's really beautiful.'

Beth felt her cheeks redden. 'Thank you.'

Keira looked over at their form tutor, who was picking up her bag ready to move on to her first lesson. 'Looks like it's time to go. I've got German now... Yuck. Maybe I'll see you at break?'

Pushing back her chair, Keira joined the others who were queuing to get out of the door. Beth looked over her shoulder to see if Carina was there, but it seemed she'd already gone. Beth's next lesson was Geography. Carina would be in that lesson too, but, for the first time in ages, Beth felt the knot in her stomach loosen. If she had someone to hang out with at break time, things wouldn't be so bad. She wouldn't need to go to the library and hide in one of the booths with a book until the bell for the next lesson rang. She wouldn't have to wish that she was anyone in the world but Beth Travis.

Sliding her homework back into her bag, she left the classroom, walking slowly along the corridor so that she wouldn't have to stand in the queue outside the geography room door with the others.

She waited until everyone was in and then seated herself in an empty seat at the back. Carina was sitting near the front with her best friend, Charlotte. They both glanced at her as they took their folders out of their bags, but their expressions were neutral and they soon looked away again. Perhaps they'd seen Keira talking to her. If they knew that someone was being friendly towards her, they might not be so inclined to have a go at her.

Buoyed by this thought, the hour went quickly. They were revising climate change and Beth found that, for once, she was actually taking it in. Maybe, when she got home, she'd have another look at her revision notes. Put in a bit more effort. That was for later, though. The lesson had come to an end and she needed to go outside to find Keira.

There was a large paved area with benches at the side of the school. When the weather was fine, the upper and lower schools took it in turns to use it. Beth got to the door just as the younger ones were coming in and stood back to let them through, watching them as they jostled and laughed down the corridor. Sometimes she thought it would be nice to be that age again, to go back to a time when things were simpler.

The last of the children had come in and Beth was just going through the door when she saw Mrs Snowdon walking along the corridor towards her. Instead of passing by as Beth expected, she stopped.

'Beth, if you've got time, I'd like to have a word with you.'

With reluctance, she let the door close again. She glanced through the window. Keira was already outside; she could see her, leaning against the wall, her bag over her shoulder. She was looking around as though searching for someone. Could she be looking for her? If only she'd look this way, Beth could wave to her or signal that she wouldn't be long.

Mrs Snowdon must have registered her reluctance to talk, for she continued quickly. 'It won't take long. I just want to talk to you about your coursework.'

Of all the break times to choose, it had to be this one. Her one chance to make a friend and it was going to be ruined. Keira was standing now, hitching her bag onto her shoulder.

'I'm not sure, I…'

'Don't look so worried. It's nothing bad, I can assure you.'

'What about lunchtime?' Through the window, she could see Keira moving between the groups of young people. She was probably going to join Carina's crowd over by the netball posts. Soon the opportunity would be lost. 'Couldn't I see you then instead?'

Mrs Snowdon shook her head. 'I'm sorry, Beth. I'm on duty lunchtime. Honestly, it will only take a few minutes.'

Beth dragged her eyes away from the window. 'Okay.'

The art room was at the end of the long corridor and it seemed to take an age to get there. Beth followed her teacher into the room and stood awkwardly as she retrieved her polythene art portfolio from a trolley at the back of the room. The art room was light, its large windows looking out onto the playing fields. It was here, during her art lessons, that Beth felt the happiest. Instead of being confined to a desk, next to someone who would, in all likelihood, rather be sitting somewhere else, she could move freely around the large table, lost in her own little world of drawing.

Unclipping the plastic handles of the portfolio, Mrs Snowdon took out Beth's paintings and drawings and spread them across the Formica surface of one of the tables.

'I've been having a look at your work, Beth, and I just wanted to say that you have a lot of talent. You've mastered some tricky techniques and you're one of the few students I've taught who seems to be happy working in any medium.'

She picked up one of the paintings and studied it. It was one Beth had done a few months ago – a watercolour and ink drawing of the head of an eagle, its yellow eyes looking straight out at whoever was looking at it. It was only on closer inspection that you could see the tiny reflection of a mountain crag in each of its pupils.

'This one in particular. I think it's very powerful. It's good to make the viewer think.' Mrs Snowdon pressed her palms onto the table and leant forward. 'I wanted to ask you whether you'd be happy for me to enter this, and two of your others, into a competition. It's called the Baxter Prize and is being run by a national newspaper for young people aged between fourteen and eighteen years of age. The theme is freedom and I thought these three pieces would fit the brief perfectly. Is it something you might be interested in?'

Beth stood with her arms folded, unable to think. 'Would you be entering anybody else's work?'

'No, it's only one entry per school.'

'Surely there must be someone better than me. What about Carina? Her work's amazing.'

Mrs Snowdon smiled. 'If we entered this, I think you'd have a good chance of doing well. I've noticed a lot of your work follows a theme, Beth. Have you always had an interest in birds of prey?'

Beth looked at the paintings and sketches spread out on the table. One was a drawing of a feather done in a fine black pen, so delicate that it looked like it would lift off the page if a breeze entered the window. Another was an abstract, the page covered in talons of different shapes and sizes, giving the paper texture as well as colour. Her favourite, though, was the outstretched wing of a bird in flight.

'I'm not sure. I think I must have.'

Mrs Snowdon walked over to the window and looked out at the distant fells. 'Do you draw them from memory or do you use a picture or photograph?'

Beth thought of her favourite place above the disused Temple Quarry. At some time in the past, someone had made a bench there from the unwanted slate that was piled up in heaps. With her back to the midnight blue water that had collected in the chamber at the bottom of the quarry over a hundred feet below, she would sit on the bench and watch the kestrels that nested in the cliffs or the sparrowhawks with their dark plumage and bright yellow legs. Often, she would see nothing but, in those moments, she would just let her imagination run free.

'Sometimes I photograph the birds, but mostly I just watch them and remember what I see.'

'But the eagles? There aren't any of those around here.'

'I know… but I know what they look like. I go onto the fells and imagine them there.'

Her teacher was silent for a moment. 'And is that what you were doing last week when you were absent from school?'

Beth went cold. She looked at the floor and tried to think of something to say. How could she know?

As if reading her mind, Mrs Snowdon carried on. 'Girls who are unwell generally aren't seen at nine in the morning waiting at the bus stop with a rucksack on their back.' She paused. 'Especially when, twenty minutes earlier, they were seen being dropped off at the school by their mother.'

Pulling out a chair, Mrs Snowdon indicated for Beth to sit, then pulled out another for herself. Beth waited in dread for what she would say next. She didn't know that anyone had seen her. Why hadn't she been more careful?

'I expect you're wondering why I haven't said anything to your parents. I certainly should have done and I'd probably get into trouble with Mrs Thompson if she knew.'

Beth chewed at a nail. 'Why didn't you?'

Mrs Snowdon shifted in her seat and glanced at the door. 'I wanted to give you the chance to tell me about it first. It's not like you to do something like this. One or two of the others, maybe, but not you. I'm thinking you must have had good reason to truant. Is there something going on I should know about? Is it problems with the other girls?'

The kindness and concern in her eyes made Beth want to cry. She'd always liked Mrs Snowdon and if she was going to say anything to any teacher, it would be to her – but she couldn't.

She just couldn't. It would make things a million times worse. So instead of telling the truth, she chewed her lip and shook her head.

'Everything's fine.'

Mrs Snowdon gave a small sigh and Beth imagined how she would be wrestling with her conscience, wondering whether to push her further or whether to report her unauthorised absence to the head. She felt guilty for putting her in this position.

They sat in silence for a while, then Mrs Snowdon pushed back her chair. The sound of its legs scraping on the tiles set Beth's teeth on edge. She watched as her teacher started putting her paintings back into the folder.

'I'm not going to say anything this time, Beth, but if it happens again, I shan't be able to turn a blind eye. I want you to know, though, that any time you need to talk, I'm always happy to listen. There are some big personalities in Year 11 and I could give you some strategies that might help in dealing with them.'

Beth stood up. 'Can I go now?'

Mrs Snowdon looked surprised. 'Yes, Beth, of course you can. I'm sorry to have made you miss some of your break time.' She picked up the picture of the eagle and looked at it for a moment before slipping it into the folder with the others. 'Oh, and about the competition. I'll understand if you don't want to submit your paintings, but it would be a shame not to. It really is a wonderful opportunity. Have a think about it.'

'I will.'

There were ten minutes of break left and, if Beth was lucky, she still might have a chance to talk to Keira. Leaving Mrs Snowdon to set up for her next lesson, Beth hurried back along the corridor. When she got outside, she stood on the top step and looked out at the sea of pupils in their maroon blazers. Where was Keira? It was a while since she'd spent a break time outside and, as she walked between the chatting groups, she began to feel more and more uncomfortable. She had nothing in common with the girls, with their expensively highlighted hair and plummy voices.

She was just about to give up her search when she spotted the back of Keira's head. With a smile, she started to walk towards her, but it was only when she got nearer that she saw Keira wasn't alone. Carina and Charlotte were with her. They were sitting on a low wall, which was why she hadn't noticed them. She stopped in her tracks, hoping that they hadn't seen her, but they had. Carina lifted her blonde head and smiled and, as if at some invisible signal, Keira turned around too.

Unsure of what to do, Beth stood there. For one ridiculous moment, she thought that Keira might help her out but, when she looked at her, Keira wouldn't meet her eyes and a telltale redness had started to creep up her neck under her ponytail.

What came next didn't surprise Beth. She saw its inevitability in the moments before it happened. Carina flung her arms out wide, then flapped them as though she were a bird.

Beth's palms began to sweat and she waited. *Just get it over with.*

Raising her voice to the soprano of a Disney princess, Carina pressed her hands to her chest and sang. 'My heart soars like an eagle when you smile.'

The crush of betrayal was too much. She'd shown Keira that poem in good faith. Unable to hear any more, Beth turned and walked away. She wouldn't give them the satisfaction of seeing her misery.

CHAPTER SEVEN

Leona

Sunlight picks out the last of the yellow daffodils that are growing on the steep slope behind the house, but the backyard is in shadow, so I've turned on the strips of fluorescent lighting in my workshop. I've got the radio on and the song I'm singing along to is something from the charts.

In front of me on the bench is the pair of silver earrings I've just finished making. They are in the shape of leaves, fine strands of silver criss-crossing to look like delicate veins. I'm just attaching the hooks when my phone rings. It's Scott.

'Hi, babe. Can you do me a favour?'

Scott's voice fades in and out. He's taken a group up to Helvellyn and I'm surprised that there's any signal at all. I remember, two years ago, hearing how a young man fell down that mountainside. His walking partner had found him unconscious six hundred feet from the path, but had been unable to use his mobile. By the time he'd found help and the rescue team had arrived, it was too late. It's a story I try to push from my mind when Scott's out on the fells.

'What is it, Scott? I can hardly hear you.'

'I forgot to take the—' All I can hear is static.

'The what?'

The phone goes dead, then after a few minutes, it rings again. 'I'll speak quickly in case we're cut off again. Would you mind taking the lawnmower round to Mum's? Her old petrol one's packed up and I said she could borrow ours until she can get a new one. I would have done it yesterday but forgot all about it.'

'Of course I don't mind. I'll go later this afternoon. I've got to make a delivery to a lady in Ambleside, so I can go on after.'

'Thanks, love.'

The phone cuts out again and I shove it back into my pocket before starting to clear up my workbench. As I do, I smile at the thought of seeing Scott's mother. I liked her the very first time Scott introduced me to her, and I know Fay has a soft spot for me too. Sometimes when I visit, she'll have baked her delicious pecan brownies specially, knowing how much I love them. It won't happen today, though, as she's not expecting me.

Picking up the leaf earrings, I hold them up to the light and inspect them. They are one of my more popular designs and, this week alone, I've made six pairs. If things carry on the way they have been, I'll soon be able to afford to rent a workshop in Ambleside – one with a small shop attached. How I'm looking forward to the day when I'll no longer be reliant on the money that goes into my bank each month. Money that Scott knows nothing about.

I carefully lay the earrings onto the pad that sits inside the little blue box I've just got out of the drawer. *Leona Designs* is written on the lid in silver. If anyone had asked me what I'd be doing when I was thirty-seven, a jewellery designer wouldn't have even been on my list, but I've taken some courses and it's something I know I'm good at. As I close the lid, I think how strange it is that it was Ria who made it all possible.

At the thought of her, my stomach clenches and the feeling of contentment leaves me. Last night I woke up again to a racing heart, sweat drenching my nightdress and that same feeling of dread I'd had before. Unable to face the darkness in the room, I'd stumbled out of bed and opened the curtains, trying not to wake Scott. I hadn't managed it though and, when he'd asked me if I was all right, I'd made up a story of a bad dream which he'd had no reason to disbelieve. He'd lifted the duvet and I'd climbed back in, resting my head against the dark hairs of his chest and feeling grateful for the warm comfort of his body. But, even as he pulled me close and stroked my hair, I knew that it would be a long time before I managed to sleep again.

'Damn you, Ria!' I hadn't meant to say the words aloud, and the sound of my voice echoes inside the empty space of the workroom. Is this how my life is going to be now? I put the boxes, containing the jewellery I'll be delivering, into carrier bags with the same simple silver writing on them, then let myself out of the workshop.

Our cottage is on the end of the terrace, the rest being holiday rentals and weekend homes. As the season hasn't started properly yet, it's the only one occupied, but in a few weeks the cottages will start to fill up. The shared grass area at the front is bare too, but by June, the holidaymakers will have unfolded their green canvas chairs and will be sitting, glass in hand, watching the sun set behind the mountains. If they see me, they'll raise their chilled white wine in greeting and I'll feel obliged to ask them about their day and listen politely as they talk about the walk they've just done or the museum they've visited. The path that runs along the outside of the cottages will be littered with their walking boots.

Scott has taken on the job of unofficial grass cutter and the lawnmower is in a shed near where my car is parked. I lift it into the boot and, as I'm doing so, a flash of white catches my eye under the hedge at the side of the drive. On closer inspection, I see it's a carrier bag and, when I pull it out and open it, I find it stuffed full of clothes: a pair of walking boots, a navy hooded top, a pair of jeans and an old walking jacket. I recognise them all as Beth's. I wonder what they're doing there.

Thinking I'll ask her later, I reverse out of my parking space and drive away. In the rear-view mirror, I watch the house with its grey slate walls and small-paned windows get smaller and, as I leave it behind, I get the feeling, once again, that the past is about to catch up with me.

Pushing the thought away, I pass through the village, then drive the three miles to Skelwith Bridge, where I take the road to Ambleside. It doesn't take long to drop off the jewellery, leaving me free to go to Fay's house. She lives in a white flat-fronted house in Birch Road and, when I get there, she's in the garden at the side of the house, taking in her washing.

'Leona. What a lovely surprise!' She greets me with a kiss, then holds me at arm's length. 'Are those dark circles I see under your eyes? I hope you haven't been overdoing things.'

I must be looking particularly rough for her to comment like that and I hope against hope that she won't start asking me any awkward questions.

'I've not been sleeping too well,' I tell her. Deliberately making my tone light. 'Mice in the roof.'

'Little blighters,' she says, with a rueful shake of the head. 'That's what comes of choosing to live in the back of beyond.'

'I'd hardly call Church Langdon the back of beyond, Fay.'

'It is to me. Come on, I'll make us some tea.'

She goes back into the house and I follow her in, taking a seat at the kitchen table. She fills a kettle and takes a couple of mugs off the mug tree. 'How's Beth?'

'She's fine. Why do you ask?'

'No particular reason,' she says, dropping teabags into the mugs. 'I just like to know my family are well and happy. Has she got a boyfriend yet?'

'Goodness, Fay, she's fifteen for heaven's sake. There's plenty of time for that. Besides, anyone interested in Beth would have to sit a three-hour exam on how to treat her well if Scott had anything to do with it. I wouldn't want to be in their shoes.'

'Scott might be a bear of a man,' Fay says, putting a mug in front of me. 'But inside he's a pussy cat.'

I laugh, thinking of how safe I feel in his arms. 'You're right there.'

It was his gentleness that had first attracted me to him all those years ago, that and his warm brown eyes and the thick dark hair he always wore a little too long. It wasn't long after I'd moved to Church Langdon from Carlisle. I was in an outdoor clothing shop in Ambleside, trying on fleeces, and Scott had been standing next to me, testing the weight of walking poles in his outstretched hands. When he'd dropped one, the clang as it hit the hard floor had made me jump and when his eyes met mine, I'd found it hard to look away again.

'He adores her, you know.' Fay is looking at me, her hands wrapped around her mug.

'Of course, I know. She loves him too. What's brought all this on?'

She looks away. 'Oh, I don't know. It would have been my anniversary today and I suppose I'm just being sentimental.'

'I'm sorry,' I say, touching her arm. 'I should have remembered.' Scott's father died when he was a boy and since that time, according to Scott, Fay has never so much as looked at another man. It's a shame as I know she'd make someone very happy.

'I wouldn't expect you to, darling. It just makes me think about you and Scott… Your situation.'

'Our situation?' I find it hard to believe she used that term. 'I presume you're talking about the fact we're not married?'

'Wouldn't you like to be?'

I can't believe she's asking me this. Doesn't she know me at all? 'No.'

The abruptness of my answer seems to shock her. 'Forget I said anything, love. It's not really any of my business.'

I force a smile. Wondering why this has come up now. 'You know we don't hold with marriage, Fay. We love each other and that's all that matters.'

'And you're certain Scott feels the same about it?'

I'm stunned into silence. He hasn't said anything to me recently and I'd just presumed he'd accepted the way things were.

'Has Scott said something to you?'

She hesitates. 'Of course not.'

Getting up from the table, she walks over to the cupboard and pulls out a cake tin with a picture of a West Highland Terrier on it. She takes off the lid and I know, from the delicious smell, what's in there.

'Would you like one?' she says, offering it to me. 'I made them specially.'

As soon as she says it, she realises her error. Her face falls and she puts the tin down on the table.

'You knew I was coming, didn't you, Fay? It was Scott who put you up to this.'

The brownies sit between us in their tin, evidence of his deception. What was he thinking of, enlisting his mother to do his talking for him?

Fay looks away, embarrassed. 'He loves you, Leona, and he wants to make it official. You can't blame him for that.'

'No, but I can blame him for not talking about it to me first.' I fight to keep my frustration in check. After all, it's not Fay's fault. 'I think I'd better go. I'll just get the lawnmower out of the boot.' I look at the car through the window, realising it probably won't be necessary.

Fay guesses what I'm thinking. 'It's true I asked Scott if I could borrow the lawnmower. He didn't make it up.'

'Well, that's something then.' I don't want to argue with her as she's the nearest thing I have to a mother now. Instead, I take a breath and smile. 'I'll put it in the garage, if you like.'

'That would be kind of you. Thank you.'

Wanting to make amends, I reach into the tin and take out one of the brownies. It's rich and chocolatey, but I can't enjoy it. Not when Scott's given me something else to worry about. Finishing it quickly, I dust the crumbs off my lap, then stand up.

'I'll see you soon, Fay.'

I'm about to put on my coat when she comes around the table and takes my hand in both of hers. She's a head shorter than me and it's hard to believe that, at six foot three, Scott is her son.

'Don't be too hard on him, dear,' she says, her forehead creased into a frown. 'He only wants to look after you.'

I don't answer but let myself out, wondering how she'd feel if I told her that I'd had enough people looking after me to last me a lifetime.

When I get back home, there's still a coil of anger inside me. Instead of going back to my workroom and getting on with something, I pace the living room, picking things up and putting them down again, seeing it through my family's eyes. There are too many cushions on the settee. Some have ruffled edges, others patchwork covers: an assortment collected from charity shops and flea markets. None of them match any of the others or the floral cover of the settee. In fact, the whole room is a hotchpotch of colours and textures. Without realising it, I've turned the small stone cottage into my own personal Aladdin's cave. Scott jokes that I'm in danger of becoming a hoarder, but every item is precious to me.

In my hand is a white china duck, its body decorated with a daisy chain of blue flowers. I bought it in a craft shop in Grasmere and it sits on the mantelpiece alongside two brass candle sticks and a carved wooden elephant. Stroking the duck's shiny back, I look out of the window wishing Beth would come home, needing her company. But her bus isn't due for another half an hour and even when she gets home, there's no guarantee what mood she'll be in.

Feeling nostalgic for the closeness we once shared, I put the duck back on the mantelpiece and go upstairs, thinking that I might sort out some washing. As my workshop takes up most of the backyard, and the kitchen is too small for a tumble dryer, clothing hangs from airers in front of the radiators. Picking up the empty washing basket from the bathroom, I take it into my bedroom and start lifting the clothes from the rails.

The window is at the front of the house and looks out across the top of Blackstone Farm to Langdon Fell. The view is the first thing Scott and I see when we wake up each morning and I never tire of it. There's a deep window seat in front of it and I sit there, trying to conjure up the feeling of peace that the view usually gives me. It won't come, though. I can't get Fay's words out of my head. They go round and round like a song I've heard too many times on the radio. *He wants to make it official. You can't blame him for that.*

A wave of insecurity washes over me. Scott's asked me before, but I've never taken him seriously, brushing it aside with a joke. If I say no too many times, is there a chance he might leave me?

The thought has come out of the blue as in the nine years we've been together, I've never doubted him. I can feel myself getting anxious – am aware of the shirt clutched in my fist. Even as I'm thinking it, I know I'm being ridiculous, but how is it I'm so certain of him? I thought I'd known Ria, but it turned out I hadn't known her at all… Or the things she was capable of.

Ria. My eyes are drawn to the built-in wardrobe at the side of the room. The urge to go over to it is strong. I try to distract myself by folding up some of Scott's T-shirts and putting them away in the chest of drawers but, like a recovering alcoholic, I'm unable to fight it. With a quick glance at my watch, I drop the last T-shirt onto the bed, then cross the room and throw open one of the wardrobe doors. Kneeling in front of it, I use both hands to push aside the bags and shoes that are jumbled on the floor below my hanging rail.

I stare at the wooden boards and the pull becomes even greater. I don't do anything to start with, then, hesitantly, I reach out my hand and ease my fingertips under the edge of one of them. My heart flutters in my chest like a caged bird. At this moment, I want to be anywhere except here, but I can't stop.

The board comes up easily and, from the dark bowels between the joists, I lift out the envelope that's hidden there. Still not certain I want to, I lift the flap, my heart racing. My hands are shaking as I pull out the contents. A photograph lies on top of some others and, even though I knew it would be there, the knowledge doesn't prepare me for the strength of the emotions that threaten to overwhelm me when I see it: sadness, shock, revulsion.

For, staring up at me, is Ria. The last photo taken of her when she was still happy. She's smiling into the camera, her long dark hair falling over her shoulders, and she looks carefree. For twelve years, I've refused to let myself look at her, but now that I have, it's like a shot to the heart.

The front door slamming makes me start and the other items in the envelope fall onto the floor. I hear Beth's voice calling me and I look at the half-open door, my hand frozen in mid-air. But, as I hear her footsteps on the stairs, I come to my senses. She mustn't see all this. Gathering everything up, I stuff it back into the envelope, then shove it back into its hiding place. The floorboard bangs into place and I've just time to grab Scott's T-shirt from the bed as Beth pushes open the door.

CHAPTER EIGHT

Beth

'What are you doing?'

Beth dropped her school bag onto the floor and stared at her mum. She was kneeling on the floor, one of Beth's dad's T-shirts clutched to her chest. Behind her, the door of her wardrobe stood open, and, inside, Beth could just see a pile of shoes and bags that had been shoved up against one of the sides.

Reaching behind her, her mum pulled the door closed. There was a faint sheen of sweat on her forehead and she looked as though she might be about to faint.

'There you are.' Her smile was bright. Forced.

'Are you okay?'

Beth watched as her mum ran her fingers through her hair, dragging it away from her face and wiping her brow with her sleeve.

'I just came over a bit dizzy, that's all.' Easing herself up from the floor, she began folding the T-shirt. When she had finished, she placed it on the bed, laying her hand over it as though it might float away. 'Anyway, don't worry about me. How was school?'

Beth picked up her bag again and lifted it onto her shoulder. All the way home on the bus, she'd been planning what she was going to say to her mum. Imagining them sitting at the small table by the window with mugs of tea in their hands and the fells falling into shadow beyond the window. She'd tell her all about Carina and how much she hated the school, and her mum would lean over and hug her and tell her that she'd sort it. That everything would be all right. She could move to Lakeside Comprehensive in September and they'd all live happily ever after.

It wasn't going to happen, though. It was all in her head. Gone were the days when, after she'd come home from school, they'd sit together in front of a TV programme neither were that interested in, mugs of tea in their hands and the empty wrappers of Penguin biscuits in their laps. It had been an excuse to chat about Beth's day, picking over the parts that hadn't gone well. Celebrating, with a clunk of china, the parts that had. Now, it seemed her mum didn't have time for her between making her precious jewellery and jumping whenever her phone rang. God, it was like their family was going crazy.

'School was fine.'

She turned away and crossed the landing to her bedroom, closing the door behind her. The bed creaked as she threw herself onto it and tried to empty her mind of everything that had happened that day. But it was impossible. However hard she tried, the pictures kept coming back into her head, making her stomach twist and clench at the memory. She'd never rid herself of the sheer hell of being the butt of the joke once again. Could you die from shame?

Rolling onto her side, she stared at the wall. Inside a glass clip-frame was a picture she'd made a few years back – a brown and black collage of birds of prey, cut out of the nature magazines she'd liked to read when she was younger. She'd begged her mum for a subscription for her birthday and, each month when the magazine had arrived, had pored over its pages, tearing out her favourites and keeping them in a folder. She still had that folder somewhere.

Now she looked at the collage through half-closed eyes. Her mum had never liked it, although she'd never said why. She hadn't wanted her to put it on her wall, but Beth had managed to persuade her. Most of the birds were in flight, their wings interweaving and overlapping to give the impression of motion. It made Beth feel restless, her small bedroom too cramped.

A glance at her bedside clock showed her it was four thirty. There would still be a few hours left of daylight. Pushing herself up, she loosened her tie, then dragged it off and threw it into the corner of the room along with the hated maroon jumper.

She was just pulling on her hoodie when she saw a carrier bag on the floor bedside her dressing table. She hadn't noticed it when she came in. Picking it up and looking inside, she confirmed what she already knew. It was the bag of walking clothes she'd stuffed into the hedge and forgotten to bring in. Her mum must have found it and put it in her room. Would she be able to tell from it that Beth had been bunking school? Walking the fells when she should have been in class? Knowing there'd be questions asked later, Beth wracked her brains for a reason she could give for why the bag should be in the hedge, but could think of nothing. Shit. Why had she been such an idiot?

Emptying the bag onto the floor, she stuffed the dirty clothes into the washing basket, then picking up her walking boots and rucksack, tiptoed to the door. Pulling it open a crack, she looked across the landing to her mum's bedroom. She had her back to the door and was folding down the airer.

As quietly as she could, Beth crossed over to the stairs and went down. When she reached the living room, she hesitated. Should she tell her mum what she was doing? Deciding she should, she called up the stairs.

'I'm going out for a walk, Mum. I won't be late.'

Without waiting to hear her mum's answer, Beth shoved her feet into her boots and went outside, leaning against the wall of the workroom to do them up. Walking behind it, she unlatched the gate in the fence and went through. The narrow path that ran along the back of the terrace, and the lower slopes of the fell that rose up behind, were in shadow, the cottages blocking out the sun. Only the top of the fell was in sunlight and, when she shielded her eyes, she could just make out the dark mound of the slate cairn at the top, silhouetted against the blue sky.

Zigzagging up the hillside was a stony track and it was this path that Beth chose to take. Being careful not to slip on the loose stones, she climbed the slope until it met up with a larger path. Either side of her, the grass had been cropped short by the sheep that grazed there, but by the sides of the little beck that trickled down the hillside, it was as long and straggly as a mare's tail.

Below her were the slate roofs of the miners' cottages, her home for the past nine years. Although she had only been six when she'd moved to Church Langdon, she could still remember quite clearly the featureless, purpose-built flat in Carlisle where they'd lived before.

Each morning, when it was school time, her mum had taken her by the hand and led her across the communal landing to the lift that smelt of piss and cigarette smoke. She had been frightened of that lift. Scared it might drop.

One day, as they'd waited for it to come up from the ground floor, the door to one of the other flats had opened and a woman had come out with a child of about her age. How desperately she'd wanted to say hello, to have her as her friend, but her mum hadn't let her. Instead, she'd put her arm around her and ushered her into the lift as the doors slid open. As she'd watched the numbers above the metal doors change from 5 down to G, she'd shouted and said her mum was mean, but her mum had told her that she must never talk to strangers. Even then, she'd thought it an odd thing to call their neighbours.

The other thing she remembered was the noise of the traffic that had passed by her window day and night, and the laughter and shouts from drunk youths as they had rolled out of the pub at the end of their street. Beth closed her eyes. The only thing she could hear now was the bleating of a lamb higher up the hill. It made her feel even more lonely, if that was possible.

Climbing higher, she felt the muscles in her legs begin to work and the tension in her body ease. It was a beautiful afternoon, the sun disappearing behind the clouds only to break out again, turning the bracken-covered slopes to gold. The climb was steep and soon Beth's breathing became more laboured. She stopped and took off her jacket, looking across the tops of the houses to the valley which spread out beyond the village. It was divided up into a patchwork of shapes by drystone walls and looked like a picture in a children's book. There was the campsite, and further on she could see two farms and the white bulk of the hotel where a lot of her dad's clients stayed, but this all disappeared from sight as the path bent around the fellside.

Now the rock-strewn track took her through a gap in a drystone wall and over the little beck before beginning its long climb to the top of the fell. Just one last ascent, past the old slate-miners' bothy, and then she'd have reached the cairn at its summit. She'd found it by chance the previous summer, at the highest point of the ridge where the hill flattened out. Apart from Temple Quarry, it was one of her favourite places.

The final scramble to reach it was over shattered and jagged rocks, but she was used to it. Arriving breathless at the top, she stood with her hands on her hips and gazed out at the ring of mountains that formed a natural amphitheatre for the lake that lay below. She took off her rucksack and sat with her back against the rough stones, stretching her legs out in front of her. She closed her eyes and felt the breeze on her face. It was just her and the sky and the clouds. Up here there was nothing to stop her believing she was the only person in the world.

'Hi there!'

Beth's eyes flew open. Coming up the hillside was a man. He was dressed in combat trousers and a faded navy T-shirt, the camera he had around his neck banging against his chest as he walked. When he got closer, he raised his hand in acknowledgement and

Beth felt a twinge of irritation; she'd been hoping to have the place to herself.

It was as if he'd read her thoughts for, as he reached the cairn, he smiled apologetically. 'Sorry. Didn't think anyone else would be up here today. I've got a godawful hangover and I thought the walk would do me good. Can't say it has, though.'

Without moving, Beth studied him. He was older than her by a few years and, unlike her dad's full beard, his was just a few days of sandy growth. His long hair was pulled back from his face in a ponytail and his blue eyes were accentuated by his tan. It was obvious he didn't work in an office.

'Are you a photographer?' She nodded towards the camera that swung from his neck.

The man smiled. 'Bit of a giveaway, isn't it? Yes, I'm freelance. Travel journalism mostly, but I've been known to turn my hand to other things if I'm desperate. Once photographed a woman's Pekingese for three hundred quid... Now that was a story.'

Taking his rucksack off his back, he rummaged inside and pulled out a lens which he fitted onto his camera. 'Do you mind if I take some photos? It shouldn't take long, then I'll leave you in peace.'

'I don't mind.'

As he lifted his camera, Beth wondered what her mum would think of her sitting at the top of the fell, talking to a strange man. She knew she ought to feel nervous, but she didn't. Instead, she watched him stand with his legs astride, the muscles of his forearms working as he twisted the lens, wishing she'd tied back her unruly hair. She must look a sight with her winter-pale skin – make-up was frowned upon at Lady Edburton.

She had expected him to take lots of photos, but instead he lowered his camera again and stood looking out across the valley. Waiting for something. Then, as if conjured up by his presence, high in the sky Beth saw a peregrine falcon. It rose on the thermals and glided effortlessly with wings spread wide, silhouetted against the blue. Aiming his camera at it, the man clicked the shutter again and again.

Why was she just sitting there? Bending to her rucksack, Beth unzipped it and pulled out her sketchbook and pencil and started to draw. Her fingers worked fast, capturing the essence of the bird – the power in its wings and its perfect symmetry. She wasn't aware that the man had stopped taking photographs. She wasn't aware of anything, just the way the pencil felt between her finger and thumb. The control she had over it.

'Bloody hell, you're good.'

His shadow fell across the page and she looked up to see him scrutinising her work.

'It's okay, I suppose.' She felt embarrassed. It was the second compliment she'd received today about her work and she was unused to it.

'Don't put yourself down. You've got some serious talent going on there. May I?'

Shyly, she handed him the book and waited as he flicked through it. 'They're just sketches I do when I'm out.'

He nodded. 'Are you at art college or something?'

The fact that he presumed she was older than she was pleased her, and she thought carefully about how she should answer. Saying she was at art college would be a lie too far but that didn't mean she couldn't bend the truth a little. Even though she'd never see him again, she didn't want him thinking she was just a silly little girl.

'No, but Art's one of the subjects I'm taking for my A levels.' There was no need to mention the school she attended; he would probably think she was at sixth-form college and she certainly wasn't going to put him right.

He nodded. 'Local, then?'

'Yes. I live in Church Langdon.'

'I know it. In fact, I've got my camper van parked in the farm campsite for a few weeks while I do some freelance work. It's a pretty place. I photographed the church for a promotional leaflet last year.'

'You live in a camper van?' Beth tried to imagine it. It would be even smaller than their Carlisle flat.

'For most of the year, yes. I like the van. It gives me freedom. I can come and go as I please. Stay in a place for as long as I like, then piss off again.'

Beth put her drawing book and pencil back in her rucksack and zipped it up. While they'd been talking, the falcon had disappeared from view and the sun had sunk behind the mountain, turning the valley below to monochrome.

'I ought to be getting back.' Her dad would kill her if she was still out on the fell when it grew dark. She'd grown up to his horror stories of what could happen if you couldn't see the path. How something as simple as a sprained ankle could leave you stranded, and how quickly hypothermia could set in if you were immobile.

'Do you want me to walk you back? I can come up here another time and finish these off.'

'No, don't worry. It'll be quicker on the way back.'

'Cool. I actually came up here to catch the sunset. The falcon was a bonus.'

Beth thought she could detect a note of relief in his voice. After all, why would he want to cut short his photography session to see her safely back? It wasn't as if they even knew each other.

'The best place to see them is at the old quarry on the other side of the valley. It's a magical place.'

He looked at her with interest. 'Is it now?'

'Well, *I* think so.' She'd never told anyone else it was where she liked to go, and she wondered if she had been wise to do so now. Picking up her rucksack, she swung it onto her shoulder. 'Anyway, I'd better go.'

She said goodbye but he didn't answer. He'd already turned back to the valley, his camera pointed towards the mountain peaks, where the sky behind was now streaked with orange. Instead of replying, he raised his hand in a form of salute, his mind now focused on his task.

It was only as Beth picked her way back down the hillside, as the sky darkened to the west, that she realised they'd not even exchanged names.

CHAPTER NINE
Leona

I lift the plastic crate onto the trestle table and start to unpack the boxes. I've brought with me some necklace stands and some black velvet ring cushions. The earrings I've chosen to keep in their boxes at the front of the table. As I open the lid of a small, square box and take out the ring that's nestled inside, I can't help wondering about Beth. When she'd come home from her walk last night, her eyes had been bright and her cheeks flushed, feverish even. I hope she's not coming down with something.

The craft fair at the Kelsick Centre in Ambleside isn't going to make me a great deal of money, my commissions bring in more, but I've always enjoyed doing them. I like the bustle in the hall at eight thirty when the sellers start setting up: the sound of boxes being ripped open and metal table legs being unfolded. Most of the stallholders know each other well and I smile as I see a hand wave or a name being called. It makes me feel as though I'm involved, even though I prefer to keep myself to myself.

The time I like best, though, is when the customers arrive, pushing through the doors at half past nine. It's as if they think by waiting a minute longer, they might miss out on something. I love to see the look on the women's faces, and the resignation on their husbands', as they pick up a necklace and hold it up to their necks. They'll look at themselves in the mirror I've placed on the table and I'll tell them how much it suits them. Nine times out of ten, after turning the small label over and looking at the price, they'll reach in their bags for their credit cards. Witchcraft, Scott calls it. I like to think of it as good salesmanship.

The stall next to mine has a collection of wooden carved bowls and spoons, and the man who has the pitch is polishing an apple made of beech until the wood gleams in the strip lighting.

'Reckon we'll be having a good turnout today,' he says, without taking his eyes off the polishing cloth.

I push a silver ring, twisted into a love-knot, into the slot in the black cushion and nod. 'Yes, it's been well advertised.'

'They've got the urn on already. Fancy a coffee before the mob rolls in?' He puts the cloth down and looks at me expectantly.

'That would be nice, thank you.'

Placing the wooden apple onto a Perspex display stand, he wanders away to the other end of the hall where a table has been set up for drinks. *Tea and coffee £1.60, Cakes £1* has been written in red felt pen above plates of flapjacks and lemon drizzle cake. As he speaks to the woman behind the table, I think of ways to avoid being drawn into a conversation when he gets back.

As I hang up the last of my necklaces, I wonder what Scott is doing. He was still in bed when I left, and will probably now be up and planning his next walking route. My phone is in the back pocket of my jeans, and I put my hand to it to make sure it's secure. Since the phone call, I've dreaded it ringing, but I need to have it with me in case Beth needs me… or Scott. I still haven't said anything to him about my conversation with Fay, or my panic attack in the shop, and I'm just wondering if I should, when the doors open and the first customers arrive. Many of them are tourists; there's something about their new walking trousers and matching fleeces that give them away. They've probably come here for the cheap coffee, but I can guarantee they'll be leaving with more than that. It happens every year.

My first sale is made quickly: a chain with a simple silver teardrop hanging from it. I hold up the matching earrings for the woman to see, wondering if I might be able to persuade her to buy them too, but when she says she'll think about it and come back later, I know it isn't going to happen.

More people come to the table and I make a few more sales. It's hot and stuffy in the hall. The windows are closed and, when I reach behind me, the radiator is hot to my touch despite the unseasonably warm weather we've been having. Finding no way to turn it down, I take off my cardigan and hang it on the back of my chair, wishing I'd worn something cooler. In the last half hour, the noise in the hall has risen and I'm finding it difficult to hear what people are saying.

A man holds a bracelet up for me to see. He's an ordinary-looking man and his wife has moved on to the next stall. I expect he wants it as a present for her, as he glances over to make sure she isn't looking before leaning across the table to speak to me. The narrow aisle between the rows of tables is full of people. Where have they all come from? A coach party maybe? Those who are looking at the stalls are blocking the way of the ones who are trying to get to the refreshments area and, although I'm safely behind my table, I imagine the press of their bodies.

The man's mouth is moving but I can't hear what he's saying. His words are drowned out by the thrumming in my ears. It takes a moment to realise it's the sound of my own blood. I try to concentrate on what he's saying, but the picture I have in my head of the red viscous liquid circulating through my body is making me nauseous.

He leans in closer and my hearing comes back. He's irritated now, worried his wife will turn around and see his purchase. 'I said, how much is this?'

I try to answer but my mouth is dry, my tongue stuck to the roof. He's too close, his thighs pressing against the edge of the table as he speaks. The sea of people is pressing in. His eyes are fixed on me.

'The bracelet,' he barks. 'How much?'

I can't answer. It's happening again. The fear is overwhelming. Paralysing.

'Is she all right?' He's turned to the man with the carved wooden bowls. In a minute, they'll both be staring at me.

The need to get away is acute. Shoving my chair to one side, I push myself away from the table and stumble along the back of the stalls towards the ladies. Luckily, no one is in there and I lock myself inside one of the cubicles, retching into the toilet until my stomach hurts, thankful there's no one to hear me.

A few minutes pass, then I hear the door open and someone comes in, a wave of sound following them from the hall. I can't go back in there. Resting my forehead on the shiny door, I try to steady my breathing as the footsteps walk to the cubicle at the end and I hear the twist of the lock. With an effort, I straighten up and wipe my mouth on some toilet paper.

It seems an age before I hear the flush of the toilet, then more footsteps on the concrete floor and the roar of the hand dryer. Only when I'm sure the room is empty again do I feel able to unlock the door and come out. I know I'll have to phone Scott.

Thankful that my mobile is still in my back pocket, I find his name, my hand shaking as I press the call button. It doesn't take long for him to pick up and I breathe a sigh of relief.

'Hi, Babe, what is it?'

'I need you to come to the craft fair and pick me up, Scott. I'm not feeling well.'

'You were okay this morning.' He sounds distracted and I know that his mind is still on the group he'll be taking out this afternoon.

'Please, Scott, just come and get me.' Despite trying, I can't stop the wobble in my voice. Scott must have heard it too, as his voice changes.

'I'll be there in fifteen,' he says, and all at once I wish he was here now to wrap me in his big arms.

Without saying more, I end the call and put my phone away before splashing cold water on my face and drying it with a paper towel. Then, resting my hands on either side of the basin, I look at my face in the mirror. If he could see me now, would he recognise me? Reflected back is a woman with dark circles under her eyes and tension around her mouth. I wish I knew what was happening to me.

Scott drives with one hand on the wheel, the other covering mine. I've told him what happened and it's a relief not to have to pretend any more. I'd thought I could deal with it on my own, but I can't. In the back of his Land Rover are my boxes of jewellery. While I waited in the car, he collected it all up and made excuses for me. He says we'll collect my car another time.

'How long has this been going on? The panic attacks and the sleepless nights?'

As the town disappears behind us, the houses replaced by fields of sheep, I stare straight ahead, thinking about his question and wondering how honest I can be. His hand on top of mine is warm and comforting and the urge to confide in him is great, but I know that if I do, our lives will never be the same again.

'They started a few days ago,' I say, turning to him. 'The feelings come over me so quickly that there's nothing I can do.'

The answer's an honest one. The nightmares I had for the first few years, and the pills I needed to take to block everything out, are so long ago now that he doesn't need to know about them. Or about the face I saw in the glass: the person from my past who started this all off.

'But there must be something that's triggered all this, Leona. People don't have panic attacks for no reason. Is there anything that's worrying you?'

I look away again. This time there's no way I can answer truthfully. If I tell him, Ria will become his problem too, and I can't let that happen. I say nothing, hoping he won't ask me again.

'I think you should see Dr Rosen. Tell him what's going on. There might be something he can give you to help you sleep.'

'No! I don't want that!' My voice comes out too loud.

'I only thought…'

'I'm sorry, Scott. What I meant is, I don't have any problem getting to sleep. Most nights I'm fine, it's just sometimes…'

How can I explain about the darkness and the terror? How it would take more than a white pill to make it go away. I don't want to talk to Dr Rosen, the kindly GP who's seen our family through throat infections, migraines and sprained ankles. I don't want sleeping tablets. I need someone who won't judge. Someone who will understand.

In my purse, tucked into a compartment where I keep my books of stamps, is a slip of paper with a telephone number on it. Since the day it was handed to me, all those years ago, I've carried it with me, hoping I'll never need it.

When I get home, I know I'll have to ring it.

CHAPTER TEN

Beth

Four days had passed and, whether at school or at home, Beth found she could not get the photographer's face out of her head. On the few occasions she went into Ambleside, she'd look at the boys hanging around the park and compare them to him. Their skin hadn't yet taken on the coarseness of adulthood, whereas his was weathered from being outdoors, and there were lines around his eyes from squinting at the camera. And although most of the boys had a shadow of hair above their lips, she doubted any of them shaved and couldn't help wondering what the feel of the man's stubble would be like beneath her hand.

After school each day, she'd climb the fell, hoping that he'd be there again, but he never was. Chances were, he'd moved on but, even if he hadn't, he probably had a girlfriend, or even a wife, back in London or somewhere. Someone who knew more than Beth did about love.

It was disconcerting to find that sometimes it would be his face that appeared beneath the soft lead of her pencil, rather than the birds or the landscape. The high ridge of his cheekbones and the furrow of his brow as he looked out across the valley. In that short time they'd spent together, maybe no more than twenty minutes, she'd studied his face, the planes and the shadows, and she knew that whether face-on or in profile, the drawings in her book were a good likeness.

Even though she wanted to, she never kept the sketches. She'd tear them into little pieces and watch them blow away across the valley like confetti, knowing she wouldn't be able to explain them if her parents were to see. Instead, she kept the feelings that stirred inside her to herself. She'd had crushes on boys before, but this was different. Even though he was older than her, it was like they had a connection. It reminded her of how she used to talk to her mum, before her mum started acting so strangely. Maybe it was because they seemed to have so much in common, or maybe it was simply because he'd come into her life at the right time. Whatever it was, for the first time in a while, up on that fellside, she hadn't felt alone.

Unable to settle to her revision this evening, she'd decided to take the path alongside the river that wound its way along the valley opposite their house. Pushing open the wooden gate that led into the field, she crossed the cattle grid and walked down the path to the stone bridge.

She tried telling herself that the reason she'd walked this way was that she was tired of the fells. Tired of climbing up their rock-strewn paths. It wasn't true, though; it was because she hoped she might find him at the campsite that lay on the other side of the bridge from where she stood now, watching the water race and tumble between the boulders. Wasn't that why she'd put on a smudge of eyeliner and some mascara before she'd come out? Not too much, just enough to bring out the colour of her eyes. When she'd looked in the mirror, she'd been surprised by what she'd seen. Not a gauche schoolgirl, but a young woman with high cheekbones and a shy smile.

Now, though, the confidence she'd felt as she'd looked in the bedroom mirror had disappeared, to be replaced with a flutter of butterflies in her stomach. She hadn't even thought about what she'd do if she saw him. How she'd explain why she was there, staring across the field at the tents and camper vans. Wracked with indecision, she did nothing, just stood on the bridge, her arms wrapped around her body.

This was ridiculous. She couldn't just stand there. Taking a deep breath, Beth stepped across the bridge and into the field. As she walked towards the first tents, she could see that most of them were zipped up, their occupants out for the day. In fact, the whole site was quiet, except for a woman carrying a plastic basin of clothes over to the wash block.

The few camper vans and caravans that were there were parked in a different area of the field, near a small copse. Some were huge and white and she could picture what they would look like inside, all chintzy fabrics and shiny appliances. Their owners wanting a smaller model of their homes when they went away.

It wasn't these that caught her eye though, it was the small bug-shaped VW camper van parked a little way from them. Its faded green paintwork was rusting in places and the curtains at the windows were bright yellow sunflowers on an orange background. There was something about it that made her guess it was his.

She moved closer. Apart from a pair of walking boots outside the door, there was no sign that anyone was in the van. What she was hoping to achieve, she didn't know, but something made her walk to the window. Cupping her hand above her eyes to cut out the reflection, she peered into the gloomy interior. There wasn't much to see: just a bench seat, a small work surface with a hob, and that was about it.

'Well, fancy seeing you.'

Beth sprang away from the window, her heart racing. The photographer was behind her. It was as if she'd conjured him up out of nowhere. He stood with his hands in his pockets, his long hair tucked behind his ears. She tried to work out from his expression whether he was annoyed or not. It was difficult to tell.

'I was just looking for a place to sketch.' Could he hear her voice shaking?

'You thought you'd sketch my van?'

'No, of course not. I was sketching on the bridge and then I remembered that you'd said you were staying at the campsite here.'

'So, you decided to look me up?'

'Well, yes… No… I just thought…'

'I'm flattered.' Although his face remained impassive, he sounded amused. 'Show me what you were sketching.'

Beth swallowed, her hand dropping to the flap of her canvas bag. She couldn't show him: there was nothing to see. 'It's not finished. I never show anyone my work until it's finished.'

She wondered if he would see through her lie.

'I see.' He stopped and looked around him. 'Now that you're here. Fancy a brew?'

'I don't mind.'

'You don't mind? That's a strange answer to a pretty straight-forward question. Either you do or you don't.'

Beth felt her cheeks redden. She was acting like a stupid child. She could just imagine Carina's face if she saw her now.

'Yes. Tea would be nice.'

'It might take a while for the kettle to boil. Are you in a hurry?'

'Not really.' When she'd got home from school, she'd found a note from her mum telling her she'd gone to visit a customer, and her dad was with a group on Scafell.

'What's your name then?' Unlocking the van, he slid the door open and reached inside, pulling out two folding chairs that had seen better days. He opened them and indicated for Beth to sit.

'Beth.'

The man nodded. 'Suits you.'

He still hadn't said what his own name was, and Beth was too shy to ask. He'd climbed into the back of the van and was busying himself with a kettle, stooping so that his head didn't bang the roof.

Beth stretched out her legs and looked across the field to the river. There was someone fishing and she wondered whether they'd caught anything.

'I was christened Darrius, but everyone knows me as David.'

She turned to look at him to see if he was joking, but his head was bent to the mug of tea he was stirring. 'Why?'

He looked up. 'Why what?'

'Why have you changed your name?'

He gave a bark of laughter. 'You're kidding me, right. Do you honestly mean to tell me you'd want to be called Darrius?'

'Well, obviously not. I'm a girl.' She paused. 'Why David?'

He put her tea in front of her. 'You'll laugh if I tell you.'

'I won't.'

'Let's just say I was a bit obsessed with Mr Bailey when I was younger.'

'Mr who?' As soon as she'd asked, she felt stupid. She should probably know.

'David Bailey. In my opinion, one of the best portrait photographers there's been in recent years. Nabbed himself some beautiful wives too – Marie Helvin for one. Lucky bugger.'

'So you named yourself after your boy-crush.' Beth put her hand in front of her mouth to hide her smile.

'Something like that. See. Told you you'd laugh.'

'I was just thinking. A few years ago, I had my room covered in Dali prints. Imagine if I'd called myself Salvador.'

'I dunno. I think it would rather suit you.'

Beth sipped her tea, trying not to stare at David's long slim fingers that were wrapped around his mug. It was nice to be having a conversation with someone other than her parents. Someone who wasn't constantly checking on whether she was doing her revision or obsessed with what she was eating.

'My art teacher wants to submit a piece of my work to a competition.' She hadn't planned to say it. It just slipped out.

David scratched his head and looked at her. 'That's a good thing, isn't it?'

'I suppose so.'

'You don't sound too sure.'

She didn't want to tell him how entering the competition would add more fuel to the fire. She could hear them now: *what a poser… she's so up herself… fucking show off.* And if she won… That was something she couldn't even begin to think about.

'I don't know if I'm good enough.'

'Bloody hell!' David leant over the arm of his deckchair and emptied the dregs of his tea onto the grass. 'How can you think that? It's a while since I've seen sketches as good as yours.'

'Really?'

'Why would I say it if it wasn't true?'

A picture of Keira came into her head. That was why. The hurt and the humiliation were still inside her.

'Hey, what's wrong?' There was a note of surprise in his voice.

Leaning over to her, he reached out a hand and touched her face. When he drew back his finger, it was wet. She hadn't realised she was crying. Feeling foolish, she wiped her face with the heel of her hand.

'It's nothing.'

'It doesn't look like nothing to me, but if you don't want to talk about it, that's up to you.' He got up and took her mug from her. 'That place you were telling me about when I met you up at the cairn. Where the kestrels nest.'

'The old quarry?'

'That's the one. I was thinking of going there to take some photographs. Fancy coming?'

The sun was getting low in the sky. Beth checked her watch. 'What, now?'

He laughed. 'No, of course not. I mean at the weekend. Unless you've got something better to do.'

'No,' she said quickly. 'No. I'm not doing anything.'

'Great, that's a plan then. Bertha and I will pick you up in the morning.'

'Bertha?'

David cocked his head towards the camper van. 'That's what I call her. I'll come by at eight.' He looked across at the row of miners' cottages. 'Which one is yours?'

'Don't worry,' Beth said quickly. 'I'll come here. Save you turning the van round.'

'Okay. Whatever. Look, it was nice to see you and all that, but I've got stuff I need to get done.' Picking up the mugs, he placed them on the floor of the van, then turned back to her. 'Are you feeling all right now? I hope it wasn't something I said. I have been known to put my size ten in it sometimes.'

'No, it wasn't you.' Beth got up and lifted her bag onto her shoulder. 'I was just being stupid.'

'Glad to hear it. It happens to us all at times.'

She smiled and thanked him for the tea, then made her way back across the field to the bridge. When she reached it, she stopped and looked back, wondering if he'd be watching her, but he wasn't – he'd gone inside the van, taking the chairs with him.

As she walked back along the road, she hummed a tune to herself. For the first time in a long while, she felt happy.

Across the road, Graham Hargreaves had put a sign outside the door of his shop, advertising local ice cream. Fancying some, Beth crossed the road and pushed open the door.

The man looked up from his paper. 'Fine afternoon.'

Beth smiled. 'It most definitely is.'

'What can I get you?'

'Just a small tub of vanilla ice cream, please.' She got some coins out of her pocket and placed them on the counter as Graham turned his back on her and rummaged in a small freezer compartment.

He slid it towards her, then rang it up on the till. 'How's your mum?'

'My mum? She's fine.'

'That's good.' He handed her the receipt. 'Gave me a bit of a scare, though, the other day.'

Beth felt a shiver of concern. 'Why? What happened?'

'Didn't she say? Probably didn't want to worry you. She had a bit of a turn, is the best way to describe it. Looked as if she'd seen a ghost. Face as white as a sheet and pulse through the roof. I wanted to drive her home but she wouldn't hear of it.'

'Oh.' Beth frowned. Her mum hadn't said anything.

'Anyway,' Graham continued. 'Glad to hear she's all right now.'

He went back to his paper and Beth let herself out, the doorbell tinkling as she pulled it open. Why hadn't her mum said something? Had she not wanted her to know? There was a time when they would have told each other everything.

She desperately wanted to talk to someone but there was no one to tell – except her dad, and she didn't want to worry him. Maybe if her mum had encouraged her to make friends when she was younger, she'd now be on the phone to one of them, telling them what Graham had said. She'd listen to their words of sympathy then, between them, they'd work out what she should do.

With a jolt, she realised the only person she wanted to tell was David, but what would she say? *My mum's going crazy and I'm scared?*

Stripping off the cardboard lid and throwing it in the bin, she dipped the little plastic paddle into the ice cream, realising, as she did, that she was no longer hungry.

CHAPTER ELEVEN
Leona

It doesn't look like a consultation room. It looks like someone's living room. There's a curved settee in a neutral beige material and a matching armchair. The walls are neutral too, with tasteful abstract prints, and on a low table by the window the thick green leaves of an aspidistra plant contrast nicely with the floaty, white curtain at the window.

I've been sitting here for ten minutes and, so far, we've done nothing but exchange pleasantries. How long it's taken me to drive here. How beautiful the countryside is looking with the bluebells out.

While we've been talking, Lisa Manning has been sitting back in her chair, her neat ankles crossed. Now, she leans forward a little.

'Why don't you tell me what made you come to see me today, Leona? Or would you prefer me to call you Leo?'

Ria's voice is in my head. *Get out of my house, Leo. I never want to see you again.*

'No,' I say quickly. 'Nobody calls me that.'

It's peaceful in this room with its tall windows. One of them is open a little and a breeze shivers the curtains. Her question has taken me by surprise; for a moment, I'd forgotten the reason why I'm sitting here.

I look at her and notice how, behind her glasses, her eyes are an unusual shade of green. I'd been expecting someone older, with iron-grey hair in a bob, or maybe even a man. Not this slip of a girl whose light brown hair is pulled back from her face and caught behind her head with a tortoiseshell clasp.

She smiles at me and it's a nice smile. It reaches her eyes and I feel myself responding.

'I'm not coping. I thought I was, but I'm not.'

She nods and looks down at her notes. I wonder what she's thinking, how much is written there.

'I'm here to help you. You don't have to be on your own through this.'

'I'm not on my own. I have Scott and Beth.'

'I know that, of course you have. It's just that sometimes, in situations like this, you need more support than your family can give you.' A strand of hair slips loose and, as she pushes it back into the clasp, I notice the shine of her clear nail polish. 'Why have you never come before? It's been what... twelve years?'

I think about this, remembering the early days. It had been hard, but I'd got through it. Everyone said I should forget her, forget Ria. That looking back would only cause me more pain. I'd done what they'd said and, in time, she'd become just a memory. A phantom who sometimes haunted my dreams.

'I've started to see her.'

'Who do you see?'

The fabric of the settee has a faint check on it. I run my finger over it, counting the squares.

'Who, Leona? Take your time.'

Tucking my hands under my legs, I look up at her. 'Ria. That's who I see.'

She picks up a pen from the glass table between us and makes a note on the pad she has in front of her.

'And how does it make you feel when you see her?'

'Scared. I'm scared she's coming back.'

'She can't come back, Leona. You know that's not possible.'

'I know she can't.' A well of sadness opens up within me. 'But despite what she did, I miss her.'

I'm trying to hold myself together but it's too exhausting. Instead, I drop my head into my hands and let the tears fall.

Lisa says nothing, just pulls a tissue from the box on the table and hands it to me. I blow my nose and push the tissue up my sleeve. 'I'm sorry.'

'There's nothing to be sorry about.'

'I've been wasting your time. I know there's nothing you can do to help me.'

Lisa looks at her notebook. 'You say you've been having panic attacks. Do they happen often?'

'I've had them in the past but now they're getting more frequent.'

I remember the panic I'd felt in Graham Hargreaves' shop and the overwhelming fear I'd had when I'd woken that night.

'Usually they happen in the daytime but sometimes they wake me up.'

'Can you describe them to me?'

I watch the curtains flutter. 'I feel a terror I can't explain. My chest is tight and I sometimes find it hard to breathe. I feel as if I'm about to die.'

Lisa slides the clip of her pen into her notebook to mark the page, then closes it and places it on the coffee table. 'During a panic attack, a lot of adrenaline is coursing through your body and it's this that is causing the physical and mental responses. But it's important to remember that feelings can't hurt us… not physically, anyway. You might feel like you're going to die when the attack happens, but the fact you're sitting here with me is proof that you didn't. Around sixty percent of people with a panic disorder experience at least one attack at night – a time when darkness can make you feel more vulnerable.'

I think of how claustrophobic the velvet darkness seems and how desperate I am to turn on a light. 'But when I get them, I haven't been dreaming.'

'A panic attack at night is pretty much the same as in the daytime. The only difference is, it happens in a less conscious manner. We forget that our subconscious is still active when we're asleep. These attacks have been found to occur during non-REM sleep and are not always a direct response to a dream.'

A fly is buzzing around the room. It lands on the arm of the settee and I feel a desire to squash it with my fist. I don't though, just flick it away.

'Why is this happening to me now?'

Lisa levels her cool green gaze at me. 'Rather than concern yourself with why it happens, I think we should concentrate on how you will respond the next time it does. It's important not to fight against it, but to work with it. I'll show you some breathing exercises you can do which will help and, if it happens at night, don't try and go back to sleep, do some ironing or read a book until the anxiety goes. Most importantly though, when you feel an attack coming on, you must try to remember that there's nothing life-threatening causing these symptoms.'

I stare at her. 'But what if there is? What if I'm in danger?'

I expect her to react, but she doesn't. Her voice is as calm and level as it was before.

'There's no danger, Leona.' Picking up her notebook again, she opens it and turns back a few pages, reading what's written there. 'I think that it would be beneficial to you to look back to when it all happened.'

My heart clenches. 'No! I can't do that.'

'I know it's hard, but until you confront your feelings and make peace with the past, you won't be able to deal with the present.'

'But I've been all right for years.'

'The subconscious is good at burying bad memories. Locking them up until, one day, something happens to turn the key and release them. Have you ever told Scott?'

'I can't. You know I can't.'

'When something traumatic has happened in the past, it's sometimes difficult to keep it from our loved ones… Even when we know we should.'

'I haven't told him.'

She steeples her fingers under her chin. 'And if you did, what do you think he would say?'

My stomach churns. I've asked myself this question a million times. 'I don't know.'

There's a vase of lilies on a polished wooden console behind me. Every now and again I catch their sweet, cloying scent. Lisa is speaking again. She's asking me to tell her about Ria. From the beginning. So that, together, we can work out what it is that makes me afraid. I wonder if I can do it.

Lisa gets up and stands by the window. She parts the white curtain and looks out. When she looks back at me, her eyes are serious.

'I know it's Ria's story, but I think it's *you* who should tell it.'

CHAPTER TWELVE

Ria

Ria leant across the table and took a strand of her friend's long fair hair between her finger and thumb.

'How is it you have such gorgeous hair when, however long I've spent on it, mine looks like a haystack?'

Leo pulled a face. 'What? The "just got out of bed" look? I'd give my right arm for hair like that. Men can't get enough of it in my experience and, if I'm not mistaken, there's one over by the bar who wouldn't mind getting his fingers tangled up in yours right this minute.'

'What do you mean?'

'His face has *I'd like to take you home with me* written all over it.'

'Stop it. You're embarrassing me.'

It was nearly seven and the bar was filling up with people on their way home from work: men in tailored suits and women in grey knee-length pencil skirts and high-heeled shoes, their voices loud and confident, their make-up just so.

Looking down at her jeans and T-shirt, Ria felt out of place. Usually, she and Leo spent their evenings in the student union bar or in the pub at the end of their road, but tonight she was working. Well, maybe not working as such, as it was only a trial. She would have to wait until after she did her set later in the evening for the manager to make a decision. If he liked what he heard, and liked what he saw in the till at the end of the evening, he'd said she could have a regular Thursday evening spot. This would be for cash, not just free drinks.

She could certainly do with it; even after buying most of her food from the value range at Tesco, and limiting her alcohol consumption to weekends, her money was never going to stretch to the end of term. It never did, but this year she'd vowed not to turn to her parents for another handout.

'Well, what do you think?' Leo said, nudging her.

'About what?'

'About him? Over there at the bar… The one who's staring at you.'

Trying not to make it obvious, Ria looked over her shoulder. There were several people at the sleek black counter, but it was clear straight away which one Leo was talking about. The man was perched on the edge of his stool, one shiny black shoe resting on the rail, and he was looking their way.

He was quite a contrast to the guys on her business studies course with their wine-coloured skinny jeans and emo haircuts. Like most of the other customers, his suit trousers looked expensive, and he'd taken off his jacket to reveal a white shirt with a faint blue stripe that fitted the contours of his body. His sandy hair was neither long nor short but combed back from his face, and his chin was showing just a hint of five o'clock shadow.

Scared he had seen her looking, she turned back quickly. 'Actually, I would have thought he was more your type.'

Leo sat back and took a sip of her wine. 'God no. Far too metrosexual for me. Anyway, I'm happy with Adam. I couldn't cope with two men.'

Ria laughed. 'That's not what I heard.'

Dodging Leo's punch to the arm, Ria drained her glass. It probably wasn't a good idea to drink before she performed but, with any luck, it would calm her nerves.

With elbows propped on the table, she rested her forehead on the heels of her hands and tried to concentrate on the songs she would be singing later. As she ran the words through her head, she could still feel the man's eyes on her.

'Is he still looking?'

'So, you *are* interested.'

'I didn't say that. I just don't like being stared at.'

The chair scraped as Leo moved it a little to see past her. 'He sure is. I wonder what he does?'

'It could be anything. There are a million different offices in this area of London. I reckon he looks like a lawyer.'

'My guess is marketing or advertising. In fact, he looks like he should be in an advert himself. He's got that David Beckham sort of look. Bet he'd rock a sarong.'

'Shush… He'll hear you.'

'What, with this racket? And, in any case, he's on the other side of the room.'

It was true. Loud chart music was playing through the speakers on the walls. It was hard enough to hear what Leo was saying, let alone anyone else.

'If this is the sort of music the customers like, my stuff's going to go down like a lead balloon. God, what was I thinking of? This really wasn't a good idea.'

Catching her hand, Leo gave it a squeeze. 'They'll love you. How could they not? Anyway, I have a feeling that you could play the bagpipes today and you'd still have one admirer.'

'Still looking?'

Leo smiled in amusement. 'Yup. Still looking. Oh, wait a minute, I think he might be leaving.'

Ria felt a stab of disappointment. 'I'll have to save the bagpipes for another day then.'

'Looks like it… Oh, no, wait a minute. He's not leaving, he's just going to the gents. Fancy another drink? I could follow him if you like.'

Ria raised her eyes in mock horror. 'Not unless you want to get yourself arrested!'

'Spoil sport. I always fancied myself as a sleuth. Anyway, what was your answer to the drink question?'

Their glasses were both empty but Ria shook her head. 'I'd better not. I'd get the words all muddled or play the wrong chords.'

'As if that's going to happen. I've heard you play enough times to know you could do it in your sleep.'

'Anyway, I've got no money.' Leaning back in her chair, Ria tried to relax, letting one song, then another, wash over her. It was only when Leo shook her arm that she came back to the present.

'Look,' Leo hissed.

Ria turned to see one of the girls from behind the bar weaving through the crowd with a bottle of white wine in her hand. When she reached them, she placed it on the table and looked back over her shoulder.

'It's from that guy over there.'

He was standing now, side on to the bar, his elbow resting on the shiny bar top. Slowly, he raised his glass and, as her eyes met his, he smiled.

'Lucky you,' the girl said, wiping her hands on her black apron. 'He's been in three times this week and half the girls who work here fancy him.'

Ria felt herself colour. She glanced at Leo. 'It might not be me he's interested in.'

'Oh, it's you all right,' the girl said, 'and, if you ask me, you might have hit the jackpot with that one. He's done pretty well for himself from what I've heard.'

With a chuckle, she picked up a couple of empty glasses from the table next to them, then walked away, pausing to say a few words to the man before lifting the flap and going back behind the bar.

Leo picked up the bottle and poured them both another drink. 'You'll be on in a minute. With this inside you, you won't care whether they cheer or boo.'

'Don't say that!'

'I'm only kidding, Ria. You'll be great. You just need to show them what a proper song sounds like.'

There was a small raised area in the corner of the room that, from the look of the small screen attached to the wall, was used for karaoke. As the music quietened, and the bar manager nodded at her, Ria felt the butterflies that had been in her stomach all afternoon multiply. Tipping her glass, she swallowed a large mouthful of wine, then stood up. Her guitar was leaning against the wall. Picking it up, she walked over to the makeshift stage and placed the strap over her neck before plugging it into the small amplifier and adjusting the microphone to the right height.

'Can you hear me all right?' Her voice sounded unnatural. Unlike her own.

If she'd been hoping for a lull in the conversation, she was wrong. One or two people turned towards her, but most carried on talking. Unsure of what to do, Ria strummed a chord and then another. Taking a deep breath, she tried to imagine she was in the bedroom of her flat, sitting cross-legged on the bed, playing only for herself. It seemed to work and, as her body and mind responded to the music, she started to relax.

Moving closer to the microphone, Ria began to sing a number by Dido. It was one of her favourites and she knew it suited her voice. As the words fell from her lips, she found she was no longer nervous. Not caring whether or not anyone was paying her attention, she closed her eyes and let the music take her. She was singing for herself and for Leo who, since the day they'd enrolled at university, had been her best friend and confidant.

But, as she opened her eyes again, she realised that there was someone else she was hoping to impress. It was impossible not to look across at the bar to see if he was watching. Her eyes scanned the men who stood there but, to her disappointment, he was no longer there.

Her voice faltered, but then she saw him. He had moved closer and was leaning against the wall to her right, a glass of beer in his hand, and the sight of him made her heart lurch. What was the matter with her? This time he wasn't looking at her, but at the floor, as though concentrating on the words.

The bar was quieter now and more people were looking her way. Some of the women were mouthing the words along with her and Ria felt her lips curve into a smile. As she did, the man lifted his head and their eyes met. He didn't return her smile, but neither did he look away. It was as if an understanding had passed between them and, in those few seconds, Ria knew that her life was about to change.

CHAPTER THIRTEEN

Beth

'You're up early?'

Beth stopped with her hand on the door handle as her father's voice floated out from the kitchen. She'd been hoping to leave the house without anyone making a fuss, but she'd forgotten he'd said he'd be making an early start that morning.

'I'm going walking… with some friends.'

Her dad appeared in the doorway, his thick hair awry and his long-sleeved T-shirt untucked from his walking trousers. 'Blimey. Didn't know teenagers understood the meaning of the word "morning". Does your mum know you're going out today?'

'Sort of.' She'd made a half-hearted attempt at telling her the previous evening, but she hadn't seemed to be listening. What her mum had been doing all afternoon Beth had no idea but, when she'd come home, she'd been even more preoccupied than usual and had taken herself off to her workshop, only coming out when Beth's dad had called her in for supper.

'And she's okay with it?'

'Why wouldn't she be?'

'Because she likes to know where you are. You know that. The fells can be dangerous if you aren't careful.'

Beth felt impatience brewing inside her. 'For goodness sake, Dad. I'm not stupid.'

He'd gone back into the kitchen and she could hear him scraping butter onto toast. '*I* know you're not and *you* know you're not, but your mother's a worrier. It's easier to indulge her. Tell me where you're headed today and I'll leave her a note or, better still, do it yourself – there's a pen and paper on the table by the window.'

Checking the time on her phone, Beth went over to the table. Grabbing the pad of paper, she scrawled: *Mum, I've gone to Grasmere with Carina and some others. Back for dinner.* At the mention of the girl's name, Beth felt her teeth clench, but she knew that if she told her Dad it was Carina she was meeting, it would keep him happy. Carina's dad was the owner of the walking company he worked for and it was easier for everyone if Beth let him believe the two of them were friends. Her mum probably wouldn't see the note until much later. Recently, she'd not even been up before Beth had gone to school. Had just called goodbye to her from her bedroom, her voice gravelly with sleep.

'And keep your phone on just in case she needs to get hold of you. Is it Carina you're going with?'

'Yes, and some others.'

'Great. Well, have a good day. You can tell me about it when I get home. It's Great Crag and Grange Fell for me today with a stag party. Wish me luck!'

Beth laughed. 'You'll need it.'

She let herself out of the house and ran down the lane. It looked like it was going to be a beautiful morning. The day had broken with a fragile beauty – the sun rising in a pale blue sky, small wisps of cloud feathering high above the peaks. David had said for her to be at the campsite at eight and she was going to be late.

Unlatching the kissing gate, Beth let herself into the first field, then ran along the stony track to the footbridge. From here she could see the camper van, but she couldn't see David. It was only as she walked through the field towards it that she saw him. He was sitting in the driver's seat, a map spread out on the dashboard. When he saw her, he smiled, his eyes crinkling. He wound down the window.

'Morning.'

Beth was out of breath from hurrying. 'Sorry I'm late. My dad wouldn't stop talking, then he made me write a note to my mum to say where I'd be.'

He raised his eyebrows. 'Did he now? Well, anyway, you're here now.'

Feeling stupid, Beth dropped her rucksack onto the ground by her feet. Why did she have to go and say that? Now he would really think she was just a silly kid.

'What does your dad do?'

The question surprised her. 'He takes groups out walking on the fells. Tourists mostly.'

David looked interested. 'Great job. Wouldn't mind doing that myself. He must know the Lake District like the back of his hand.'

'He does. There aren't many parts he hasn't been to, and he's walked all the major peaks. Mum says Wainwright should be his middle name, but we gave it to the cat instead.'

'There's nothing like earning money from doing something you love. I should know.' Leaning across the passenger seat, he opened the door, then turned back to her. 'Getting in then?'

Beth walked round to the other side of the camper and climbed in. She had expected it to be untidy inside, clothes and camera equipment strewn everywhere, but when she looked behind her, everything was neatly stowed away. It smelt of warm leather and a faint citrus smell that, as David leant across to help with her seat belt, she realised was coming from his skin.

His face was close to hers. 'The belts in Bertha are old and knackered. If you don't tug them just right, they refuse to budge.'

His nearness made her heart beat a little faster. Apart from her dad, she was rarely in close proximity to a man. She sat on her hands, ignoring the impulse to reach out and touch his cheek.

'Poor old girl,' he continued. 'She may not be all that pretty, but she serves me well, so to speak.'

Unsure of what to say, Beth decided to say nothing. She watched him struggle to get into reverse.

'I may have to take back that last comment,' he said, his smile wry. 'You'd better not let me down today or it will be the scrap heap for you next week.'

Beth laughed. 'Poor Bertha.'

David reversed the camper van onto the track, the stones crunching under the wheels, and they headed for the gate at the far end of the field. When they reached it, Beth jumped out. She opened the gate wide enough for the van to pass through, then hopped back in, holding her breath as David leant over her, yanking the temperamental seat belt to free it.

'Damn belt,' he muttered, as he sat back and touched his foot to the accelerator. The van rattled as they passed over the cattle grid that separated the campsite from the main road. 'So, do you want to give me directions or are you happy for me to follow my nose?'

Beth turned towards him. She'd only ever walked to the quarry from the bus stop and, as she didn't drive, she realised she had no idea how to get there.

'I… I'm not sure of the way.'

'Don't look so worried.' David swung a right, the hedgerow brushing the side of the van. 'I looked it up on the map before you arrived.'

Beth looked away. Was he making fun of her? She really hoped he wasn't.

'I also read up about it,' he continued. 'The mine was worked from the nineteenth century until the early 1960s. I thought it might be popular with divers or climbers now, like some of the other disused slate quarries, but apparently, the whole place is too unstable. A couple of divers have lost their lives there.'

'I didn't know that. Maybe you shouldn't have told me.' Beth shivered, thinking of the makeshift slate bench, high above the circle of dark water, where she liked to sit and draw. The water that had taken those lives. 'What I like is how peaceful it is there. I hardly see anyone.'

'That's how I like it too,' he said, with a smile.

Unlike her mum's Mini, the seats in the camper van were high up, giving her a better view, and Beth found she was enjoying their drive through the countryside. David had turned onto a road signed for Coniston. It wound between fields of Herdwick sheep, their white heads contrasting with their grey bodies. One day, she should draw them.

'Have you brought your sketchbook?' David asked.

She nodded. 'I hardly ever go anywhere without it. What about you? Got your camera stuff?'

'Camera stuff? I'll have you know, my *equipment* is worth several grand.'

'Really?'

'Yes, really. You forget, this is my job. You don't get your photographs accepted in *British Wildlife* magazine using a disposable camera from the supermarket.'

'Oh, I don't know. I seem to remember taking a rather good photo of my mum's ear with one when we lived in Carlisle.'

'You lived in Carlisle?'

'Not for long. Just a couple of years.'

'Did you like it there?'

'I don't remember much about it as I was only little, but I don't think so, no... apart from the castle. I remember Mum taking me there once on my birthday. I liked the pictures that had been carved into the stone walls of the keep: knights and mermaids and animals. They were original fifteenth-century graffiti and I made my mum wait while I tried to copy them on the back of the guidebook with a crayon.'

She didn't tell him how her mum had hovered over her, giving the evils to anyone who looked like they just might come over to compliment her on her drawing. Or how she'd dragged Beth away before she'd finished.

'So, you were interested in sketching even then.'

Beth smiled. 'I suppose I must have been.'

David pulled the camper off the road into a lay-by. 'If you're up for it, I'd like to walk from here. It will give me a better idea of the geography of the place. I like to put my pictures into context.'

'I don't mind.' She'd put on her walking boots and trousers that morning just in case.

'Just let me get my stuff.' Walking round to the side of the camper, David unlocked the door and slid it open. Under one of the seats was a drop-down locker. Reaching inside, he brought out his camera bag. He unzipped it, checking the contents to make sure he had everything he needed.

Beth undid her seat belt and jumped down. 'Do you want me to carry anything?'

David shook his head, hoisting the bag onto his shoulder. 'No, you're all right... Me Tarzan!'

He sprang away from her, beating his chest, and Beth couldn't help but laugh. 'You're completely mad!'

'You haven't seen me when it's a full moon yet.'

Checking his phone for directions, David crossed over the road and walked along its edge until he came to a fingerpost, Beth trailing behind. 'It's this way.' He climbed over the stile and waited for Beth to join him, then together they followed the footpath up the hill towards a farm.

Beth checked the time. It was nearly nine and, although sunny, the air was fresh. She pulled at the zip of her fleece, glad she'd decided to wear it. On reaching the farm, they walked between the house and the barns, petting a dog that had run out to meet them, before turning right onto a trackway signposted to Temple Quarry.

The path rose again steeply, and Beth was surprised and pleased when David offered her his hand. But as soon as the ground levelled out again, he let it go and she couldn't help the rush of disappointment she felt.

'Nearly there.'

The track passed through a gateway into an area of woodland and then continued on until the trees opened up to reveal a wide-open space.

'Bloody hell.' David stood with his hands on his hips, staring out at the scene. In front of them was a massive excavation of light-green coloured slate, sheer-sided and unfenced. Like bands of green abseilers, small firs clung precariously to the ledges and fissures in the rock face.

'It's amazing, isn't it?' Beth moved closer to him, keen to share her love for the place.

'How deep do you think that drop is?' He stared down at the dark green water of the flooded workings. 'One hundred… one hundred and fifty feet?'

Beth watched him, enjoying the way his eyes widened in wonder. Proud that it was she who had told him about this place. Knowing he wouldn't be here now if it hadn't been for her.

David took a step closer to the edge. 'I can see two openings down there. Any idea how to get to them?'

'I've heard my dad say you can reach them from the lower road, but I've only ever been to the top of the quarry.' She looked around at the slate spoil heaps.

'There's got to be a path leading down somewhere. I'd like to take a look. Want to come? I've got a torch.'

'I'm not sure.' It was only now, as she looked into the depths of the quarry, that a thought came to her. She was here, on her own in the middle of nowhere, with someone she hardly knew. A cloud passed over the sun, turning the lake below a darker green. Did she want to go down there? It felt safer up here, watching the shadows move across the patchwork fields below and listening to the shiver of the newly unfurled leaves of the silver birches that circled the rim of the quarry.

'Stay here if you prefer.'

She pushed away her unease. 'No, I'll come.'

There was a sign over to their right and, further on, Beth could make out a faint path through the undergrowth. 'I think that might be the way down.'

David parted the branches that threatened to choke it. 'I think you're right. Doesn't look like it's been used for a while.'

Beth joined him and looked at the sign. Its message was clear.

DANGER!
Steep unfenced rock faces and deep water
Strictly NO abseiling, climbing or diving

'Is it safe?'

'I'm not proposing taking up extreme sports, though I have to say diving quite takes my fancy. We're just going to take a look in some of the tunnels. I might get some interesting shots.'

'All right.'

David pushed his way through the tangle of branches and Beth followed. The path ahead looked impossibly steep. It descended through the trees for a way, then opened out again to run beside the gaping chasm, its bare edge formed of starkly defined and naked rock.

Not wanting David to see how scared she was, Beth made herself go on, making sure her eyes were on the path ahead, not on the sheer-sided quarry walls. When they'd almost reached the bottom, their path joined with another. Although she couldn't see it, she could hear a car.

David laughed. 'This must be the path that comes in from the Langdon road. It would have been a much easier way to get here!'

In front of them was a red and white striped barrier. It blocked the entrance to the wide mouth of a cave.

David stood for a moment looking at it, then ducked underneath.

'What are you doing?'

'What does it look like? I'm going to see what's happening inside this bad boy. You don't have to come.'

'Yes... yes, I will.' Beth ducked under the barrier. The last thing she wanted was to look like a coward.

The ceiling of the cave was high, the floor covered with loose slate. David switched on his torch and at once the striated rocks came to life. With the light to guide them, they made their way across the shifting, uneven surface towards the back of the cave where there was a smaller tunnel.

Squatting down, David directed the beam of light at the narrow opening. 'There's light at the end of the tunnel, so to speak. Come on.'

They had to bend almost double and, as they made their way slowly down the tunnel, the torch lighting their way, Beth could see that the slate under their feet had become shiny with water.

David turned back to her. 'Be careful you don't slip. I don't fancy carrying you back up that hill.'

The small circle of light that Beth had seen when she entered the tunnel was now much larger. They were nearing its end. David switched off the torch.

'Almost there.'

Beth shivered. It was cold in the tunnel and she couldn't wait to get back into the sunshine.

As they stepped out of the darkness into the daylight, David gave a low whistle and, as she joined him, Beth saw why. They were standing at the bottom of a chasm, vertical walls of slate rising up on all sides from a deep, green pool of water, jagged rockfalls reflected in its mirrored surface.

Tipping back her head, she could just see the quarry top, with its overhanging trees, where they had been standing earlier. It was hard to believe that they had climbed down so far. Sunlight shimmered on the water and it felt as though they were a million miles from anywhere.

'It's beautiful.'

David took a step forward. 'Haunting is the word I'd use. That water is thirty-two metres deep. It's where the mineshaft flooded. There are other tunnels that can only be reached from under the water.'

Crouching, he unzipped his bag and pulled out a tripod. Taking each of its carbon legs in turn, he extended them until they were the right length, then placed the tripod onto a flat slate slab at the edge of the water. When he was happy with its position, he fixed his camera onto it.

'Why is it so low?' Beth asked.

David sat on his haunches and squinted at the camera. 'Good reflection shots need to be taken as close to the water as possible.'

Adjusting the lens, he took a series of shots and Beth watched the muscles of his back work beneath his T-shirt, wondering what they would feel like under her hand.

'Yodel-oh-ee-dee!'

David's voice sounded strange, enclosed as they were by the echoing rock face, and Beth hugged herself. Looking back towards the tunnel, she realised that, despite the eerie allure of the water, she wanted to be out of the place.

It was as if David sensed how she felt. Maybe it was her face that had given her away. Whatever it was, he straightened, unclipped the camera from its stand and put it back inside his bag.

'You know, I've changed my mind,' he said. 'This place gives me the creeps.'

CHAPTER FOURTEEN

Leona

'How have you been since I saw you yesterday, Leona?'

Lisa Manning smiles encouragingly. Today, she's wearing a sheer floral blouse with a navy camisole underneath. Her slim legs are encased in black linen trousers.

'I've been all right, but I'm glad you were able to see me again today.'

'Just all right?'

I take Beth's note from my back pocket. 'I found this, this morning. It's from my daughter.' Reaching over, I hand it to Lisa.

She looks at it, then back at me. 'It's good, isn't it?'

'I don't like her taking herself off to God knows where.'

Lisa smiles. 'I think you might be overreacting a little, Leona. Beth says she's gone to Grasmere. Besides, she's not alone. She's with friends.'

I rub the side of my neck, willing her to understand. 'Beth is sensitive. She finds it hard to interact with others. She's found making friends difficult.'

'Do you think that it's all of her own making?'

'What do you mean?' I feel myself bristle.

'I just meant that, after everything that's gone before with Ria, it would be natural for you to want to keep her… well… close to you.'

How much easier it had been when Beth was younger. When it was just her and me. When I could make those decisions for her. Now she's growing into a young woman, I see how much she wants the company of others, not just mine.

Lisa hands me back the note. 'What about this Carina?'

'I don't know. Scott works for her father, but I've never thought Beth was very keen on her.'

'We can't always see what's inside our children's heads, Leona. Probably just as well too. Your daughter's a young adult. I think you should be happy that she's spreading her wings a bit.'

She leans back in her chair and laces her fingers together, a gesture I've come to recognise as one that heralds a change of subject. 'What about the panic attacks? Have you had any since I saw you yesterday?'

I reach into my bag for my notebook and open the cover. I've decided to do what Lisa suggested: log each attack and note down what I was doing prior to it. 'I had one last night. I woke up at three thirty feeling as though my heart might pound its way out of my chest.'

Lisa makes a note on her pad. 'Can you think of anything you did that might have made you anxious?'

Today the window is closed, the gauzy curtain not moving. The room feels a little warm. 'No, nothing. Apart from coming here, of course, but I'd actually felt quite relaxed once I'd got home after our session.'

'And Scott and Beth – how are they?'

I frown. 'They're fine. Why?'

'It's just that sometimes the anxieties of loved ones can be passed on without them realising it. If something is bothering either of them, it might make your own anxiety worse.'

I think of Beth. Last night she'd seemed happier. Helping me make the supper and teasing Scott like she used to. Their relationship is a good one and it warms my heart to see the two of them together, messing about like a couple of kids.

'They're both good,' I say, still guilty that it was Scott who noticed that Beth has not been herself recently. At least she seems happier now. I don't tell Lisa that sometimes I catch Beth looking at me and I'm sure it's worry I see in her eyes.

'Just remember, Leona, I'm here as a sounding block for you. You can talk to me about anything that's concerning you, even indirectly. The fact that you've started to struggle after so many years of calm is unusual but not unheard of.'

'But my fears are so irrational. It's hard to explain them.'

'Although you can't put your fears into words, after what you've experienced, any worries you have are not irrational. In fact, they are perfectly understandable. Did you find it useful to talk about it yesterday?'

'About Ria?'

'Yes.' Lisa's gaze is steady. Her voice calm.

I look down at my hands. 'I think it helped, yes. I appreciate the time you've given me. If it was just a regular counselling session, I know I wouldn't be able to see you this often.'

'It's why I'm here. It's good you're finding it helpful.' Lisa smiles and settles herself in her seat. 'Maybe we should continue.'

CHAPTER FIFTEEN
Ria

Ria opened her eyes and tried to remember where she was. There was a gap in the grey striped curtains and a shaft of morning sunlight fell across the matching duvet cover. This wasn't her flat. Moving her arm tentatively beneath the covers, she was relieved to find that she was alone in the bed. It would give her a moment or two to sort out her thoughts.

As she stared at the black and white prints on the wall and the mirrored wardrobe that spanned the entire width of the room, it all started to come back. The cheering of the punters as she'd finished her set and taken a bow, the feel of the man's hand on her wrist as she'd walked past him. The compliments he had paid her and how good it had made her feel.

She'd invited him back to their table and the three of them had finished the bottle of wine he'd bought earlier, and started on another. His name was Gareth and he worked as a broker in one of the tall glass and steel buildings in Liverpool Street. He'd been charming and attentive, asking her questions about her singing and her studies while, all the time, taking care not to make Leo feel excluded. The squeeze of her best friend's fingers under the table signalled approval, and when the apology came – *Sorry, Ria. I've got to go. I've a nine o'clock lecture tomorrow and I'm bushed* – Ria's eyes relayed her thanks.

It had been almost inevitable that she would go back with him, despite her self-imposed rule not to have sex on a first date. Ria stretched her arms out above her head, remembering the way they'd fallen through the door, impatient to take off each other's clothes. Not waiting until they had got to the bedroom but finding the leather settee instead. She blushed at the thought of what they'd done. How abandoned she'd been. When she got back, Leo would be expecting a blow-by-blow account of what had gone on, and she would have to give an edited version.

A clearing of the throat brought Ria back to the present. Gareth was standing in the doorway in his boxer shorts, a tray in his hands. At the sight of his smooth bare chest, she swallowed, remembering what it had felt like against her lips.

He smiled at her. 'I thought you might like some breakfast.'

'Thank you, I'm ravenous.'

'I'm not surprised,' he said, and Ria felt her cheeks redden further.

Walking to the bed, Gareth placed the tray on the grey striped cover. 'I've made you some porridge, and there's some toast and jam. Hope you like coffee.'

'Coffee's good, thanks.' She pulled herself up, tucking the duvet under her arms, ashamed of her nakedness.

'A bit late for shyness, don't you think?' Sitting on the edge of the bed, he pinched the cover between finger and thumb and pulled it down. 'I don't think you realise how beautiful you are?'

He ran a finger down her breast and she shivered, finding the tattoo that curled around his wrist unsettling, but before she could say anything, he'd pulled the cover back up again and put the tray on her lap.

She stared at it. There was just one cup and one bowl. 'Aren't you having anything?'

'I ate earlier. I'm not one for lying in.'

Going to the mirrored wardrobe, Gareth slid it open and took out a pair of jogging bottoms from a hanger. He pulled them on over his boxers, then selected a light blue T-shirt from one of the shelves. 'I'm going out for a run. You enjoy your breakfast.'

Pushing his feet into some running shoes, he kissed her on the forehead and made for the door.

'But I…'

It was too late; he'd left the room and she could hear his footsteps in the narrow hallway. When she heard the front door close, Ria put the tray to one side, then pushed back the covers and walked to the window. Parting the curtains just enough so she could see through them but not be seen herself, she watched him as he stood at the edge of the road waiting for a break in the traffic. She waited, wondering if he would look back, but he didn't – just jogged across the road, then turned right along the street. When he'd disappeared from view, she dropped the curtain.

Unsure what to do next, she got back into bed and pulled the tray onto her lap. She took a mouthful of porridge. It was thick and creamy, exactly as she liked it. The coffee was good too, freshly ground, not instant from a jar as she was used to. When she had finished the porridge, she spread her toast with butter and jam from the little china pot Gareth had placed on the tray, intending to only have a few bites. It was so delicious though that, before she knew it, she'd finished it.

Wiping her mouth on the neatly folded serviette, she lay back against the pillows and closed her eyes. *I could get used to this.* She couldn't wait to tell Leo, already committing the items on the breakfast tray to memory like the game she and her parents used to play at Christmas. Deciding to send a text, Ria scanned the bedroom, wondering what she'd done with her bag. She couldn't see it, or her clothes either. She must have left them in the living room. Trying to remember coming to bed, she found she couldn't. She must have been more drunk than she'd thought.

Not wanting to walk around his apartment naked, Ria went to the wardrobe and slid it open. The clothes that hung there were stylish, grouped according to their colour. Reaching in a hand, she slipped a mint green shirt off its hanger. That would do.

As she did up the buttons, she studied herself in the mirrored doors, enjoying the feel of the crisp cotton against her bare skin. The colour suited her, the dark hair that fell across her shoulders contrasting with the pale material. Her legs were tanned from a cheap Greek holiday she'd had with Leo, and she felt happy with her reflection.

Walking back to the bed, Ria picked up the tray. She was about to carry it to the kitchen when she heard the front door open. She froze, aware of the push of her breasts against the shirt, realising she'd never thought to ask if anyone else lived in the apartment. What if Gareth had a flatmate?

There was the sound of keys being thrown onto the table and then footsteps on the wooden flooring of the hallway. Scared she might be seen, Ria remained where she was, the coffee cup rattling softly on its saucer. Whoever it was, was coming towards the bedroom.

She held her breath, then let it out again in relief as Gareth appeared in the doorway.

'So, you decided to get up then.' It was a statement rather than a question.

'Christ, Gareth, for a horrible moment I thought you had a lodger you'd forgotten to tell me about. You weren't gone long.'

His grey eyes considered her. 'Long enough for you to go snooping.'

Unsure of whether he was joking or not, she looked down at the shirt she'd put on. 'I'm sorry, I couldn't find my clothes. I didn't want to walk around without anything on. I didn't think you'd mind.'

A smile hovered over his lips and Ria closed her eyes in relief. Taking a step towards her, he leant forward and kissed the tip of her nose. 'Of course I don't mind. I was only kidding.'

When he reached out his hands, she thought he was going to take the tray from her, but he didn't. Instead, he gripped the bottom of the shirt and drew it up until it was bunched around her hips. He looked down and, with the tray in her hands, there was little she could do about it. It felt strange to be so exposed but also exciting.

'Stay here with me today,' he said, slipping his arms around her, his hands resting on the curve of her back, his fingertips grazing her buttocks. 'I'll make you dinner, or we could go out.'

'I can't. I have an assignment that's due in on Monday. I'm behind as it is.'

Stepping back, he took the tray from her and put it on the floor. Then, taking her hand, he led her back to the bed.

'I'm sure I have ways of persuading you,' he said.

CHAPTER SIXTEEN

Beth

'You're looking happy. Good day?'

Beth watched her dad pull off his walking boots, holding on to the wall to keep his balance.

'Yep.'

'You've caught the sun on your nose. Did you put any cream on? It can be deceptive when there's cloud around. You need to be careful.'

Going over to the mirror, Beth turned her head one way then the next. He was right, the bridge of her nose was a little pink, and the sun had brought out the freckles on her cheeks. One more thing for the girls at school to laugh about. For the first time in a long time, though, she didn't care, for as David had dropped her off at the entrance to the campsite, he had asked whether she wanted to come over later. Three friends of his from London were staying the night at the campsite on their way to Scotland. They'd be having a barbeque and a few drinks and she'd be welcome. The more the merrier.

She hugged the memory to her. Okay, so it wasn't a date, but it proved that he liked her a bit. Why else would he invite her?

'Where's your mum?' Opening the front door again, her dad placed the boots outside.

'She wasn't here when I got back. I think she's gone into Ambleside.'

'Ah, yes. She probably mentioned it, but I've got a head like a sieve.' Padding through the living room in his walking socks, he went into the kitchen and Beth heard the kettle being switched on.

He came back into the room and perched on the arm of the settee. 'I don't think your mum's been herself lately. Have *you* noticed anything?'

Beth glanced at the clock. A conversation about her mum wasn't what she wanted at the moment. She needed to get ready. Think of a way to make herself look less like Rudolph and more like someone David would want to kiss.

A frisson of excitement ran through her at the thought. She was fifteen years old and had never been kissed properly. Not by someone she cared about. Maybe now her time had come, unless her parents mucked it up. In some ways, it was good that her mum hadn't come home yet.

'She seems fine to me.'

Her dad scratched at his beard. 'She's not said anything then?'

'Not to me. Why would she?'

'I don't know. She just seems drained. On edge. These panic attacks she's been having…'

He stopped and Beth realised it was because he was afraid he'd said too much. He didn't want to worry her.

'Graham mentioned what happened in the shop.'

He looked relieved. 'There have been other times too. I wish I knew what it was all about. She looks tired, don't you think? If she was ill, she'd tell us, wouldn't she?'

'Look, Dad. I know you're worried, but I'm sure she's all right. Maybe it's her age… The menopause or something.'

'She's thirty-seven, Beth. Don't they teach you anything in your biology lessons?'

She glanced at the clock. If she didn't ask him now, she never would.

'Dad?'

'That's me.'

'There's a new girl in my class called Emma. She's invited me over this evening with Carina and some of the others. Can I go?' At least this way, they couldn't check where she was.

Her dad raised his eyebrows. 'But you've been with Carina all day. Won't you be sick of the sight of each other?'

If she could just get him on her side, she knew he'd be able to persuade her mum.

'Please, Dad. I don't want to be the only one who isn't allowed to go. I won't be late back, I promise.'

'And how will you get home?' he asked. He got up and went into the kitchen. There was the sound of water being poured into mugs.

'I'll get a lift from Keira's dad. They have to pass this way.'

She hated lying, but she knew there was no way he would let her go if he knew the truth. She saw it through his eyes: an older guy, a camper van, people she didn't know. When put like that, it didn't sound too good.

He reappeared with two mugs of tea and put them on the coffee table. 'I don't know, Beth. You'd better wait until your mum gets—'

'Dad. I'm fifteen, not five.'

'I know that and you know that, but your mum's a different kettle of fish altogether.'

'You're as bad as Mum. You don't want me to have any friends.'

He didn't reply, but Beth could see from his face that she'd touched on something.

'If you go,' he said, 'I want you back by ten thirty. No later… And if there's any problem, ring me.'

'There won't be.' Jumping up, she went over to him and kissed him on the cheek. 'Thanks, Dad. You're cool.'

'Don't I know it.' He laughed.

He reached over and ruffled her hair, but her thoughts were already on the amazing evening she was about to have.

CHAPTER SEVENTEEN
Ria

Ria stood in the bathroom, staring at the blue line. She'd been feeling rough for a few days, but it had been Leo who had persuaded her to buy the test. Closing the lid of the toilet, she sat down and placed a hand on her stomach, wondering how she felt about it. That she loved Gareth she had no doubt, but it was all too soon. They'd only known each other a few months.

She looked at her watch. Gareth would be home soon and she needed time to think about what this would mean for their relationship. She wasn't exactly living in his apartment – most of her clothes were still in her flat – but they'd got into a routine where she would let herself in after her lectures had finished and would be waiting for him when he got home. Usually, he'd cook for her, but today, for a change, she'd decided to make something nice for him, remembering to pop into the supermarket on the way home. Feeling queasy, Ria swallowed the saliva that had filled her mouth at the thought of eating the salmon she'd bought earlier.

Closing the bathroom door behind her, she went into Gareth's bedroom and sat down on the bed. On several occasions, he had asked her to move in with him, but she'd always resisted. It wasn't that she thought anything would go wrong, it was just that having her own flat gave her a safety net. She looked around her, wondering if she could ever live here permanently. It was a very masculine apartment, but maybe she could do something about that. She took in the uncluttered floor, the clean lines of the black melamine fitted drawers and the mirrored wardrobe. She blushed at the thought of what had been reflected back at them the previous night when they'd made love.

Taking out her phone, she rang Leo's number. It answered straight away.

'Well?'

Ria felt her heart racing. 'It's positive!'

She heard Leo's intake of breath. 'Oh my God! What are you going to do? Are you pleased?'

'I don't know. I think I'm still in shock.'

'Have you told Gareth yet?'

'No, he's not home. I think he said he was having a drink with some of the others after work.'

There was amusement in Leo's voice. 'I guess it won't be long before you're calling it your home too. What will you do about uni?'

That was something Ria hadn't thought about. 'I don't know. Carry on, I suppose. I know Mum would help out, and there's a crèche.'

'Well, you don't need to think about that now. What about Gareth? You reckon he'll be happy about the baby?'

Ria frowned. 'Why wouldn't he be? He loves me.'

'No reason. It's just that you're still in the honeymoon period, and having a baby will change things big time. Since the two of you got together and became joined at the hip, I hardly ever see you.'

'That's not true, Leo. I see you every day in lectures.'

'I know, but it's not the same as going out. I miss it. I can't do next week. How about the one after? Friday? A girly night out, but you'll have to forgo the Chardonnay. All the more for me.'

Ria tried to remember if she was doing anything; Gareth wouldn't be happy if she changed any plans they'd made. She couldn't think of anything though, and Leo was right, in the last few months they hadn't seen nearly as much of each other as they used to. Maybe if Gareth and Leo's boyfriend, Adam, had got on, it would have been easier, but the one time they'd met up with them both for a drink, Gareth had made it clear he'd thought Adam an idiot. They'd never done it again.

'Friday might be all right. I'll check with Gareth when he gets in.' There was the sound of a key in the front door. 'In fact, I think that might be him now.'

'If you're having to ask permission, Ria, I'll take that as a no.' The irritation in Leo's voice was clear.

'Don't be like that. Just because Adam couldn't care less where you are or what you're doing.' Sometimes she wondered whether Gareth might be right when he called their friendship 'clingy'.

There was a pause at the other end and Ria wondered if she'd gone too far.

'Leo?'

'I'm sorry, Ria. Forget what I said. It's nice you've got someone who cares for you. And you're right, Adam could probably take a leaf out of Gareth's book when it comes to making a girl feel special. Let's not argue when you've got bigger things to think about. Go and tell Gareth the big news. You can let me know about Friday when I see you tomorrow, if you like. And, honestly, it really is great news.'

Ria was relieved. 'Thanks Leo. Look, I'd better go. I'll see you tomorrow.'

Putting the phone back into her pocket, Ria smoothed the bedspread, then went out into the hallway.

Gareth was standing by the front door, looking through the post, his tie loosened and his pinstripe shirt stretched across his broad back. His sandy hair, usually so carefully gelled, was ruffled where he'd run his fingers through it. Watching him, Ria felt a wave of desire. Sometimes she found it hard to believe that someone like him wanted to be with her.

He didn't look up. 'I'm expecting something from the Inland Revenue. Have you seen it?'

Ria went up behind him. Slipping her arms around him, she rested her cheek on his back, feeling the tautness of his muscles under his work shirt. 'I picked everything up and put it on the table.'

He shook her off. 'It should be here. Now I'm going to have to ring them.'

Ria stood with her arms at her sides. He hadn't even said hello to her. The happiness she'd been feeling at seeing the little blue line was disappearing fast. 'Is it that important?'

'Of course it's important,' he snapped. 'I wouldn't be asking you about it otherwise.'

When she said nothing, he looked at her and his face softened. 'Come on, sweetie. Don't look at me like I'm some sort of ogre. I've had a bad day, that's all.' He drew her to him and kissed the top of her head. 'You sit down and I'll make you a cup of tea. You look shattered. Are you feeling okay?'

It was the perfect moment to tell him, but for some reason she couldn't. Instead, she went into the living room, with its polished wooden floor, and sat down. Gareth followed.

She picked up the textbook she'd been trying to get her head around earlier, then put it down again. 'Yes, I'm tired. After back-to-back lectures on international business and marketing communications, who wouldn't be?'

'Poor love. Maybe you've chosen the wrong course.'

'I'm two years in, Gareth. It's a bit late to be thinking that now.'

'Yes, I suppose it is.' Gareth went over to the black ash sideboard and poured himself a scotch; he seemed to have forgotten about the tea. 'Who did you see today?'

Ria was puzzled by the question. 'What do you mean, who did I see?' She smiled. 'There are over fifty students on my course. Shall I name them all? There's Rosie, Cas, Nick…'

He stood with drink in hand, regarding her. 'Don't be ridiculous. It's just that when I'm not with you, I miss you. It helps if

I can picture what you're doing… Who you're with.' Taking out his phone, he looked at it. 'You didn't answer my calls.'

Three times, she'd seen a missed call message on her phone. She'd meant to ring him back but had forgotten.

She searched for an excuse. 'I was in a tutorial, Gareth, and my phone was on silent. I didn't realise.'

'On silent.' Gareth swirled the amber liquid around the whisky glass, then took a large mouthful. 'Of course it was.'

Ria waited, wondering why she was so on edge. The air in the room felt static.

Then, as quickly as it had arrived, the tension dissolved as Gareth's face broke into a smile. Walking over to her, he kissed the top of her head. 'You take it easy. I'll make a start on the dinner.'

Ria smiled and got up, trying to ignore the wave of nausea as she thought of the pink flesh of the fish. 'You don't need to do that. I thought I'd do the cooking tonight for a change. It's about time I took a turn.'

Putting his drink on the glass coffee table, Gareth stared at her. 'Are you saying you don't like my cooking?'

'Of course not.'

'That's good, because it wasn't the impression you gave when you were stuffing your face with my lasagne last night.'

Ria flinched. 'That wasn't what I meant, Gareth.'

'What did you mean then?'

Ria's head was starting to ache. Too often, their conversations headed in this direction, but it was hard for him. His work was stressful, and it must be difficult coming home to a girlfriend who drifted into college for her few lectures and then came home again. 'I just meant that you look after me so well, it would be nice to do something for *you* for a change.'

She touched his cheek. The stubble felt rough beneath her fingertips and it made her skin tingle. Bringing up her other hand, she drew his face down until it was level with hers, touching her lips against his. Feeling their warmth.

'Please don't be cross. I've something I need to tell you. Something good... Well, I think so, anyway.'

Gareth pulled away. 'Can it wait? I've some important calls I need to make, and then there's the dinner.'

'No, I don't think it *can* wait. I've had butterflies in my stomach since I found out.'

With a sigh, Gareth sat down on the leather settee, propping his feet on the coffee table, his black brogues reflected in the glass. 'Don't tell me: Leo has finally dumped that dickhead, Adam.'

Unsettled by his tone, Ria sat down next to him and took his hand. She ran her thumb over the gold signet ring on his little finger. 'It's not about them. It's about us.'

'What about us?'

Suddenly, her mouth felt dry. What if he wasn't pleased? What if he wanted her to get rid of it? He'd had a bad day; maybe this wasn't the time.

But he was looking at her differently now, his pale grey eyes locked on hers, drawing her in. It reminded her of the night they first met, when she'd felt she'd be happy to look into those eyes forever.

His tone had changed too. It was loving, coaxing. 'Come on, sweetheart, you can tell me anything.'

'I'm... I'm having a baby,' she stammered. '*We're* having a baby.'

She watched his face, trying to read it, but it was as though he was wearing a mask. Her heart was clenched like a fist. 'Say something, Gareth. I know it's a shock, but I need to know what you're thinking.'

'What I'm thinking? I'm thinking that this is the best possible news you could have given me.'

Lowering himself off the sofa, he knelt down and wrapped his arms around her waist, pressing his cheek against her stomach. When he looked up, Ria was amazed to see his eyes had filled with tears.

'We're going to have a baby,' he said. 'A little person who will tie us together. How could I be anything but happy?'

She studied his expression, scared to find sarcasm written there. Finding none, she carried on. 'But it will affect everything… My studies… Where we live… What we do. You don't mind?'

Putting an arm around her shoulders, he pulled her towards him so that her head was on his shoulder, the crisp cotton of his work shirt smooth beneath her cheek.

'I'll take care of you, Ria. We'll get married and you won't have to worry about a thing. I'll be the best husband anyone could ask for.'

Tilting her face, he kissed her, and Ria responded, feeling she might die of happiness.

CHAPTER EIGHTEEN
Beth

It had started to rain. Large drops that soaked into Beth's top and stuck her jeans to her legs. She didn't care, though. She didn't care about anything any more. As the tail lights faded into the distance, she ran for home, hoping her parents wouldn't smell the alcohol on her breath. She was sober now. The euphoria she'd felt earlier had left her, replaced by a growing realisation of what she'd done. It was no different to school – she'd made a fool of herself. Would he be laughing at her? Or worse still, pitying her?

The evening had started off well. She'd arrived at the campsite a little later than the time David had given her, not wanting to be the first there. As she'd crossed the field, she'd been surprised to see only two camping chairs set out beside the camper van and no one else in sight – not even David. Where was everyone?

A bottle each of red and white wine stood on a low fold-out table in front of the van. There were also some cans of coke and small bottles of beer, two of which were empty.

As she got nearer, David appeared from around the back of the camper, a sausage pronged on the end of his fork. 'Had to put the barbeque round here to get it out of the wind. Help yourself to a drink; there's wine… beer…'

'Wine's fine.' She stood where she was, feeling awkward. 'Where *is* everyone?'

David shrugged his shoulders. 'Cried off. Decided to drive straight up to Edinburgh without a stop. Mad, if you ask me. I thought it would be a shame to waste a lovely evening, and anyway, I'd already bought the sausages.' He nodded to the wine. 'Go on… I'm not going to serve you.'

He disappeared again, and Beth went to the table and unscrewed the top from a bottle of red. She didn't particularly like the taste of wine but, if she poured herself a coke, she'd look stupid. Next to the bottles were some plastic cups. She picked one up, unsure of how much to pour herself. Deciding that half a cup looked about right, she went over to one of the green camping chairs. It rocked on its spindly legs as she sat down, slopping wine up the sides of her glass.

'Sorry, these chairs were the best I could do,' David said, handing her one of the two paper plates that he'd balanced on his arm like a waiter. On it was a rather overdone sausage, a burger, a pile of coleslaw and some salad leaves. He sat down next to her in the only other chair, and she couldn't help wondering where the others would have sat.

'It's fine.'

'That's good, as there's nothing else.' Putting his plate on the grass, he tipped the bottle of beer he'd been holding in his other hand to his lips and drank. 'I still feel as though I don't know much about you, and I want to know everything. For a start, you've not told me how long you've lived here?'

Beth stared at the sausage on her plate, unsure of how to eat it without cutlery. 'About nine years.'

'It's a nice place,' he said. 'I could quite happily live here myself. Church Langdon, I mean – not this crappy campsite. Although I'm becoming increasingly fond of it, especially when the couple in the tent over there decide to shag by lamplight. Do you reckon they know how translucent the canvas is?'

Beth felt her cheeks burn. She took a large gulp of wine. To her inexperienced palate, it tasted dry and slightly acidic. Not pleasant at all.

'I can see Blackstone Farm and the campsite from the house.'
She stopped, unsure why she'd told him this.

'Then you'll be able to see me when I pop outside for my early
morning cup of tea in my boxers.' He chuckled and reached behind
him for a plastic bag of seeded buns, taking one for himself and
offering one to Beth.

Beth looked away, embarrassed. 'I can't see the camper van, just
the tents in the first part of the field near the barn.'

David handed her a tub of margarine and a knife. 'Of course,
you can't. Don't look so worried... I was only kidding. Anyway,
I'm rarely up before ten and when I am, I like to drink my tea
in the buff!'

It was hard to know how to respond to his jokes, so she said
nothing. Instead, she buttered her bun and slotted her burger
into it. Balancing her plate on her lap, she bent and picked up
her plastic cup from the ground, then took another gulp from it.

It was a beautiful evening, a line of cool shadow creeping up the
mountains in the distance until just their summits were alight. It
was strange to be here with him alone, but any feelings of unease
melted away when he smiled at her and she felt her heart beat faster.

The wine was warming her, giving her a confidence she didn't
usually have. 'It's a shame they couldn't make it.'

David looked up from his plate. 'Who?'

'Your friends,' she said. 'The ones from London. How long
have you known them?'

He squeezed a dollop of ketchup onto his burger, then took a
large bite. She thought he wasn't going to answer but, after he'd
swallowed, he smiled.

'Not long. A couple of years maybe.'

'What are their names?'

'Their *names*? What is this, the Spanish Inquisition?' He looked
uncomfortable.

Beth looked down at her plate. 'I'm sorry.'

She was beginning to sound just like her mum. Worse even, as she'd only just met the guy. If only she could explain to him that she'd give anything to have friends to share things with: jokes, clothes… secrets. A thing that could never happen with her mum always breathing down her neck. Asking her interminable questions. *Where does she live? What do her parents do?* Even if she knew their whole sodding life history, her mum wouldn't be content. People were wary of her and who could blame them with a mum like hers.

David was looking at her strangely. 'What's up? You look as if you're about to murder that sausage, rather than eat it.'

'Sorry.' Beth took another mouthful of wine, only to find her cup was almost empty. How had that happened?

'If you're really interested, my friends are called Ewan and Cas,' he said, eyeing her over his bottle of beer.

'And the other? I thought you said there were three.'

'Zara,' he said, after a moment's hesitation. 'She's called Zara. I met them at one of the magazines I've worked on. We have fun. Hang out.'

It was an odd choice of words, reminding Beth of how she'd reply if her dad asked if she'd had a good day at school.

'It's a shame they couldn't be here.'

'Yeah. Still,' he said, gesturing to the food and drink. 'All the more for us. Anyway, it gives me the chance to get to know you better.'

He gave his lovely smile and everything seemed normal again, but there was something she didn't understand. Why would he be interested in someone like her when he knew women in London with names like Cas and Zara? If they worked for a magazine, they'd be features editors or advertising executives – maybe even models.

With his blue eyes and wild, sun-bleached hair, David could have his pick of sophisticated women in the city, while Beth's only experience of the opposite sex had been a quick fumble in a bus stop in Ambleside with a boy who'd taken her to the cinema. A boy with acne, who'd forced her hand to his bulging crotch as a bus pulled in, swearing at her when she'd pulled it away in horror. It hadn't been the best experience, and the girls all seemed to have heard about it the next day at school. *Frigid*, they'd called her.

'I think it's nice that you have such good friends,' she said eventually.

'What? Oh, yeah.' His face went serious. 'Haven't you?'

'Not really.'

David tipped her cup and looked inside. 'I don't think you should drink any more. I don't want to get into trouble.'

How stupid that made her feel. 'You're telling me you didn't drink when you were seventeen?'

'No, I'm not saying that. It's just that you don't seem used to it.'

Beth drained the plastic cup, then picked up the half-empty bottle David had put on the ground between their seats, pouring herself some more. 'I'm enjoying myself – there's nothing wrong with that.'

David took a bite of his burger, rescuing a piece of lettuce that had escaped onto his lap. 'No, there's nothing wrong with enjoying yourself. Just take it easy, that's all.'

'You sound like my dad.'

'Well, that's better than sounding like *my* dad,' David replied quietly. 'He's been dead for five years.'

Beth stared at him. Despite his questions about her life, it was the first time he'd revealed anything about his own. What had made him open up like this? Maybe it was the moonlight… or the wine… or simply that it was just the two of them here together.

'I'm sorry,' Beth replied, sensing his pain. She wanted to reach out and hold his hand, make him feel he could carry on, but she didn't want to stop him either.

David dragged his fingers through his long hair and looked across to Langdon Fell, which was now just a purple ridge against the darkening sky. 'Don't be. He was an arsehole. Made my mum's life a misery. Whoever said you have to love your parents is a liar. The day he died, I gave thanks to God. Not that I believe in one.'

Beth was shocked. 'You don't mean that.'

'Oh, I do. Believe me. What about *your* father? What's he like?'

'He's not my real dad. He's my stepdad – although, strictly speaking, he's not that either, as he and mum have never married. He's kind and funny. When I was younger, he used to walk around with his underpants on his head to make me laugh, and he knows what to say when I'm down… Or rather, what not to say. Mum just seems to make things worse.'

'I expect that's because she cares about you.'

The second glass of wine was slipping down nicely. 'I know that.'

Nobody, other than her parents, had talked to her like this before. As if they were truly interested. It made her glow inside.

David leant forward and reached out a hand. Gently, he cupped her face and looked at her. For one amazing moment, Beth thought he was going to kiss her, but instead he turned her head until she was looking away from him. The touch of his fingers on her skin made her shiver.

'You have a lovely profile. I'd like to photograph you.'

Beth turned back to him, a challenge in her voice. 'Don't say things like that if you don't mean them.'

He looked baffled. 'Why would I say something I didn't mean?'

'Because that's what people do.'

'Well, I don't. I believe in the principle that if you can't mean what you say, then you should say nothing at all.'

She felt embarrassed. 'I'm sorry. I don't know what made me say that.' The wine that earlier had made her feel happy and carefree, now seemed to be having the opposite effect.

'Don't worry about it, but I meant what I said. I'd like to photograph you. There's a staggeringly beautiful tarn I found when I was out and about a few weeks ago. It would make a great backdrop. What do you say? We could go one day next week in the golden hour.'

'The golden hour?' She'd never heard of it.

'It's the time just before sunset, or after sunrise, when the angle of the sun creates long shadows, adding extra dimension. It's when I take my best shots. You must have days at college when you have a later start? I could pick you up on one of those days.'

Whenever he was talking about his work, he became more animated, and it was catching. The thought of being alone with David when the sun rose was exciting. Thrilling. So what if it meant missing school? It would be worth it.

'I'd love to.'

'Great. I'll give you a call and I'll let you know when I think the weather will be right.'

As they swapped numbers, she thought she would burst with happiness. This evening, David had made her feel that she might be pretty... Beautiful, even. The world was lovely. Everything was lovely.

It was almost dark now and she could only just make out David's face in the moonlight. Without thinking, she reached over and took his hand in her own. It was the bravest thing she'd ever done. His skin felt warm against hers and her stomach clenched in anticipation.

Instead of returning the pressure of her fingers, though, David pulled his hand away. Without a word, he got up from his chair and started picking up the dirty plates from the grass. He didn't look at her. Wouldn't.

Beth's humiliation was complete.

Grabbing her bag, she struggled up from her chair and walked quickly away across the field, blinded by tears. When she reached the bridge, she ran, and it was only then that she felt the full effect of the alcohol she'd drunk. She stopped and leant against the rough stone wall. The mountains, which were nearly in darkness, were moving in a circle around her and she knew she was in danger of being sick.

She heard a shout. Someone was running across the field after her. Without looking to see who it was, she stumbled along the path to the kissing gate that led onto the road, struggling with the latch to get it open. She could no longer stop herself. Bending double, she retched into the hedge, straightening again as a car drove by, its headlights picking out the white of her blouse against the drystone wall.

And that was when it started to rain. Big fat drops that soaked her in seconds, but she felt nothing. Her life wasn't worth living. Especially now that she'd realised whose forehead had been pressed against the passenger window as the car passed.

CHAPTER NINETEEN
Ria

Ria's mother stood in the middle of her living room, her hand to her throat. 'Oh my goodness, Ria. A baby! Are you sure?'

Ria put down her mug, the inside of it tanned from years of stewed tea. 'I did three tests. You can't get much surer than that.' She felt a rush of love for her mum, glad that she'd taken it so well. 'Have you had your hair done, Mum?'

It looked newly highlighted and she was wearing it a little longer than usual. The effect was one that Gareth would call 'brassy', but Ria thought it suited her.

'Yesterday.' Her mum lifted a hand to her hair. 'Do you think it's all right? I asked Geraldine to make it a bit lighter, but I think she might have gone rather overboard. Not that your father would notice. Sometimes I think he wouldn't say anything if I dyed it green. Anyway, why are we talking about me when you've just given me such lovely news?'

'You promise you're not just saying that?'

'Goodness me, no. I know I should be telling you that you're far too young, but what would be the point of that? It wouldn't change anything. Has Gareth told his parents yet?'

'He doesn't speak to them,' Ria said, remembering the way his face had set the first time she'd asked about them. How he'd left the room and slammed the door behind him. She hadn't asked again.

A flicker of disappointment crossed her mum's face. 'That's a shame but, never mind. We'll be here for you both.' She held out her arms, her smile wide. 'Bringing a baby into the world is the most wonderful thing. I should know. Come here.'

Pulling her daughter into her arms, she gave her a hug and Ria felt her shoulders sag with relief. Her mum was only the first hurdle, though.

Walking over to the window, Ria pulled back the net curtain. Her dad was down the bottom of the garden in his blue mechanic's overalls, squatting beside his motorbike, a frown of concentration on his face. 'You'd think he'd be sick of the sight of engines after a week at the garage.'

Her mother smiled. 'You know your dad.'

As they watched, he put down his spanner and stood up. He looked towards the house and, when he saw the two of them at the window, raised his hand in greeting.

'What do you think he'll say, Mum?' Ria dropped the curtain.

'He'll be as thrilled as I am. And if he's not, I'll give him what for.'

Ria laughed. She'd been dreading telling her parents for fear they'd think she'd let them down but, with her mum on her side, she knew that everything would be all right.

'Gareth wanted to come over with me today, but he wasn't feeling too good. Man flu, probably. He sends his love,' she said, embarrassed at having to lie. All the way here, she'd been trying to think of an excuse for him and that had been the best she'd come up with.

'That's a shame. I was hoping we'd get to meet him at long last.'

'Yes, we're beginning to think the lad's got three heads or something.' Her dad stood in the doorway, wiping his hands with a rag that was now covered in grease. His wiry dark hair had a peppering of grey in it that Ria hadn't noticed before.

Popping open his blue overalls, he slipped his arms out of the sleeves and stepped out of them. Underneath, he was wearing his favourite Def Leppard T-shirt and a baggy pair of jeans.

'So, what brings you over here this sunny afternoon? We haven't seen much of you lately.'

'Don't make a fuss, Brian, or she won't come at all… And get those dirty overalls off my living room carpet.'

'It hasn't been that long, Dad.' In her head, Ria tried to work out when she'd last visited the small semi in Clapham which had been her childhood home. She was shocked to realise it was almost two months ago.

'Well, you're here now,' he said, 'and I suppose that's all that matters.'

Ria went over to him and gave him a hug, smelling the motor oil that permeated his clothing, pleased to feel the squeeze of his arms in return. 'The thing is, Dad, I have some news.'

'Oh, yes?'

She swallowed. There was no easy way of saying it. 'Gareth and I are going to have a baby.'

Her dad stood back and scratched his head. 'You're joking, right?' He looked at Ria, and then at her mother, for any sign that this wasn't really happening.

'No, Dad. It's not a joke.'

Pulling out a chair, he sat down heavily. 'You're only twenty, for goodness sake. What about your studies?'

Ria bit the inside of her cheek. 'Gareth decided… *we* decided… that it would be best if I give this year a miss, take a break and then maybe carry on with it when the baby's older.'

'*Maybe?*' Getting up again and walking over to the sideboard, her dad picked up a photograph from the collection that jostled for space on the veneered surface. The frames were mismatched and had been picked up by her mother at car boot sales. The photograph he was looking at now was of the three of them on a caravan holiday in France. 'You've worked damn hard for this degree. You've only one year left. Don't throw it all away.'

He put the photograph back with the others, then turned and looked at her. 'Did you plan it?'

'You can't ask her questions like that, Brian. It's none of our business.'

'She's our daughter. Of course, it's our business.'

'No, it wasn't planned.' Ria looked away, her neck reddening as she remembered the night it must have happened. She'd forgotten to take her pill that morning, but Gareth had refused to wear a condom. *It will be all right*, he'd said, pushing her down onto the bed, and she'd believed him. It was only now that she realised the risk they'd taken.

'And you can afford a child?'

'Gareth's got a good job. I told you that last time I was here.'

'So you did. And what was it you said he did exactly?'

Ria looked away, embarrassed that she wasn't entirely sure. Whenever she asked him about it, he would tell her that he made money and that was all she needed to know. 'He's a broker… in the city.'

Her father's face softened. 'I'm sorry for giving you a hard time, love. I just want to know my little girl is okay.'

'I'm fine, Dad.' Her hands moved to her stomach. 'In fact, I couldn't be happier.'

Taking her face in his hands, he kissed her cheek. 'Then I couldn't be either. That's all I needed to hear. Why don't your mum and I come over sometime and we can meet this young man of yours? What about on your birthday? We could go out for a meal, or your mum could bring something over. Whatever you want.'

'Thanks, Dad. That would be nice. I'll check with Gareth.'

'It's *your* birthday, love. *You* decide what you'd like to do.'

Her mum gave him a stare. 'Brian.'

'It's all right, Mum. Dad's right. Of course you must come, and we'll go out if you're happy with that. There's a great Italian around the corner from the house.'

Her dad nodded, his eyes remaining on hers. 'That's a plan then.'

When she got home, Gareth was in his study, his eyes fixed on the screen of his computer. 'Good day?'

There was no apology for not having come with her to share their news. For ducking out at the last minute.

Dropping her coat and bag onto the floor, a habit from child-hood she'd never managed to break, she went over to him. He swivelled his chair to face her and, as he did, she knew by the way his face hardened that he'd noticed her things on the floor. Part of her wanted to go back and hang them up, but she forced herself not to. If they were going to live together permanently, he was going to have to relax a little more.

Wondering what he'd do, she sat on his lap and kissed him, relieved when she felt his hands slip under her blouse. 'Yes, I had a nice time. Mum makes a great shepherd's pie. It was a shame you couldn't come with me. I missed you.'

Pulling back the collar of her blouse, Gareth kissed her neck. 'Then I'd better make up for it now, hadn't I?'

She put her arms around his neck and rubbed her cheek against his. 'They're going to come over on my birthday next week so that they can meet you. I thought we'd go to that Italian on the corner.'

Gareth moved his head away from hers. His voice was cold. 'I hope you don't mean on the actual day of your birthday?'

'Yes, for lunch. Why? Is that a problem?'

Pushing her from his lap, he swung the office chair towards the computer again. 'No. Why would it be?'

'Because of the way you said it. What's the matter, Gareth? Don't you want to meet them?'

His eyes were fixed on the screen. 'You do what you like. I'll probably be working, anyway.'

'On a Saturday?'

'Of course on a Saturday. The world doesn't stop just because of your fucking birthday.'

Ria stepped back, her eyes filling with tears. He'd never sworn at her before. She tried to control the wobble in her voice. 'No, of course it doesn't. That wasn't what I meant.'

Leaving him in the study, Ria went into the living room and curled up on the leather settee. It was firm, the leather stretched tightly over the padded frame, and she wished there was a cushion to give her comfort. She closed her eyes. Her pregnancy and the emotions of the day had left her exhausted and, in a few moments, she felt herself drifting into sleep.

'I'm sorry, baby.' Gareth's voice cut into her dream. Opening her eyes, he came into focus. He was standing beside the settee, his arms folded. Even in jeans and a T-shirt he looked as though he'd given thought to his clothes.

Knowing how difficult he found it to apologise, she loved him for it.

'It's all right.'

Gareth knelt beside her. 'I didn't mean to get cross, but sometimes you say the stupidest things and I can't help it.'

Once again, he'd spoilt it. Ria rolled over so she was facing the back of the settee, not wanting another argument. What was it she'd said that was stupid? That her parents wanted to meet him, or that she was surprised he might want to work on a Saturday?

'The truth is,' he continued, running his hand down the length of her body. 'I was disappointed.'

She turned to look at him. 'Disappointed?'

'I'd planned to take you out somewhere special… Just the two of us. I wasn't going to tell you as I wanted it to be a surprise.' His hand rested on the curve of her waist. 'But now you've made me.'

Feeling guilty that she'd misjudged him, Ria reached over and took his hand. 'I'm so sorry, Gareth, I didn't realise. You should have said. It's a lovely idea, it really is, but I can't let my parents down. Besides, they're beginning to wonder if I've made you up. Please say you understand.'

'It doesn't sound as if they like me much anyway.'

'How can you say that? They've never even met you. When they do, they'll love you every bit as much as I do. Probably more, knowing my mum. Why don't we go out the following week?' She raised his hand to her lips and kissed it. 'You can choose where we go and I'll pretend I didn't know anything about it. Please don't be upset with me, you know how I hate it.'

Gareth stood up, his face giving nothing away. 'I'll check when I'm free.'

He went out to the kitchen and came back with the calendar he'd bought to keep track of their comings and goings. Running his finger along the week, he stopped when he reached Friday.

'That seems as good a night as any.' Taking a pen from behind his ear, he noted it down. Ria smiled.

'That's a date then.'

It wasn't until she checked later that she saw it was the night she was supposed to have been going out with Leo.

CHAPTER TWENTY
Leona

'How would you describe him, Leona?'

'Describe who?'

For a moment, I'm confused, thinking she means Scott. I've been staring at the rows of books on Lisa Manning's shelf, trying to imagine what it must be like to be her. Day after day, unravelling people's lives and piecing them back together in a better order. I picture my little family like the squares in the game I used to have as a child – the pieces being moved around each other inside the plastic edge until they form a picture. Some days we're in the right places; sometimes we're stuck in a corner unable to move.

'Who do you mean?' I ask again.

Lisa's expression is neutral. 'Gareth. Describe him to me as a stranger might. Someone who didn't know him.'

I put my hands in front of my face to help me think. 'He was charming. Charismatic. Polished.'

'Polished?'

'Yes. He always looked perfect. Well-groomed, as though people might judge him if he had a hair out of place. He was good-looking too. We couldn't take our eyes off him the first time we saw him in the bar.'

Lisa nods. Today, she is wearing a dress rather than trousers. I recognise it from White Stuff; I've got one similar.

'Was anyone concerned about him? Apart from you, of course.'

'People only saw what he wanted them to see.'

There's a pause. A siren wails in the street outside, becoming fainter. 'And what about Ria? What did she think?'

I stiffen. I don't want to talk about Ria this morning. The panic attacks I've been having have become less frequent and I'm scared that by talking about her, they'll come back.

Lisa waits. She knows that eventually my need to talk will overcome my fear of the consequences.

'Ria loved him.'

'Love or infatuation?' She runs a finger down her notes. 'She was very young when she met him.'

'Oh, it was love all right. She didn't see what he was doing and, when she did, it was too late.'

'What do you think he was doing, Leona?'

'He treated her like a princess, but he was grooming her to be what he wanted her to be. Compliant, dependent. He eroded her self-confidence and self-worth.'

'How did he do that?'

'Just little things at first, like telling her she'd loaded the dishwasher wrongly or saying he wasn't hungry the one time he allowed her to cook for him. She stopped singing too. Even though the bar manager had offered her a regular Thursday night slot, she hadn't taken it up, believing Gareth when he told her she wasn't that good. Apparently, it had been her vivid blue eyes that had attracted him to her, not her singing.'

'You must have felt helpless.'

'I did.' I bite back the tears. 'But there was nothing I could do to stop it.'

'Why was that, do you think?'

'Because of the negative comments he made about her friends. They were using her… They didn't care about her like he did. Things like that. She saw them less and less and then, once she'd dropped out of uni, she stopped seeing them altogether.'

'And how does that make you feel, Leona?'

'I feel angry.' My nails are digging into my palms. 'She couldn't see it was because he wanted to keep her all to himself. His possessiveness snuck up and took a hold of her, while she was busy believing it was love.'

CHAPTER TWENTY-ONE

Beth

Beth picked up her phone. There were four missed calls from David. She hadn't answered any of them; she never wanted to see him again.

Dragging her sketchbook from under her bed, she opened it to a blank page, then, taking a thin black marker from the basket on her bedside table, she started to draw. She did it without thinking, without caring, and when she had finished, she threw the book across the room and buried her face in her pillow. This had been the worst evening of her life. Carina was right: she was pathetic.

As she remembered the way David had pulled his hand from hers, she burned with embarrassment. She'd thought he liked her. Never would she let herself be made a fool of again. Turning onto her back, she stared at the water mark on the ceiling that had always reminded her of a whale, and when she could stand looking at it no longer, she folded her arms over her eyes and let the tears run down the side of her cheeks into her pillow.

There was a knock at the door. 'Beth? Can I come in?'

It was her mum. Reaching for her pillow, she put it over her head. 'Go away.'

'Let me come in, darling. I hate seeing you like this.'

As soon as the front door had opened, Beth had run inside, ignoring her parents' exclamations at the bedraggled state of her. Without answering their questions, she had run up the stairs and locked herself in her room, relieved when they hadn't come after her. Now, though, as her mum knocked again, she could just imagine their conversation. *Should I go up? Just leave her for a bit. Let her calm down.*

'If you don't unlock this door, I shall get Dad to force it open.'

'Do what you like. I don't care.'

There was a pause, and then her mum's voice again. Gentler now. 'Please, Beth. I just want to help. There was a time, once, when you could tell me anything.'

Beth took the pillow away from her face. It had been true once, but she'd only been a kid then. Sometimes she wished she still was. Taking a tissue out of her pocket, she blew her nose. She missed those days.

The door handle rattled and she pictured her mum outside, her eyes creased in worry. Maybe she should let her in – she didn't want to be the cause of another one of her mum's anxiety attacks. But, if she did…

Beth pushed the heels of her hands into the sockets of her eyes. She wanted to tell her what had happened. Wait for her to say she'd done the right thing – that she hadn't made a compete idiot of herself. She couldn't, though. Her mum had been so distant recently that Beth was frightened of what she might say. Could she be having problems with Dad? Did she have cancer, like the mother of the girl Beth sat next to in Food Tech?

She couldn't bear to think of it and, if she didn't let her in, she wouldn't have to find out now. She was scared to know what it was – despite what she'd said to her dad, she was worried about her mum. But her need for her mum at that moment was greater than all these fears. Wearily, she swung her legs over the edge of the bed, then walked to the door and unlocked it.

'Are you all right?' Her mum stood in the doorway, her eyes scanning the room as though there might be someone in there with her.

'Yes.' Beth stood her ground. 'And now you know, you can go away.'

'Not until I know what's going on.' Beth could see her mum taking in the soaking wet hoodie and jeans she'd pulled off and thrown into a corner. Then she saw the sketchbook that lay open on the floor where it had landed. Some of its pages had twisted away from its binding and there were splatters of tea on the cover from the mug that was lying on the carpet beside it.

'There's nothing going on.'

'Then how do you explain all this? Your sketchbook, Beth. What have you done to it?' Pulling a tissue from the box on Beth's desk, her mum dabbed at the cover. 'And the tears… It's not like you at all.'

'How do you know it's not like me? You don't know anything about me.'

'I know that something's happened – that you're angry and hurt. I just want to help.'

Sitting on the edge of the bed, her mum flicked through the pages of the sketchbook. Pages filled with eagles and kites and buzzards. As she did, something in her expression changed. There was no longer concern in her eyes but something akin to fear. It was Beth's turn to be worried.

'Why do you draw these, Beth? When you could draw anything else in the world?' She jabbed a finger at the page. 'Why this?'

The question surprised Beth. She pushed her hair back from her wet face. 'I don't know.'

'Don't lie to me. You must know. What do you remember?'

'I don't know what you're talking about.'

Her mum took her wrist, her fingers pressing into her skin. 'Ria… What do you remember about Ria?'

'Stop it, Mum. You're scaring me.'

Then as quickly as it had happened, the moment passed. With a look of horror, her mum dropped her hand. 'Oh, darling, I'm so sorry.' She pulled Beth into her arms. 'I don't know what's the matter with me.'

Beth looked at her white face. 'You're not well, Mum. I think you should see a doctor.'

'Everything okay in here?' Her dad stood in the doorway, rubbing at his beard. Beth wasn't sure how much he'd heard. She glanced at her mum, who was staring at her as though willing her not to say anything.

'Yes. Everything's fine.'

'That's good then. It's late and I could do with my bed. Coming, Leona?'

He offered his hand and her mum took it. As she got up, the sketchbook slipped onto the floor. Neither of her parents looked at it as they went out. Beth picked it up. She stared at the eagle's feet she'd drawn in the black marker. The talons sharp and deadly. She hadn't lied to her mum; she didn't know why she had drawn them.

Closing the book, she got into bed. It was late before sleep would come, and when it did, it wasn't David she dreamed about. It was a faceless woman called Ria.

CHAPTER TWENTY-TWO
Ria

Ria could hear voices in the square outside the apartment. Putting down the baby book she'd been reading, she went to the window. Her mum and dad were standing in the street, studying the brass numbers on the houses. Satisfied they'd got the right place, they climbed the steps to the front door.

'They're here.' Getting no answer, Ria went into the hallway. 'Gareth, I said they're here?' The last time she'd seen him, he'd been in the study doing something at his computer, but she could see, from the open doorway, that he was no longer in there. Where was he?

Hurrying to the front door, she felt the nerves begin again. What would her parents make of the apartment? It was nothing like the student flat she'd shared before moving in with Gareth. Neither did it resemble her parents' rather chaotic semi with its cheap mismatched furniture and dining room table covered in motorcycle parts.

Opening the door, she was greeted by her mum's cheery smile. 'Happy birthday!'

'Thanks, Mum. How was your journey?'

'We got the bus. Fifty minutes door-to-door.'

Her dad was running his hand down the stucco pillar that supported the first-floor balcony above. 'Not bad, this.'

Giving them both a kiss, Ria ushered them inside, taking their coats and hanging them on the black coat stand. As she showed them into the living room, she couldn't help seeing the place as if through their eyes: the blond wood flooring and the black ash furniture with its clean minimalist lines. No cushions and no knick-knacks or photographs like the ones that graced her parents' mantelpiece. The only artwork was a huge frameless black and white photograph of a New York skyscape that hung on the wall above the black leather settee.

They stood awkwardly in the middle of the room and Ria felt as though she was showing clients around a show home.

'Sit down and I'll get us a drink. What would you like? Sherry? Whiskey? Or there's some chilled wine in the fridge.'

Her dad looked at his watch. 'Go on then, you've twisted my arm. It's not as though I'm driving. I'll have a whiskey.'

Ria could see he'd made an effort, exchanging his usual uniform of oil-smeared jeans and jumper for a pair of cord trousers and a shirt. Her mum was wearing a dress Ria hadn't seen before and she wondered whether she'd bought it specially.

'Place must have cost a pretty penny.' Her dad took the drink she handed him. 'South Kensington's a decent area to live. Hob-nobbing with royalty, if you please.'

It wasn't far off what Ria had thought the first time she'd seen the white flat-fronted terrace, with its pillared porches, in daylight. It was situated in a leafy square, its wide bay windows looking out onto private gardens enclosed by black railings, and was a million miles away from the semi where she'd grown up.

'Yes, it's very nice,' her mum agreed, joining her dad on the settee. 'You must have had a good tidy-up before we got here; the place is immaculate.'

'Gareth doesn't like a mess. It's made me realise what a slob I've always been.'

Her dad stopped flicking through the pages of the shiny hardback he'd found on the glass coffee table. 'I don't remember it bothering you before.' He closed the book and touched a roughened finger to its cover. '*Vanity Fair – A Century of Iconic Images*. What's that all about?'

'It's Gareth's. He's interested in that sort of thing.'

'Is he now?' He looked at the door. 'Where is he, anyway?'

Ria couldn't admit to not knowing. 'He just popped out to get some wine. He won't be long.'

'Thought you said there was some in the fridge.'

She was beginning to feel flustered. 'He wanted to get another bottle in case we ran out.'

'The man must think we're bleeding alcoholics.' Ria was relieved when he laughed. 'Probably not far off the truth. What are you having, Pamela?'

'I'd better have some of that white wine, now they've gone to so much trouble. Anyway, happy birthday again, darling. What's it like being twenty-one?'

Ria laughed. 'Not much different.'

'It's being a mother that will change you. How are you feeling?'

'Not too bad. A bit sick in the mornings, but I'm twelve weeks now and it's got a lot better.'

'Well, you're blooming. Unlike me when I was carrying you. I was as sick as a dog for most of it. That's part of the reason we decided to stick to just the one.'

'That and the fact that you thought it meant you'd be able to avoid any more "how's your father" for the next thirty years.'

'Stop it, Brian.' Ria's mum gave him a slap. 'Or I'll leave you at home next time.'

Glad that Gareth wasn't there to hear their conversation, Ria went to the kitchen to get the wine. Where was he? Looking around for a note or some other indication of where he might be, she found nothing. She glanced at the clock on the wall and saw it was twelve ten. They didn't need to be at the restaurant until twelve thirty, but he'd known what time her parents were arriving. Taking the bottle of white wine out of the fridge, she unscrewed it and filled a glass, then poured herself some orange juice. Trying to hide her frustration, she went back into the living room.

'Here you are, Mum.'

'Thank you, love.' Her mum raised her glass. 'To you. I've got a present for you in my bag. Do you want it now, or shall we wait for Gareth?'

'I'll have it now, if that's okay.' She knew what her mother's presents could be like and she'd rather open it while they were on their own.

Reaching into her bag, her mum brought out a package wrapped in bright red paper. 'It's not much, but I made it myself. I hope you like it.'

Ria took the parcel and sat down next to her. There was a label on it and she turned it over. In her unruly hand, her mother had written, *Something for your new home*. Ria's heart sank a little. She couldn't imagine Gareth approving of anything her mum would choose, let alone make. Slowly, she pulled off the paper, trying to put off the moment. What she saw inside confirmed her fears. It was a white cushion on which her mum had appliqued pink gingham hearts. Below them, she had embroidered *Home Sweet Home*.

Her mum looked around uncertainly. 'I'm sure you'll find a place for it.'

Ria forced a smile. She couldn't let her think she didn't like it. Leaning over, she kissed her cheek. 'I will, Mum. It's lovely, thank you.'

They drank and made small talk, and all the time, Ria watched the clock. If Gareth wasn't back soon, they would have to go without him. By the time she heard his key in the door, she was near to tears.

He came into the living room and stared in surprise. He was wearing his jogging bottoms and a running shirt that was covered in sweat.

'Brian... Pamela... you're early.'

Her parents exchanged a look. It was clear Gareth hadn't been out to the off-licence. Her dad rose and held out his hand.

'Good to see you, mate. We thought you had emigrated.'

Ria stood up, frustration and anger overwhelming her. He would need a shower and a change of clothes before they could go. She felt like a child who'd had her day spoilt. 'Why didn't you tell me you were going for a run, Gareth?' She couldn't be bothered to pretend any more. 'We're going to be late. What were you thinking?'

Sitting down again, it was impossible to stop the tears bubbling to the surface. Gareth was by her side at once. 'Sweetie, don't cry. It's just a misunderstanding. Remember, we changed the time of the booking to one o'clock to make sure you were properly over your morning sickness before your mum and dad arrived?' He turned to her parents. 'Ria said she'd let you know. I'm guessing she forgot.'

Ria looked up at him, wet-eyed. 'We never said that, Gareth. We didn't talk about changing the time.'

He swept her hair out of her eyes and kissed her forehead, the gesture reminding her of something her dad might have done when she was a child. 'The pregnancy hormones are making you forgetful. Never mind. No harm done.'

Feeling ridiculous, Ria took a tissue out of her pocket and blew her nose, sensing her mum's look of sympathy. She was sure they hadn't changed the time, but Gareth was right, recently she'd been getting quite forgetful, misplacing things and having to be reminded of appointments she hadn't remembered making.

'Anyway, I won't be long getting ready.' He wiped a finger under Ria's eye and whispered in her ear so that only she could hear: 'Pull yourself together, Ria. You're embarrassing me.'

CHAPTER TWENTY-THREE
Leona

'And her family, Leona. What about them? Weren't they concerned?'

Like mine are about me? I haven't told Lisa about my meltdown in Beth's bedroom. About the way both she and Scott have been tiptoeing around me, in case they say something that might set me off again.

'I don't think so. After Ria got pregnant, I think they were just relieved that he was going to stick by her. They were quite traditional like that. I reckon they liked the fact he was looking after her. If they were worried that he didn't let her do anything or that they saw less of her, they didn't let on. They probably passed it off as concern for her pregnancy. But a wedding without your family and friends… Is that normal?'

Lisa doesn't answer, but pushes the water jug towards me. I shake my head. I want to get this over with – tell the story to the end, and then perhaps I can get back to some sort of normal life. Not that I've lived a normal life since it happened. On the outside, maybe, but not in my head. I just want it all to be over.

'When the baby was born, did things change for Ria?' Lisa pours herself some water and takes a sip, leaving a perfect imprint of her pink lipstick on the glass.

'For a bit, yes. Gareth loved Lily – that much was obvious. I stopped being concerned.'

I should have known better.

CHAPTER TWENTY-FOUR

Ria

The doorbell rang and Ria looked up, wondering who it might be. They weren't expecting any packages and the health visitor had stopped visiting a while back. She'd grown used to the days being just her and Lily, seldom going out. Even the trips to the supermarket, which she'd once enjoyed, had been replaced with online shopping. It would be too much for her, Gareth said, with a baby to take care of.

Checking the Moses basket to make sure the baby was still asleep, she went to answer the door, surprised to find Leo standing there holding a big pink balloon.

'I decided that if you weren't going to ask me over, I'd have to just come uninvited.'

'I'm sorry, Leo, it's just that…' Ria looked behind her, anxious to get back to the sleeping baby.

'I just wanted to see her before I become a pensioner.'

Ria laughed. 'It's only been a few weeks.'

'Three months actually.' Folding her arms, Leo gave Ria a mock frown. 'Anyway, aren't you going to invite me in? I'm skiving lectures as it is.'

'Of course. I'm sorry.' Seeing Leo's open arms, Ria stepped into them, the warmth and familiarity of her friend's body making tears well in her eyes. She'd missed this.

'Hey, don't cry. You're a new mother. You should be happy.'

'I am,' Ria said, taking a tissue from her pocket and dabbing at her eyes. 'I don't know what's got into me. It must be the hormones. Come in, I'll make us some tea.'

Leo's ripped-at-the-knee jeans and unruly hair looked out of place in the apartment. It made Ria feel that she'd moved on. Left her old life behind.

'Goodness. She's gorgeous.' Leo bent to the Moses basket. 'And so tiny.'

'You should have seen her when she was first born.' Ria stopped, feeling her face redden. She knew Leo would have been round like a shot had she asked. Camped out at the hospital if necessary – but, in those first days, Gareth had said it should be just the two of them – their own little family. Even her parents had had to wait a few weeks to meet their first grandchild. Although her mother had offered to come and stay, Gareth had said they didn't need her. He would take care of them both.

'You look tired, Ria. When was the last time you had a break?'

'A break?'

'From the baby… From domesticity.'

'You say it like it's a dirty word. I like my life. I'm happy.'

Leo stood up and flung an arm around Ria's neck, pulling her cheek close and kissing it like in the old days. 'I'm sorry. I didn't mean it to come out like that. I just mean that Lily is Gareth's baby as well as yours. Is he doing his bit?'

'Of course he is.'

Ria had been pleased when Gareth had agreed to take some time off when the baby was first born, surprised at the bond that seemed to have formed between father and daughter. In those first few weeks, he'd taken his turn to change Lily's nappies and got out of bed to fetch her from her Moses basket when she needed a feed at night. He'd been considerate of Ria's feelings, not pressuring her for sex when she was clearly exhausted.

Then, one night, a month after Lily was born, things had changed. Lily had been fractious all day, not wanting to settle, and at ten o'clock Ria had fallen into bed, craving sleep. Gareth had been out with some clients and when he'd climbed into bed, she could smell the drink on him. She'd felt his hand slide around her body, cupping her breast, and she'd taken it and kissed it. Moving it to her hip. Sure he'd understand.

The next night, he hadn't come home, and she hadn't asked where he'd been. Afraid of what his answer might be.

The ringing of her mobile phone made her jump now, and she snatched it up from the coffee table. Turning away so that Leo couldn't see her face.

'Hi, Gareth… What am I doing?' She glanced at Leo and moved away into the hall. 'Nothing much, just some housework while Lily naps.'

Tucking the phone under her chin, she went into the kitchen where she couldn't be heard. Lifting the teapot from the cupboard, she added a heaped spoonful of tea from the caddy. It was a long while since she'd bought tea bags. In the background she could hear voices, the sounds of Gareth's office.

As she listened to what Gareth was saying, her hand hovered above the teapot. 'I didn't know you were going to be away tonight.'

Peering at the calendar on the wall, she saw nothing written there. 'There's nothing on the calendar. Are you sure you told me? No, I'm not calling you a liar, Gareth. Of course, I realise one of us has to work.' She paused, embarrassed. 'It's just that I've got no money. My bank card's not in my purse. I must have left it somewhere. Yes, I do need it. It's Mum's birthday and I thought it would be nice to take Lily to see her tomorrow. I'll need money for the bus and I want to get her a present.'

In the other room, the baby had started to cry. Moving to the door, she listened to hear if Lily would settle without her going to her, and was relieved when the crying stopped as quickly as it started.

'Yes, I've looked everywhere.' Why was he being so difficult? 'No… No. Please don't get cross. I understand. No, there's no one here. Why would there be? Of course I love you. I'll see you tomorrow evening.'

Wondering why she'd lied, Ria switched off the phone and pushed it away from her. She sunk her head into her hands. It was the fourth time Gareth had called her that day.

'I'll lend you the money. How much do you need?'

Leo was standing in the doorway, holding Lily, the baby's sleeping face half-obscured by her fair hair.

'You don't need to do that. It's fine.'

'Your husband's happy to leave you with no money and you think it's fine? Don't you have any other cards, Ria? What about a credit card?'

Ria took Lily from Leo's arms and kissed her, embarrassed to answer the question. 'Gareth has one. He doesn't think we both need one and I agree. It would only be a temptation to spend, and things are a bit tight at the moment.'

Ria looked at the kitchen, seeing what Leo was seeing: the large kitchen island and the shiny black cupboards with their marble worktops. Her words sounded ridiculous. 'He's not always like this.'

Leo held out two twenties. 'Take it. You can pay me back when you next see me. Go and see your mum, Ria, and talk to her.' There was a pause. 'Are you sure you're all right?'

'Of course I am. Why shouldn't I be?'

'You just seem different somehow. Not the happy-go-lucky Ria who used to go clubbing with me on a Friday night. I haven't forgotten how you blew me out that time.'

'I told you what happened. Gareth had planned something special for my birthday. I couldn't let him down.'

'But you were happy to let *me* down. You've dropped your friends, given up your singing… What other parts of your life is he controlling, Ria?'

Ria felt her hands clench. 'Nothing. Gareth's right. You never liked him.'

Leo looked shocked. 'That's not true, Ria. It's not him I don't like. It's what he's doing to you.'

'He isn't doing anything. You're just jealous because we've made a nice life for ourselves. A lovely apartment. A baby. What have you got? A rented flat and a boyfriend who's a waste of space.'

Ria stopped and bit her lip, wondering what had come over her. She'd never spoken to Leo like this before.

'Listen to yourself, Ria. Listen to whose words these really are. I don't for one minute believe that's what you think, but, if it is, then I'd better go. Don't bother giving me the money back. Gareth probably wouldn't let you come round anyway... That's if you even dared to tell him.'

The need to defend Gareth was stronger than her friendship with Leo. Nobody understood him like Ria did. Nobody saw what she saw when he was in one of his good moods. She drew herself up. 'How dare you talk about my husband like that? You don't know anything about my marriage. If you can't be civil about him, get out of my house, Leo, and don't bother coming back.'

'If that's what you want.' Placing the money on the worktop, Leo turned and walked out of the kitchen, leaving Ria wondering if they'd ever see each other again.

Ria had been watching television when the front door slammed. Pointing the controller at the television, she muted it.

'Gareth?'

He appeared in the doorway, swaying slightly. 'Who else would it be?'

'It's just that you said you wouldn't be home tonight.'

Folding his arms, he leant against the door frame, a smile on his lips. 'Aren't you pleased to see me?'

Ria's heart started to beat a bit faster. He was unpredictable when he'd been drinking. She'd only just got Lily to sleep and she didn't want a row. 'Of course I am. I'm just surprised, that's all.'

He held her gaze a moment, then turned and went into the hallway. She heard his footsteps as he went into the kitchen and found she was holding her breath. She hadn't done anything wrong, yet she felt guilty. There was the sound of the dishwasher being opened and the rattle of crockery as the wire racks were pulled out in turn. It was then that she realised what he was doing. He was checking. In the silence that followed, Ria imagined Gareth counting the cups and plates; working out how many they'd used since the previous evening. She could see the mug with the blue and white stripes around the rim – the one they only used for visitors – sitting with the others, and knew what he'd be thinking.

She was right. He strode into the sitting room, the mug in his hands.

'Who the fuck used this?'

His voice was low. Menacing. There was no point in lying. It would only make things worse. 'It was Leo.'

'You're lying!'

The mug smashed against the wall by Ria's head, chips of white china covering the wooden floor like confetti.

Ria bent to pick up the pieces, her hand shaking. 'I'm not lying, Gareth. Why would I?'

He stood over her and she could sense he was deciding whether or not to believe her. 'Why was Leo here?'

'To see Lily. Why else?'

'Even though we agreed…'

'No. I never agreed to anything.' Indignation made her brave. She stood up and faced him. 'Leo is my friend… About the only one I have left.'

He moved so quickly, she didn't have time to react. She felt the pressure of his thumb and finger as he grabbed her chin. 'Come to talk about me behind my back, more likely. I bet the two of you had a fine old time discussing what a sorry life you have. How you'd have been better off if you hadn't met me.'

'That's not true. Why would we do that? Stop it, Gareth, you're hurting me.' Pushing his hand away, she glanced at the door, praying Lily wouldn't wake.

As if thinking the same thing, Gareth stepped away and Ria felt her body unclench. Relieved that the storm had passed. But it hadn't. Without warning, her husband's fist flew towards her face, making contact with her jaw. She fell back against the wall, the shock stopping her from crying out.

Almost immediately, Gareth was beside her. Crouching next to her, he pulled her to him, rocking her backwards and forwards in his arms.

'Baby, I'm sorry. Sometimes I think you want me to lose my temper. It will never happen again. I promise. I love you. You must believe me.'

Ria felt his tears on her face and she knew what it had taken for him to apologise. It was her fault. She should have told him about Leo, been more sensitive, not let him find out the way he had. Even though the pain in her jaw was excruciating, she reached up a hand and stroked his face.

He loved her and it would never happen again.

'Let's go to bed,' she said.

CHAPTER TWENTY-FIVE

Beth

Beth had hoped that by arriving late, she would avoid Carina, but as she went through the gates and the wide wings of Lady Edburton came into view, she knew it was never going to happen. Most of the students had gone in, but Carina was leaning against the wall by the steps. There was no doubt in Beth's mind that she was waiting for her as, ever since she'd seen her in the car, she'd known it would only be a matter of time before Carina would use what she'd seen to her advantage.

This morning, unusually, Carina wasn't surrounded by her girlfriends, but was standing on her own. Maybe she could go in one of the side doors and avoid her, or push into one of the last groups of girls who were going in, and hope she wouldn't be seen? It was hopeless, though. From her vantage point on the steps, there was no way Carina wouldn't see her as she walked up the drive. Beth would just have to face what was coming to her. Get it over with.

Ducking her head, Beth walked as quickly as she could, hating the sound of her feet on the gravel as she walked towards the entrance. A few stragglers were climbing the steps and she slipped in behind them. As they jostled forward, one of the girls stopped and said something to Carina. This could be her chance. Only a few more feet and she'd be able to duck into the school. Taking her bag off her shoulder, Beth unzipped it and pretended to be looking for something. If she was lucky, she might just get past.

It wasn't to be, though. Just as she reached the door, she felt a hand on her arm, the fingers pulling at her maroon jumper.

'Beth. How are you? I've been worried about you.'

Carina's smile was friendly, her tone concerned, but Beth wasn't taken in by it. Sometimes she thought she preferred it when Carina was openly hostile; at least, then, she knew where she was with her.

Beth pulled her arm away. 'You don't need to be.'

'It's just that I haven't seen anyone that sick in a long time. What was it? Tummy bug? Food poisoning? No, don't tell me... You just can't take your drink.'

'It's none of your business.'

She tried to move forward, but Carina caught hold of the strap of her rucksack and pulled her back. 'I wonder what Mummy and Daddy would think if they knew their precious daughter was out drinking. Do you think they'd be pleased to hear she vomited most of it back into a hedge?'

'It wasn't that bad.'

'If you say so. Lucky for you, Dad was too busy watching the road to notice. He might have felt the need to mention it to your dad this morning otherwise.'

Beth decided to bluff it. 'Even if he did, my dad wouldn't care.'

'Maybe not.' Carina narrowed her eyes. 'But they might care if I told them who you were with.'

'I wasn't with anyone.'

'So I was imagining the fit-looking guy with the long hair, was I? The one who looked so worried about you. You've kept *him* quiet. Wonder what he sees in you. It can't be your magnetic personality, that's for sure.'

'Fuck off, Carina. You don't know anything.' Beth pressed the bridge of her nose with her finger and thumb. David must have followed her out onto the road. She'd been drunk; she hadn't realised. All she remembered was the rain and the misery. How, after wiping her mouth on her sleeve, she'd run back home, believing he hadn't cared.

'How old is he anyway?

'He's twenty-four, if you must know. It's not that old.' Carina was right, though. Her parents would go ape-shit if they found out. Her mum was overprotective enough as it was. 'Anyway, I'm not seeing him. He's just a friend.'

'If you say so. I wonder whether the other girls would agree with you?' Carina gave a wave to Keira, who was just going in, and Beth felt self-pity wash over her.

Her shoulders sagged in resignation. 'Don't tell them, Carina.'

'I'd have thought you'd have wanted them to know, *Jessica*. Something to be proud of.' Carina pushed herself away from the rail. 'You never know, you might even get another nickname. I wonder what they'll come up with? On second thoughts, they'll probably just use the good old standard that everyone recognises. *Slag*.'

With a laugh, she turned her back on Beth and pushed her way into the building.

Beth folded her arms across her chest, wishing she could disappear. She hated her... Hated all of them. The only person who'd seen her for who she really was, was David.

And now she'd blown that too.

CHAPTER TWENTY-SIX

Leona

'Gareth did hit Ria again, of course. Men like that always do.'

I'm looking at a small stain on the carpet, near the coffee table, wondering what has made it. Was it an accident? Was it deliberate? It makes me think of all the faceless men and women who have sat in this very chair, turning their lives inside out for Lisa to view.

'But, of course, you'd know that, wouldn't you,' I continue. 'You must see hundreds of people in your job with the same story.'

'Not hundreds,' Lisa says, her fingers steepled under her chin. 'But enough. Do you feel able to carry on?'

'Carry on? I suppose so.'

After all, it's something I've been doing for the last twelve years. Since Ria made her choice and turned my world upside down. Since the monstrous thing she did.

'Ria became more and more cut off from people. Gareth's version of her became who she was. Boring, stupid.' Lisa is studying my face. She will have seen the contempt I've been unable to hide. Hear the disdain in my voice. I continue anyway. 'She became dependent on him for everything. Especially money. He'd come home with clothes and toys for Lily, but, if she wanted anything for herself, she'd have to time it carefully. Think about what to say and when to say it, so as not to make him angry.'

Standing, I walk to Lisa's shelf of books, running my finger along the spines.

'And when he wasn't threatening her, he ignored her. His weapon was silence. Cut off from her family and friends like she was, she needed his love. Life became all about making him happy.'

I think of Scott. His easy-going nature and the ironic smile that's never far from his lips. Ria wouldn't have known what true love was. Would only have known a hand raised in anger, not in tenderness. One that left a bruise, rather than the shiver that lingers after a caress.

'There was Lily, of course, but she was just a baby. Poor Ria. She was little more than a child herself when Gareth came into her life.'

Lisa nods and writes something in her notes. 'It's the first time you've shown sympathy for her, Leona. That's a good thing.'

'Is it? I'm not sure.'

It's the anger that's kept me sane as I've tried to come to terms with what happened. It's what's helped build the wall around me. One that I've only allowed Scott and Beth to breach. But where there's been anger, there has also been fear. Remembering Ria is taking me to places I had hoped to leave behind. Unlocking rooms in my heart that I had hoped would remain secure.

I think of my outburst in Beth's room. How my paranoia has affected our relationship more than I could ever have imagined.

'Last night I mentioned Ria to my daughter.'

Lisa shows no surprise. 'And what did she say?'

'She doesn't remember, she was too young, but I was scared and I lost my temper when I began to question her. It frightened me. A child should never have to fear her parent.'

'No, they shouldn't.'

We sit in silence and I know we're both thinking about the same person.

'Did Gareth ever hurt Lily, do you think?' Lisa asks eventually.

The question shocks me. 'Never. She was a sweet child. Despite the way he treated Ria, he adored her.'

'Do you think she knew what was going on?'

'I don't think so. She was only little. When it all ended, she was still only four.'

'Children absorb more than you think. They might not understand all that's being said, but they can recognise the emotion behind the words… Anger… Fear… Even if it's not directed at them.'

'I know what you're doing. You're using Ria's daughter to excuse what happened.' I turn to her and realise I'm shouting. 'Nothing can excuse what she did. Nothing.'

If Lisa is concerned by my outburst, she doesn't show it. Instead, she gets up and walks over to the other side of the room where there is a low table. On it is a tray with two cups and saucers. A kettle is plugged into the wall and she flicks the switch to turn it on. I watch as the bubbles, in their stripe of clear Perspex, rise as quickly as my anger did just now. When the water has boiled, the bubbles calm. I try to steady my breathing.

'I'm sorry. I didn't mean to shout.'

'You don't need to apologise, Leona.' She smiles at me. 'Your session isn't over yet, but I think you could do with a break. Would you like some coffee or tea? I have camomile. It might help.'

I sit down, exhaustion washing over me. I've kept things bottled inside me for so long that I worry they'll explode out, like the contents of a soda siphon. Whatever I say can never be taken back. The thought scares me.

'That would be good. Thanks.' I wait while Lisa pours boiling water over the tea bag. She doesn't make a drink for herself. Coming back to where we've been sitting, she puts the cup on the table in front of me.

'I'm worried Beth's being bullied.' I've no idea why I've said that. The words have come from nowhere.

Lisa sits down, placing her hands in her lap. 'What makes you think that?'

I think of Beth's closed face. The way she avoids questions. Her defensiveness. I've seen these things before. Seen them in Ria.

'Call it a mother's instinct. She's never been happy at her school, but recently things have got worse. She doesn't want to go out any more. Just stays in her room, drawing. Ria was the same. She used to be the life and soul... until Gareth. He changed her into someone I didn't recognise and there was nothing I could do to help her. What if I can't help Beth?'

'You can't hold yourself responsible for everything, Leona. Beth is an adolescent. Mood swings are par for the course.'

I'm not listening, my mind worrying over the facts. 'I think she may be skipping school too. It's happened before.'

'I see.' Lisa looks concerned and it makes a shiver run down my spine. 'Have you spoken to the school?'

I shake my head. 'Not yet.'

'I think you should... as a first step.'

'You're right, I suppose, but why is she doing this? I sometimes wonder whether I should talk to her about what happened in the past. Maybe I'm the cause of whatever it is that's troubling her.'

'No, Leona. That wouldn't be a good idea. There's a chance it could make things worse for her if she knows. If she remembers, it mustn't cloud how she feels about you.'

'Shall I go on with the story?'

Lisa looks at the clock on the wall. 'We could extend the session by thirty minutes if you like. I think it's important we talk about how it all ended, don't you?'

My heart is beating a tattoo in my chest, but I know that I have to go on. The only problem is... which story to tell?

CHAPTER TWENTY-SEVEN

Ria

The house was quiet when Ria let herself in, just the murmur of the television coming from the living room. As she stood in the hallway, she tried to work out how she felt. Was it excitement that clawed at her stomach, or fear?

Trying to control her emotions, she put her head around the door of the living room. It was empty, but there were signs that her babysitter, Abbie, had been there: the throw from the back of the settee had been left in a heap on the floor and the empty cover of a box set sat on the coffee table. Abbie was the teenage daughter of the family who lived next door and, although it had taken Ria a long time to pluck up the courage to ask her, she'd been more than happy to look after Lily for a few hours.

On the television, a police officer was escorting a youth to a panda car, placing his hand on his head as he pushed him down into the back seat. Another stood on the pavement, writing something in a notebook. Ria stood in the doorway, watching the flashing blue light as the car moved away into the night. It wasn't the sort of thing she ever watched.

Going back out to the hall, Ria could hear a kettle being filled in the kitchen and the clatter of a mug on the marble worktop.

'I'm back, Abbie,' she called. 'I'll be with you in a minute – I'm just going to check on Lily.'

She was about to take off her coat when she changed her mind. The black dress she was wearing was an old one from her student days. Although quite plain, it was short and not exactly the thing she'd wear to see her parents. That was where she'd told Abbie she was going when the girl had arrived earlier – a precaution in case Gareth discovered she'd been out. Not that there was any reason why he would. These days, if he went out, he didn't come home until the small hours, if at all, and, as far as she knew, he never spoke to the neighbours. No, her secret was safe.

Crossing the hallway to Lily's room, she pushed open the door. The light from the hall cast a white stripe across her daughter's bed and she could just make out her sleeping figure. Lily lay with her duvet clutched in her small hand, her sandy hair, so much like Gareth's, falling across her face. Kneeling beside the bed, Ria gently pushed Lily's hair away from her cheek and kissed it, breathing in the smell of her. She stayed there for a moment, her arm around her, watching the rise and fall of her chest, feeling the warmth of her breath on her cheek.

Without warning, a picture came into her head, the memory too strong to push away. A different child. A tiny hand, so cold. So very, very cold. Ria's heart clenched in a vice-like grip and tears pooled in her eyes. What if she couldn't keep Lily safe?

Feeling Lily stir, Ria forced herself back to the present. She stood and gently pulled the duvet up around her daughter's shoulders, then she turned and, in the half light, took in the room: the jumble of soft toys piled up at the end of the bed, the moon and stars mobile that had hung from the ceiling ever since Lily was a baby, and the doll's house in the corner that Gareth had bought her for her fourth birthday.

It was hard to believe that tomorrow they would be leaving all this. That she and Lily would be starting a new life. She felt a wave of nausea at the thought of what she was going to do. She could still see the dismay on Leo's face as she'd shown her the fresh bruises at the top of her arms. The wine they'd been drinking had made it easier to talk. To tell the secret she'd been keeping for the last four years. But her words had come as no surprise to Leo.

As she'd pulled her cardigan back over her shoulder, and felt her friend's tears against her cheek as she was pulled into a hug, she'd known that she couldn't take any more. It would break her heart, but she had to leave Gareth. For too long she'd been like a caged bird, with Gareth holding the key to the door. Leo was right. She needed to break free. If not for her own sake, then for her daughter's.

Ria's hand moved to her bag. The piece of paper, with the solicitor's number Leo had given her, would be her way out. Once she was in the safety of her parents' house, she'd ring him.

She looked at the sleeping child, a rising tide of guilt lapping at her. The bond between Lily and her father was strong. What if Lily hated her for taking her away from him?

Tonight, Gareth was at a work do, a corporate event at a smart hotel near St James's Park, all black tie and cocktail dresses. He hadn't wanted her with him – couldn't trust her not to embarrass him, he'd said – but how could she have gone anyway, with the marks from his fingers still visible on the tops of her arms? She took a shuddering breath. What would he do if he knew what she was planning?

With a last look at Lily, she left the bedroom, leaving the door ajar. This time she had to be strong. She'd tried to leave before, but always she'd backed out. Scared of what he might do if he found her. Scared of his threats. Not this time, though. This time she would do it.

Abbie was putting her coffee cup and biscuit plate into the dishwasher. Ria could hear the clink of china and the rattle of the cutlery as she slid the tray closed.

'Leave that, Abbie. I'll do it later…'

She stopped. Her body rigid. It wasn't Abbie who leant against the kitchen counter, arms folded. It was Gareth.

She felt the breath leave her body. 'You're home.'

'One of us is.' His pupils were glassy. 'Where the hell were you?'

She swallowed. 'I went to see my mum and dad.'

'So that kid from next door said.' His eyes bored into her, seeking out the lie, paralysing her. Pushing himself away from the counter, he walked unsteadily towards her.

Forcing her limbs to move, Ria took a step backwards, the stainless-steel bin rocking as she made contact with it.

'I haven't seen them for nearly a year. I didn't think you'd mind.'

He'd reached her, his hand grabbing at the lapel of her coat. He forced it down over her shoulder. 'So you went to see your parents dressed like a whore?'

Ria looked at her black dress, remembering how good it had felt to wear it – taking her back to a time when things were simpler. Before the nightmare began. Now the dress was just a symbol of her guilt.

'I'm sorry.' The apology was automatic.

Gareth's head was close to hers now. She could feel his breath… smell it. He grabbed her face, his finger and thumb digging into the skin of her cheeks. 'Where have you been?' He squeezed harder. 'And don't fucking lie to me.'

His forehead had a film of sweat on it and damp patches had begun to bloom under the armpits of his expensive blue shirt.

'I told you. I went to see my parents.' She was gambling with his patience, but she couldn't let him know the truth.

Letting go of her face, he smiled. Once, it would have melted her heart. Not now. 'Why don't you empty your bag?'

'No.' Ria placed her hand over the zip as if that might be enough to stop him. Inside the bag was the solicitor's number. He mustn't see it.

'I said empty your fucking bag!' Grabbing the bag off her shoulder, he fumbled at the zip, turning it over and emptying the contents onto the floor.

A lipstick rolled under one of the bar stools and Ria watched it, steeling herself for what was to come. Swaying slightly, Gareth pushed at the few things with the toe of his shiny black shoe. There was her purse, her brush, her mobile phone. The paper with the number on was not amongst the items scattered across the tiles.

With relief, Ria remembered that she'd tucked the piece of paper into one of the inside pockets. With luck, he wouldn't find it. But even as she thought it, his hand was inside the bag, probing and pulling.

He held the piece of paper between his thumb and forefinger like a prize. 'What's this?'

'It's nothing.'

Reaching a hand behind him to steady himself on the kitchen island, he read it, then put it down on the shiny counter. His voice was icy. 'Andrew Clearly. Who the fuck is that?'

Ria wondered whether she could make a run for it. Get out onto the street and bang on Abbie's door. Tell her she was married to a madman. She backed away, hoping to get out into the hall, but it was only when her back came up against the sharp edge of the marble worktop that she realised she'd misjudged it.

His gaze hardened. 'If you're having an affair, I swear I will kill you.'

Ria was near to tears, but she knew of old that if she broke down in front of him, it would only make him angrier.

'I'm not, Gareth. You've got to believe me.'

'Why would I believe you when you're nothing but a jumped-up whore? If I hadn't picked you up from that sleazy cesspit of a bar, nobody else would have touched you. Just look at you. You're ridiculous.'

Hard though she tried, Ria couldn't stop the tears from falling. She glanced behind her. 'You'll wake Lily.'

'And what if I do? Don't think she doesn't know what her mother gets up to when her dad's not here. How many others are there sniffing around?'

'It's not like that.' She edged her way along the worktop, hoping to reach the door, but in two strides, Gareth was there, blocking her way. She would have to tell him.

'Andrew Clearly is a solicitor.'

'What do you want a solicitor for?' He leant against the door frame, his voice calm now, but his words were like a net closing in. Slowly, he rolled up his sleeves and she knew what was coming. She could lie or tell the truth. Either way, she'd lose. The truth was easier. 'I'm leaving you, Gareth. I've had enough.'

The words hung between them, knife-sharp. Ria waited, trying to read his body language for clues, but could find none. His face was impassive now, but she knew how his mind worked. She wasn't fooled.

His laugh was empty. 'Are you stupid enough to think that if you left, I wouldn't find you? You have no idea of the power of money. People owe me.'

'I wasn't going to run away. Just stay at my mum and dad's for a while. You'll be able to see Lily when you want.'

'You wouldn't dare leave me,' he said, the sneer in his voice evident. 'I'm all you've got.'

Lurching forward, he pushed up against her, pressing his body hard onto hers so that her spine bit into the worktop. Taking her face in his hands, he tried to kiss her, but she turned her head away, repulsed by the smell of whiskey on his breath.

He drew her face back towards him. 'Don't tease.'

The hands she had once loved to feel on her skin, now made it crawl. She screwed up her eyes. 'Please don't.'

'It's a bit late to play hard to get, isn't it?'

Grabbing her by the hair, he tipped her head back and forced his mouth onto hers, crushing the underside of her lip against her teeth. There was the unmistakeable metallic taste of blood. With his free hand, he reached down and pulled her dress up over her thighs, shoving his hand between her legs.

Over the years, she'd felt she'd lost the right to say no, but now she fought to get away, fear making her brave. 'If you touch me, when Lily's older, I'll make sure she knows exactly what her father is. A rapist and a wife-beater.'

The force of his hand knocked her to the floor and, through the blinding pain, she realised her error. His eyes were cold, his lips a thin line as he stood over her.

'And I will make sure she knows your dirty little secret.'

Her fear was overwhelming. Paralysing. He would kill her. She knew it. With blood hammering at her temples, she pushed herself away from him across the floor, but he was quicker. Grabbing her by the throat, he forced her to stand. He was too big. Too near. She could feel the press of his fingers on her neck.

Gareth's face was as hard as if it had been stamped on a coin. Though it was close to hers, she could barely recognise him, anger making his smooth features ugly. She was shocked to see the hatred in his eyes, and it was then that she realised he had probably never loved her. Not really.

He pressed harder, his eyes never leaving hers. Ria pulled at his hands, but he was too strong. She was struggling to breathe. The room was blurring.

He would kill her.

Reaching out a hand blindly, Ria grabbed at anything that was there. Her fingertips met with the heavy pasta jar. As she brought it down, the cold glass making contact with the side of his head, there was only one thought in her mind.

It would end badly. But at least it would end.

CHAPTER TWENTY-EIGHT
Beth

'I was beginning to think you weren't going to come.' David pushed the door of the camper van closed and walked over to her. 'That you've been avoiding me. I'd been hoping I might bump into you on the fells, but the chances of that were pretty slim.'

Although the bench where she was sitting was uncomfortable, cold and damp with dew, Beth remained where she was. It was not yet dawn, but there was the sensation that day was at hand. Despite the pale moon that hung over the church, the sky to the east was already lightening. She could hear the occasional bleat of a sheep from a nearby field and, in an hour or so, Graham Hargreaves would be trundling down the lane in his van to open up his shop in order to receive the morning papers.

'I wasn't going to come.'

He folded his arms. 'What made you change your mind?'

'I woke up this morning and thought, you know what, if he's going to be a dickhead, then I might as well get up at some ungodly hour and find out why.'

She wasn't going to tell him how hard it had been not to answer his calls. How the idea of seeing him again, once planted, had become too strong to ignore – even if it meant she would be embarrassed all over again. What made her wake last night and see his text, she didn't know, but there had been something romantic about his request to meet her at dawn. Like pebbles thrown at a window in a movie.

'I see. A dickhead's what I am, is it?' His surprise at her choice of words had turned quickly to amusement. 'Well, you're probably right. I wouldn't win any contests for diplomacy.' Shoving his hands into his pockets, he looked at her. 'I would have explained it all to you, only you ran off and then never answered any of my calls.'

'You could have messaged me, like normal people do. Not wait until last night to do it.'

For once he was serious. 'What I had to say, couldn't have been said in a message. Anyway, who's to say you wouldn't have ignored that too?'

Beth looked away. 'I'm here, aren't I?'

'You are... and I appreciate it. I didn't mean to upset you.'

'I wasn't upset,' she said, hoping he wouldn't see through her lie. 'I was angry. So, what was it that made you treat me like a leper? My sweaty palm? The fact that your girlfriend wouldn't like it?'

'My girlfriend?' He looked confused.

'The one who should have been going to the barbeque.'

'The one who...?'

'Zena or Zara or whatever her name is.'

David frowned. 'Oh, her. Why would you think she was my girlfriend?'

'I just had a feeling.'

'Well, for your information, she isn't. Anyway, what's the big deal?'

Beth swallowed. Despite everything he'd said, it was clear he didn't care what she thought. She was moments away from getting up from her damp bench and taking the lane back to her house, but if she did, she'd never know how she'd managed to read the signals so wrongly. If she didn't find out, there was every chance she'd make the same mistake with someone else.

'So? Are you going to tell me or shall I just go home? I know what's looking like the better option at the moment.'

'I will – only just not here.' He sat down next to her. 'Did I tell you I've had another commission?' Her expression gave him his answer. 'No, of course not. You haven't been speaking to me. Anyway, I have.'

'What for?' Beth tried not to sound too interested.

'A local magazine. They want me to do an article called "Country Haunts".' He made quotation marks with his fingers in the air. '*A series of photographs capturing the mysterious bleakness of the wilder areas of the county.* I'm not going to tell the editor that the title is a fucking cliché and that I know any photographs I take will be just a vehicle for yet another trite article on the ghosts of the Lake District.'

Beth looked towards the churchyard. 'I've lived here most of my life and I've never seen a ghost.'

'Me neither. It won't matter, though. The readers will look at the photographs I've taken – all dark slate, rugged mountains and misty tarns, and their imaginations will do the rest. Speaking of which, that tarn I told you about… Fancy going to see it?'

'What, now?'

'Why not? I've checked the forecast and the weather should be perfect for the photographs I want to take. If we leave now, we will have timed it perfectly.'

'For the golden hour?'

'You've got it. Well remembered.' He got out his keys to the camper van and jiggled them in his hand. 'Anyway, what do you say? Fancy a jolly?'

Behind her, the church bell tolled the hour and she wondered whether her parents would have woken yet. Whether they'd gone into her bedroom and seen she wasn't there. No, of course they wouldn't have. It was much too early. Later, they would though, and then all hell would break loose. There would be questions from her mum about who she'd been with and what they'd talked about. A lecture on how people couldn't be trusted. That you never knew what their motives were. She'd heard it a million times before – in the lift in their old block of flats, as they'd stood in the entrance hall on her first day at Lady Edburton, when she'd suggested she'd like to join the drama group that ran on Saturday mornings in Ambleside. All the sodding time, in fact.

'I'd better just send a text to Mum. She'll only freak out if she finds I'm not there.'

And ask Beth questions about people she'd never even heard of in a voice that sent shivers down her spine.

'No problem. You can do it while we're driving. Hope she won't mind me whisking you away so early.'

Beth looked at the phone in her hands. 'She won't.'

That was because she wouldn't be telling her anything about him. She'd say she'd decided to get the early bus in order to go to breakfast club to revise. Her exams were only a few weeks away and, with any luck, her mum would believe her.

David held the door of the van open for her. 'Come on, then.'

She got in and he reversed into the lay-by, then pulled out onto the road. As they drove, he didn't speak, but instead, reached over and turned the radio on. The reception wasn't good, the hissing and crackling masking the country music that was playing. He fiddled with the dial and then, finding nothing better, turned the radio off again.

'Bloody reception.'

Beth said nothing. The early start had left her sleepy and, as the van drove through the countryside, she felt her eyes closing.

After what only seemed a few minutes, she felt a gentle shake on her arm. 'Beth. We're here.'

She opened her eyes, wondering where she was. Then she remembered. She was out on the fells with David. She ran a hand across her mouth, hoping she hadn't dribbled in her sleep, and looked out of the window. They had left the road and were in some sort of car park. Apart from David's camper, there was only one other vehicle – a Land Rover that was parked at the far side. A couple of early hikers were preparing for their walk. The woman was bending down, lacing her walking boots, a Labrador beside her, and the man was studying a map with a torch. Beth was disappointed. She wanted this to be *their* place. Not something to be shared with others.

David climbed out and raised his hand to them in greeting. 'Morning.' He turned to Beth, who had joined him. 'Looks like someone else has had the same idea.'

'Maybe they won't be going the same way.' Beth hoped it was the case. It had suddenly become important to her that they were alone.

'Maybe.' He slid open the door of the camper and took out his rucksack of camera equipment. 'We'll go this way.'

A ladder stile took them out onto the rough grassland of the fells. Immediately, there was a choice of paths, but David pointed to the one straight ahead.

'That's the way.'

Beth stood with her hands on her hips and looked up. In the milky light of dawn, she could just make out the path snaking its way up the mountainside, hugging its contours before disappearing into a copse of trees.

'It looks steep.'

'It looks worse from down here. You'll be fine and it certainly beats Striding Edge on a bank holiday. Believe me, it will be worth it when we get there, and then you'll thank me for dragging you out of your cosy bed.'

He led the way, his feet picking out the safest path. At first, it was fairly level. It passed behind a white farmhouse with thick, rough-cast walls on the flank of the hill, but then it started to climb. They gained height quickly and soon the slopes on either side of them fell away, pleated by a curtain of shale.

Beth looked down. They hadn't been climbing long but already it seemed they had left civilisation far behind. Wisps of mist still clung to the lower slopes and lingered in the valley. It was ethereal and beautiful.

'Doing all right?'

Beth nodded, unzipping her jacket as she grew warmer. To either side of the path the fells were covered in ferns, young fronds showing their shepherds' crooks.

'A chameleon's tongue.'

'What was that?'

'The ferns. They look like chameleons's tongues.'

David looked down. 'I suppose they do. That's the artist in you speaking.'

Beth was pleased. It was like they had shared something. The track was steep and rocky, the feeling of remoteness increasing with every step. As they climbed higher, new layers of peaks came into view and, as the sky lightened from navy to palest blue, their craggy summits stood out in dark relief against it.

Beth stopped and listened. A loud hissing and shushing had come from nowhere. 'What's that?'

'It's where we're going next. Peter's Ghyll.' David climbed onto an outcrop of rock and pointed. Reaching out a hand, he pulled Beth up to join him. She stared. They'd been following a little beck for some way, but what she saw in front of her was different. Here, the water rushed down the slope in an ever-increasingly deep gorge, tumbling in a series of waterfalls to the valley far below. It was wider, more urgent, than what they had seen before.

'To reach the tarn, we have to cross it. It's not far now.'

The path across was nothing more than rocks and slabs poised above the cascade. Beth felt her palms go clammy. They'd been chatting as they'd walked, easy conversation about their favourite part of the Lakes and which fell they liked the best, but now she fell silent.

David looked at her. 'What's up?'

'Is it safe?'

'You don't think I'd risk my camera equipment if it wasn't, do you?' He gripped the straps of his rucksack tightly. 'Put your feet where I do and you'll be fine. Not scared, are you?'

'Of course not.'

Beth watched as David crossed and then, taking a deep breath, she followed, wobbling her way across the stones, trying not to look at the rushing water that plummeted from the hillside below her. When she reached the other side, David smiled his approval.

'Crossed like a true professional.' He clapped her on the back. 'Just through the plantation of silver birches up ahead and we'll be there, but we mustn't hang about.'

Beth checked her watch. It was nearly six thirty. The sun would soon be up. Walking faster, they wound their way through the silver-white skins of the naked trees until they emerged from the gloom. And there it was – the tarn David had been telling her about. Completely still. Reflecting its surroundings.

'You took me to your special place, so I thought I'd take you to mine.' David took his rucksack off his back and opened his arms wide, as if to encompass all he saw. 'This is why I do what I do.'

Beth was mesmerised. The scene before her was as beautiful as any she'd ever seen. There was nothing but the sky and the fells and the shining water. Most noticeable of all, though, was the silence. Not an eerie one, but one that filled her with a sense of peace.

David smiled at her. 'What are you thinking?'

'I was wishing.'

'Wishing?'

'Yes, that life could be this simple. Just me and the sky and the peaks. No people to have to please or tiptoe around or worry about. Does that sound stupid?'

David shook his head. 'It's not stupid. I feel like that whenever I come here.'

Crouching down, he unzipped his rucksack. Today his hair was loose and it fell about his face as he lifted out his camera. 'You know, I've never brought anyone here before. I've never wanted to.'

To the east, the sky had turned pink with streaks of orange. A shepherd's warning. Beth pushed the thought away. Nothing was going to spoil this perfect moment.

'Yet you brought *me*.'

'Yes.'

Beth moved closer and put her hand on his shoulder. She wondered if he might shrug it away, but he didn't. 'Why, David? Why did you want to bring me here?'

Twisting his body, he looked up at her. 'Because you're different. Because you get me... You get all this.' Turning back to the camera, he took off the lens cap. 'And because I like you.'

'You like me?' No one had ever said that to her before.

'Don't sound so surprised. You're beautiful and talented and sensitive... Too bloody sensitive, if you ask me.'

Beth put her hands on her hips. 'Are you making fun of me?'

He laughed. 'See... exactly what I was saying.' Placing the camera strap around his neck, he pushed himself up. 'But you're right. I am making fun of you a bit. It's how I am when I'm feeling awkward. Sorry.'

The sun had been rising steadily over the distant peaks, and the shadows of the birches behind them cast long stripes across the short springy turf. The tarn, which had been a navy mirror when they had first arrived, was now a lighter blue, and, as they watched, the dark shadow of a bird of prey passed across it.

Beth looked up, watching the bird soar in the thermals, wings spread wide. She shivered.

'Are you cold? Here. Have my fleece?'

'No, I'm not cold. It's just that sometimes when I watch them, I get the weirdest feeling.'

David looked at her. 'What sort of feeling?'

'I don't know. Like someone's stepped over my grave. My mum asked me what my obsession with them was.'

'And what did you tell her?'

'I said I didn't know.' She watched the hawk glide effortlessly in the clear morning sky. 'It's the truth. Do you think I'm odd?'

'A bit, but I like it. Come and sit with me. I need to explain what was going on in my head last Saturday.' Sitting down, he stretched his legs out in front of him and leant back on his arms. 'Don't worry. It's not wet.'

Beth sat down beside him. She said nothing.

'The truth is, I was worried.'

Beth tilted her head back. The sky above was ridged with white clouds. 'What about?'

'I like you, Beth… I already told you that. But you're only young. I'm not sure what people would think.'

'I'm seventeen. I don't care what people think.'

'Well, I do. Not just for your sake, but for mine. I'm seven years older than you. You're still doing your A levels, for God's sake. I don't want people saying stuff.'

'What stuff?'

'You know what people can be like. Getting the wrong idea.'

Beth thought of Carina and shivered. She knew exactly what he meant. 'We don't have to tell anyone.'

David reached over and touched a lock of her hair, running it through his fingers. 'How many boyfriends have you had, Beth?'

She felt herself blush. 'A few.'

He looked out across the water. 'A few. Now, why do I not believe you?'

Tears pricked the back of her eyes. 'All right, so I've never had one. What bothers you more? That I had the audacity to hold your hand… or that I wouldn't know what to do after?' She got up. 'I'm sorry if I'm not the experienced, sophisticated girl you're obviously looking for, David. Maybe I'll just go round the block a few times and come back to you when I start to forget all their names.'

David stared at her. 'Don't be ridiculous. That's not what I meant at all.'

Covering her face, Beth felt tears bristling. She wished she was anywhere now but here. With him.

'Look at me, Beth. Do you really think so little of me?' His hands were warm on hers as he lowered them from her face. 'I didn't mean to upset you. I just didn't want to do the wrong thing.'

Placing a hand either side of her face, he drew her head towards him and kissed her forehead. The touch of his lips like a brand.

'Look, Beth. It's the golden hour. I should take some photos.'

He didn't move, though. Didn't bend to pick up his camera. Instead, he folded his arms around her and she felt his chest rise as he drew a breath. Beth rested her head against his shirt, breathing in the smell of him and, as she did, she saw the sun had bathed everything in a halo of light. She didn't need a camera to capture this moment – it was etching itself on her memory.

It was clear he was struggling with himself. Lifting her head, Beth looked into his eyes.

'It's not the wrong thing. How could it be?'

Cupping his face in her hands, she pulled him towards her, touching her lips to his. It was a tentative kiss, and at first, he did nothing. Then, just as she thought the same thing would happen again, she felt his lips part and his fingers tangle in her hair.

CHAPTER TWENTY-NINE

Leona

'Are you happy to go on, Leona?'

I hear Lisa's words as if from a great distance. Opening my eyes, I see, by the clock on the wall, that we are almost at the end of our session.

I nod. 'I'd like to go on, yes.'

It's only by getting to the end of Ria's story that I know I'll be able to move on.

The room is warm today, sunlight filtering in through the gauze curtains. Reaching my hands behind my neck, I capture my blonde hair between my fingers and twist it into a heavy knot, fixing it with a clasp I've found in my bag. Maybe, one day, I'll have it cut regardless of what Scott thinks. It's my hair, after all.

I look at Lisa. Despite the warmth, she is cool and composed in a cotton dress, her hair hanging loose for a change. There's something about her manner that relaxes me. A way she has of giving me space to breathe. To revisit the past in my own time. To be myself. Not just Scott's wife, or Beth's mother. It might be something she's learnt in her training, but somehow, I doubt it. Some people just have a natural empathy.

She leans forward. 'I'd like to ask you a question, Leona.'

'What is it?'

'How do you feel about what Ria did? Angry? Shocked?'

Through the open window, I can hear a blackbird singing. Its sweet melody makes me want to cry. 'I feel disappointed in her.'

'Disappointed?' Her surprise is hard to disguise.

'Yes. Things could have been so different, if only she'd realised what he was doing to her. His need and his anger, sucking the life from her. She used to be so bright… so strong. But, little by little, he whittled away at her self-confidence until there was nothing left.'

'That's very sad.'

I think of Scott and the encouragement he has given me since I started my jewellery-making business. The miles he's driven to exhibitions and craft fairs with boxes of my silverwork in the boot of his Land Rover. The way he tells everyone he meets that my work could grace the window of even the smartest jeweller's in Windermere. That's real love.

'If you're told you're worthless enough times, you start to believe it. If only Ria had listened to her head and not her heart, it might not have ended the way it did.' I feel sick inside. 'She could have killed him.'

'I know it's hard for you, Leona, but it's important that you understand that Ria had no choice.' Lisa thumbs through the notes on her lap. 'The strangulation marks on her neck show that Ria could have lost her life if she hadn't fought back. It was done in desperation. In light of the severity of Gareth's attack on her, the police accepted her plea of self-defence and no action was taken. You must accept it too.'

It's all there in front of her. The computer printouts neatly filed in her ring-binder. Lisa has been busy. It's all in there. What happened.

The problem is, sometimes a lie is easier than the truth.

CHAPTER THIRTY
Ria

The letterbox clattered shut and there was a thud as the envelope hit the wooden floor. Ria's mother looked up from her ironing.

'I thought the post had already been?'

'It has. It comes earlier on a Saturday,' Ria said, putting down the picture book she'd been reading to Lily. Lifting her from her lap, she went to the window and pushed back the net curtain. The street was empty except for a couple of kids on bicycles doing wheelies along the opposite pavement. How different the street was to the wide avenue of her home with Gareth, with its private gardens, enclosed by the black metal railings, where she had sometimes sat with a book.

'I'll go and see what it is when I've finished this.' Ria's mother bent to the washing basket and pulled out one of her husband's faded T-shirts, spreading it out on the ironing board.

'It's all right. I'll go. You help Nanny by handing her the clothes, Lily.'

Ria went into the hall. The envelope that lay on the doormat was large, with a white address label on the front. Bending to pick it up, Ria saw that it was her name that was printed on it.

Inserting her finger under the flap, she opened it and pulled out the catalogue that was inside. Her first thought was that it was a holiday brochure, as the picture on the cover was of a woodland. Sun filtered through the trees and a woman with white hair stood looking out over a lake. But then she noticed the flowery white script at the bottom.

In this your time of loss.

Puzzled, Ria flipped through the pages. What she saw there made her shudder. Inside were pictures of coffins in all types of wood, caskets made of willow and wreaths of lilies.

'What is it, Ria?' her mother called.

She stood rigid, her eyes glued to the page. Memories crowded in. A silent chapel. A tiny coffin, one spray of baby's breath adorning its pale wood. There was no doubt who was behind this. Only Gareth knew the truth. The brochure was a reminder, but also a warning. Even from his prison cell, he had the ability to mess with her mind.

'Ria?'

Dragging her eyes away, she glanced at the living room door. She needed to pull herself together. 'It's nothing, Mum. Just a holiday brochure. A friend must have dropped it round.'

It was a ridiculous thing to say. What friends did she have? Since the trial, the only person she had seen was Leo, but their relationship wasn't the same as it had been. Where there had once been fun and laughter, there was now a reservation that had not been there before.

Feeling nauseous, she went into the kitchen, then let herself out of the back door. Round the back of the house, in the garage compound, were the recycling bins and a rough plot of unclaimed land where people sometimes parked their cars to avoid having to put money in the meters. Being Saturday, there were a number of vehicles there already.

Lifting the blue lid, she pushed the brochure down underneath an empty box of Rice Krispies and an old copy of *The Sun*. Her hand was shaking. Somehow, from his prison cell, Gareth had made sure that this thing would never end. His hold over her was as strong as it always had been and it was something he would never let her forget.

People owe me. She shivered as she remembered his words.

Some nights, as she lay in her single bed, in the room she'd slept in all through her childhood, she'd remember what had happened in the weeks and months after it had all come to an end: the kindness of the female police officer who had been first at the scene, the professionalism of the photographer who had recorded her bruises, and the respectful way she had been interviewed. She also remembered the people who had come forward to give evidence on her behalf and the previous girlfriends who had found the courage to tell their own stories. All these things comforted her, but then, as her eyes finally closed, she'd feel again the press of her fingers on the paper as she gave her prints, the sweep of the DNA swabs in her mouth and the click of the machine as it was turned on to record her words. More than that, she remembered her fear that she wouldn't be believed.

All these things would fade as her mother woke her in the morning with a cup of tea, just as she used to all those years ago. The one thing she couldn't get rid of, though – the thing she carried with her as she struggled to get through each day – was the steely look in Gareth's eyes as she'd given her evidence. A look that had changed to incredulity as he was handed his sentence.

Slamming down the lid of the recycling bin, she leant against it, covering her eyes with her hands. The police had said it was over. That she was safe now. But she knew she wasn't. Somewhere, buried under paper and cardboard, was the picture of the coffin in the undertaker's brochure. It was clear Gareth wouldn't rest until he had taken his revenge.

She was just turning to go back through the gate when she caught sight of a white van. It was reversing out from between two parked cars. To start with, she didn't pay it much attention, but, as it pulled into the forecourt, she heard its engine rev. Her eyes widened in fear as, with wheels spinning, the van drove towards her at speed.

Rooted to the spot, Ria stared in horror. There was nothing she could do. It was going to hit her. And then it was as if some primal survival instinct kicked in, unlocking her limbs.

Throwing herself down behind the bins, she curled into a ball and prayed.

CHAPTER THIRTY-ONE
Ria

Detective Inspector Dayton linked his fingers and looked at Ria across the desk. She'd told him what had happened and, when he'd asked if it was an isolated incident, she'd told him about the funeral parlour brochure, the dead rat on her parents' doorstep and the pizza deliveries that had arrived unordered the following week.

'It's going to be hard to prove that your husband is behind all this. Do your parents know what's going on?'

Ria shook her head. They had been out the night of the pizza deliveries, and the rat she had managed to get rid of by shovelling it into an old shoe box and throwing it into the skip in the supermarket car park.

'I haven't told them. I don't want to worry them.' The interview room was small and airless and she wished she could open a window.

DI Dayton bent his head to the file in front of him. 'It looks like our Mr Curtess has some friends who are happy to do his job for him. It's not surprising, considering the circles he moved in. He must have pulled in a few favours.'

'You said I'd be safe if I testified. You promised.'

'I'm sorry, Ria.' He had the decency to look embarrassed. 'It seems he had quite an influence on the outside. That's the power of drug money.'

Ria swallowed. Until the trial, she'd had no idea what Gareth had been involved in. How could she have been so naive? It explained a lot: the changes of mood, the cash, the secrecy. The job in the city had been nothing but a smokescreen. It had been years since he'd been a broker. Years since the finance company he'd worked for had shown him the door. A blind eye could be turned when cocaine use by their employees was confined to after-hours, but when it affected their judgment during the day, it was another matter. Especially when it lost them money.

'I'm scared of what might happen next. I don't think he'll ever forgive me for what I did.'

DI Dayton poured a glass of water from the jug and handed it to her. It was an action that should have been ordinary, but it was weighted with the enormity of what he was about to say.

'There *is* something we can do. A way to keep you and Lily safe.'

Ria felt weak with relief. 'Really?'

'Yes, but it's not a decision I expect you to take lightly. Have you heard of the Witness Protection Scheme?'

The clock on the wall seemed to be ticking very loudly. 'Yes, I think so.'

'If we take you onto the programme, we can give you a new home… a new identity. That way, no one will be able to find you. Gareth's serving a sentence for your attempted murder and it's also clear he's able to influence, pay or intimidate people to continue to put your life at risk. This real and immediate threat puts you in the high-risk category and therefore makes you eligible for our protection.'

A fly that had been buzzing around the room, settled on the table. Ria watched it until DI Dayton flicked it away. The way he'd put it made the danger all the more real.

'But what about my parents? What would I tell them?'

'You would say that you had decided to go away for a while, that London held too many bad memories. It's understandable that you would want a new start with your daughter somewhere else.'

'Lie to them, you mean?' Ria could feel the blood leave her face. She bit her lip to stop from crying. The idea was unthinkable. 'How could I do that?'

As soon as she said it, she felt a wave of guilt. It would not be the first time she had concealed the truth from them. Her lie before had been a much greater one.

'It wouldn't be far from the truth, would it? Not if you are truly worried about your safety... and that of your daughter.'

'Gareth wouldn't do anything to Lily. I know he wouldn't.'

DI Dayton leant forwards. 'Can anyone really predict what a person will do when they are desperate?'

He'd chosen his words carefully. She, more than anyone, knew that it was impossible to know how much Gareth might be capable of.

'Couldn't I just move away... Be taken off the electoral roll?'

'You could do that, but if you did, you would leave yourself vulnerable. The Witness Protection Scheme is the only way we could guarantee your safety and, even then, it would depend on you. It would be a secret you would need to keep forever. If you told anyone about your previous identity, we would no longer be able to protect you. You'd have to live a life in the shadows, being careful not to bring attention to yourself... but you'd be safe.'

It didn't seem real. It was like something out of a police drama. She responded as if on automatic pilot. 'What would I have to do?'

'You would be assigned a witness protection officer and be asked to sign a memorandum of understanding.'

'What's that?'

'It's a document that lays out what is expected from both parties. In a nutshell, it defines the terms of your new life. You would be given a new name, a new home and enough money to live on until a job could be found for you. In return, you would be agreeing to cut off contact from everyone from your former life, to never return to your home town, and not to tell anyone of your former identity.'

'What about my parents? Would they be moved too?'

He looked grave. 'We can't protect every member of a witness's family. It's you and Lily who are most vulnerable.'

A terrible thought gripped her. 'Would I ever see them again?'

His silence gave her the answer she'd been dreading and the tears she'd been holding back now fell freely.

DI Dayton's face softened. 'It's the price you would need to pay for Lily's safety. It's something that might be possible in the future but it would take a lot of manpower and we don't recommend it. I'm sorry.'

'Then I won't do it.'

He levelled his gaze at her. 'If Lily is put at risk, there is the possibility that social services could get involved.'

There was a hollow pain in her chest. 'You mean they'd take her away from me? They can't do that.'

'They could if they truly believed you were endangering her by keeping her here.'

'Oh, my God!' She covered her face with her hands. The thought was terrifying. Lily meant everything to her. Leaving her parents would be heart-wrenching, but could she live her life always in fear? It was bad enough now, but what about when he came out? The thought made her blood run cold.

She had no choice.

'All right.' Her voice was little more than a whisper. 'I'll do it.'

DI Dayton's face was calm, but she could tell that he was thinking. 'Where is Lily now?' he asked. 'And will the house be empty when you get home?'

'Yes. Mum and Dad are both at work and I left Lily with Tessa next door while I came here. I told her I was going to the doctor's.'

DI Dayton nodded. 'That's good. Will she be able to stay a little longer?'

'I suppose so.'

'Good.' He pushed his chair back. 'I just need to make a call.'

He was gone for over fifteen minutes and when he returned, his manner was brisk. 'I want you to go home and pack a suitcase or a bag. When you've done that, collect Lily and wait for my phone call.'

'You mean it's happening now? Today?'

'It's how it has to be, Ria.'

It was at that moment, Ria knew that her life was going to change forever.

CHAPTER THIRTY-TWO

Beth

Life had settled into a comfortable routine for Beth. After school, David would pick her up in Windermere and take her with him to wherever it was he would be photographing that day. She would sit and draw and he would roam the area for interesting shots to take.

Not wanting them to know what she was really doing, she would tell her parents she was staying late at after-school prep club to revise, or that she was going to a friend's house to study. Any guilt she felt soon disappearing as she saw the faded green camper van parked at the end of the road.

Beth had persuaded David that it might be better if they meet in secret. That they tell no one they were seeing each other. He'd been unsure at first, uncomfortable with the idea of deceiving her parents, but, anticipating this, she had used his own argument against him. People wouldn't understand. They'd talk. He didn't want that, did he? Reluctantly, he'd agreed and they'd fallen into a pattern of seeing each other most days.

'You look happy.' David's voice broke into her thoughts.

'That's because I am.'

'Will I see you tomorrow?' He shifted in his seat. All afternoon he had seemed distracted. Out of sorts. They'd been to Temple Quarry again and were now parked up at the entrance to the campsite, the place Beth liked him to drop her so she could walk the last few hundred yards home without being seen.

'Not tomorrow. Maybe Friday.' She really needed to get some revision done. 'I'll text you.'

'Friday would be good.' David tapped his fingers on the steering wheel and stared out of the windscreen. His mood was unsettling.

Beth stroked the golden hairs on his forearm. 'Is something wrong?'

'Yes and no.'

She felt her stomach tighten. 'I'm not sure I like the sound of that. Maybe I should have the no part first.'

'The no part is easy.' He took his hand off the steering wheel and placed it on her own, which was resting in her lap. 'I've fallen for you big time.'

Beth's heart sang. She'd been waiting to hear him say something like that. 'But that's a good thing, right?'

'Not when it makes you feel like crap. There's no easy way to put this, Beth. I'll be leaving Church Langdon in a week or two. I've got another assignment down in Cornwall.'

She felt numb. 'Cornwall. But that's…'

'Miles away, I know. All the time we were at Temple Quarry I've been wondering how to tell you.'

'How long will you be there for?'

'As long as it takes.'

'And then you'll come back?' Beth knew she was grasping at straws.

David ran his thumb across the back of her knuckles. 'I've got to be honest with you, Beth. I could be anywhere after that. It's my job. You knew that when you met me.'

She had known it and yet, somehow, she had conveniently forgotten it during the weeks they had been together. It was easier to believe they would live happily ever after.

'It won't be so bad. You'll have left college soon. The world will be your oyster. Which uni did you say you were going to?'

Beth squirmed in her seat. She hated having to lie to him. It seemed that was all she was doing nowadays – lying to the people she cared for the most. 'I didn't say. I thought I'd have a year off. Time to think about what I really want to do.'

David looked relieved. 'There you are, then. That will make it easier to hook up.'

'Hook up?' The expression sounded so casual... so temporary. Picking up her hand, he kissed it. 'You know what I mean.'

A well of sadness had opened up inside her, but she wasn't going to let him see it. 'Yes, I know exactly what you mean. Look, I've got to go. I'll see you on Friday.'

Without kissing him goodbye, Beth opened the door to the camper and jumped down. As she walked to her house, she didn't look back, scared that her face would mirror the emptiness she was feeling inside.

When she got home, she saw her mum's car in the shared parking bay. It would mean she'd have to change. Quickly, she ducked round the side of the terrace and unzipped her bag. Dragging out her maroon jumper, she forced it over her head. Her skirt was more difficult. Taking off her walking boots, she leant against the wall of the house for balance, then pulled the skirt on over her jeans before wriggling out of them. Her black school shoes were next. It was a ritual she went through most days, and she was only thankful it hadn't rained in that time.

Shoving her clothes into her bag, she let herself in. She stopped in the lobby and listened. Ever since her mum had had that turn in Graham Hargreaves' shop, it was impossible to know what mood she'd find her in. Some days she'd be waiting in the sitting room for Beth, wanting to know about her day and what she'd been up to, but on others, she'd be in her studio and wouldn't come out until well after dark. On those days, her dad would come home and look in the fridge before attempting to rustle up something from the little there was in there.

Today, her mum was neither in the living room nor the workshop. Dropping her bag at the bottom of the stairs, Beth went to look for her. Her own bedroom door was closed but her parents' door stood open. Popping her head round the door, Beth saw that it was empty.

'Mum?'

The sound of a toilet flushing was her answer. She waited, expecting her to come out, but she didn't. Instead, there was the metallic clink of the wastepaper bin closing, then the sound of a tap running. It wasn't this that surprised her though, it was the unmistakeable sound of her mother crying.

'Mum?' Her own voice was quiet. Childlike. Memories bubbled. A bed with a beige duvet cover. A lamp above her head with a fringe that cast spider legs of shadow onto the wall behind it. She'd been afraid of that shadow; she remembered that. There'd been the drone of traffic outside the window. Another sound too. Someone next to her in the bed, crying into their pillow. Her mother... She was sure of that now.

What was this place she was remembering? It wasn't Carlisle. There, she'd had her own small bed with an Ariel duvet cover and a bedside table with a white anglepoise lamp on it. As she lay in bed, she'd liked to reach out and bend it, this way and that, until her mum told her to stop. No. It wasn't there.

As the lock on the bathroom slid back, Beth ducked into her room. She sat on her bed and waited until she heard footsteps on the landing and the click as her parents' bedroom door closed. There was nothing else until she heard the clunk of wood on wood. What was she doing?

Hovering outside the door, Beth wondered if she should go in and ask her what the matter was. What had made her cry as though her heart would break. She'd heard her cry before, but not like that... and it frightened her. Raising her hand to the door, she hesitated, then dropped it again, unsure. What if she didn't like the answer?

As she went back downstairs, the family pictures on the wall above the handrail blurred with her tears. She'd wanted to tell her mum about David. Tell her that she'd fallen in love with him and how he was going to be moving on. She'd wanted to feel the warmth and comfort of her mum's arms as she pulled her into a hug. Hear her voice telling her that everything was going to be okay. For things to be as they once were. Before David had said those things. Before she'd heard her mum crying and a thread of memory had loosened. But it wasn't going to happen. There was something going on that she didn't understand. Beth stood in the middle of the small living room, feeling as if she was in a boat set adrift on the sea with no one to captain it.

Pressing her knuckles into her eye sockets, she tried to blank her mind. Scared of what other memories might unravel if she pulled that thread.

CHAPTER THIRTY-THREE
Ria

The hotel room was small, the double bed taking up most of the floor space. The plain-clothed officer who had driven them there had told Ria it was the best he could do at short notice. That had been three weeks ago. Now, she was waiting for the next move to a temporary flat in another town further away. It was there that she would be able to build up her story so that when the final move came, she would legitimately be able to say it was where she had come from.

Outside the window, Ria could hear the rush-hour traffic, a soft drone through the double glazing. It was oppressive in the room. She hadn't worked out how to turn down the radiators and the window only opened a few centimetres. Pressing her hands against the window, she looked out at the cars that circled the roundabout. There was a small business park off one of the interchanges, and behind one of the straggly trees, she could see the black and orange sign of a Halfords.

On the other side of the roundabout was the cheap and cheerful carvery she and Lily had gone to on their second night. A meal bought with the cash Colin had given her. Colin Peterson was the witness protection officer who had been assigned to her. Her 'handler'. It was he who had brought round the document to sign, and he who had explained how things would be from now on. He'd been kind and patient in the face of her distress, bringing a bag of toys for Lily and some books for Ria. Her laptop too. Any links with her past eradicated in just the click of a ballpoint pen.

Ria looked at the blue holdall she'd brought with her. Hidden underneath the nylon-covered cardboard that gave the base of the bag its rigidity, were things that Colin knew nothing about. Things she had grabbed in a desperate bid to cling to the life she was being torn from. If he knew about them, they would be removed and destroyed. She couldn't bear the thought of that.

A strand of hair had escaped from the towel she'd wrapped around her newly washed hair. It dripped down her back, soaking into her blouse. She looked at Lily, wondering what her daughter would say when she plucked up the courage to take the towel off. The little girl lay on her stomach on the double bed, her Pocahontas doll, with its shiny black hair and fringed dress, clutched in her hand. She was dancing her up and down the coverlet.

'All right, darling?'

Lily looked up. 'When are we going home? When can I see Nanny and Gramps?'

Ria turned back to the window and leant her forehead against the glass, desperate to find the words that would help her daughter understand that they'd never be going home. That she'd never see her grandparents again. It was impossible.

With a last look at the slow-moving traffic, Ria went over to Lily, the loose headboard banging against the wall as she sat down next to her on the bed. The coverlet was beige, the same as the curtains and the rather worn carpet. There was nothing to make this hotel room stand out from any other except for the matching lamps on the walls either side of the bed, whose fringes cast black spider legs of shadow when the main light was off. The room mirrored how her own life would be from now on. Anonymous.

She brushed her daughter's fair hair from her face. 'This is exciting, Lily. We're going on an adventure. Just you and me.'

'Like *Dora the Explorer*?'

'Yes, just like *Dora the Explorer*.'

'Then we'll go back to Nanny's.'

'We don't want to go back too soon or we'll have nothing exciting to tell her.'

Despite her brave words, Ria was struggling. With nothing to anchor her to her past, she felt weightless. The night they'd left London, they'd driven for half an hour to a rendezvous point with another car. Then they had driven for another three hours. Lily had fallen asleep almost immediately, but Ria had sat, wide-eyed, as the familiar roads had turned unfamiliar and then they were on a motorway heading North. The driver had said little and she'd been glad. There were no words that could take away the weight of sadness inside her chest. The guilt at leaving her mum and dad without a word.

The following day, Colin had handed her a sheet of writing paper. She could write to her parents and explain why she'd left so suddenly… She and Lily needed a holiday – time to plan the new chapter of their life away from memories of Gareth. She knew they wouldn't believe it, though; would be unable to accept that their daughter had left like a thief in the night without saying goodbye. But there was nothing else she could do. It was her only way of contacting them and Colin would make sure they got it. Her mobile phone had been taken when she was at the police station, DI Dayton explaining how the mobile network was the easiest way to trace someone, but she was glad she couldn't speak to them. She would never have been able to keep it together if she had.

There was a knock on the door and Ria went to open it. Colin stood in the corridor, a bag over his shoulder and an apologetic smile on his face. She wasn't surprised to see him: he was the only person who had visited her since the day she'd arrived.

He looked at her towel-covered head. 'Is this a good time?'

It was a strange thing to say in this place, where one hour was the same as the next. Where her days were spent reading and playing games – counting down the hours until they could close the curtains on the dismal scene outside and go to bed. Sometimes, when the four walls got too much for her, they'd leave the hotel and walk around the block, past the garage with its small shop, where she would buy essentials, and on to the scrap of green space with its swings and red dog bin. Despite the change of scene, she didn't like these outings. Afraid she'd be recognised, even though she was nearly two hundred miles from home.

'Come in,' she said, standing back. It would be nice to have some adult company for a change.

Colin nodded and stepped into the room. He was a pleasant-looking man, his hair greying even though he could only be in his forties. Despite his serious eyes, he had a nice smile and a casual manner that put her at ease.

He squeezed her shoulder, then looked over at Lily. 'Hi, Munchkin. I've brought you a comic. Do you like animals?'

Lily didn't answer. Since they'd left London, she'd spoken little. It was hardly surprising when her whole world had been turned upside down.

'Well, just in case you do, I got you this.'

He placed a copy of *Animals and You* onto the bed beside her and Ria was relieved when Lily took her thumb out of her mouth and pulled it closer. It was a little old for a four-year-old, but she appreciated his kindness.

'Look, Lily. It's got cats in it.' Reaching out, she ran a hand down her daughter's thick hair. 'You like cats, don't you?'

Lily nodded and put her thumb back into her mouth. It was a habit Ria thought she'd grown out of.

'I'll read you some of it before bedtime. Maybe one day, we'll have a cat of our own.'

It was a wild promise, but it had the right response. Lily widened her eyes. 'Really?'

'Really... and I'll even let you name him.'

'Or her,' Colin said, with a laugh. 'And remember, I am a witness to that.' The choice of words was unfortunate and the smile left his face.

Feeling sorry for him, Ria carried on. 'Then it seems we'd better find a place that will accept kittens or I won't be winning Mother of the Year any time soon.'

Colin looked relieved. 'I'll see what I can do.'

Ria picked up the kettle. 'Now you're here, do you fancy a drink?'

'I wouldn't mind. Here, I'll do it.' Taking the kettle from her, he went into the bathroom. There was the clunk of plastic against china and then the sound of running water. When he came back out, flipping the lid of the kettle back down, he was smiling.

'I see you did what I suggested.'

Ria knew he'd seen the empty bottle she'd left on the side of the bath, and the box with its photograph of a woman with a bright smile and wavy blonde hair. As she'd waited for the liquid to do its job, she'd been reminded of another bathroom. Another wait. Only that one had been fraught with tension. Gareth had told her he hadn't wanted another baby. If only she'd believed him.

Despite a thorough rinsing, the ammonia smell from her hair was still with her. She touched the towel. 'I haven't looked at it yet.'

'You'll soon get used to it. When you're ready, I'll need to take a photograph for the new passport.'

Flicking the switch on the kettle, Colin tore the top of the coffee sachet with his teeth and emptied it into one of the functional white mugs before repeating the process with the other. His easy manner, in these strange circumstances, made Ria wonder if he had a wife… children, even. He never talked about himself, and it was clear he didn't like to mix work and personal life. She couldn't blame him, but sometimes it would be nice to talk about something other than a future she could barely comprehend.

'Today is an important day, Ria.' Colin handed her the mug of coffee. 'It's my job to make it as easy for you as I can.'

Bending to the bag he'd left on the floor, he pulled out a large padded envelope.

'What's in there?'

Colin looked at her, running his finger under the sealed edge. 'It's your new life.'

With his elbow, he pushed aside a basket containing a shoe-shine kit, some nail files in a cellophane pack and a packet of needles and thread, then emptied the contents of the envelope onto the shiny veneered surface.

Ria moved closer. She stared at the bank card and cheque book that lay there. The sheaf of bank statements, and the medical cards. Picking up the cheque book, she smoothed its cover.

'Go on.'

With trembling fingers, she lifted the dark blue cover and looked at the name of the bank. Lloyds TSB – she'd never banked there. It wasn't this, or the unknown account number that made her heart miss a beat, though. It was the name printed at the bottom. Even though she knew it was ridiculous, she'd somehow been expecting to see her own name written there. Instead, there was the name of someone else. The person she was to become.

She stared at it, the words blurring as tears filled her eyes.

Colin was looking worried. 'Are you okay?'

Determined to be brave, Ria nodded. Maybe if she said the name out loud, it would become real.

She looked at Colin, her throat tightening as she spoke the words.

'Leona,' she whispered. 'My name is Leona Travis.'

CHAPTER THIRTY-FOUR

Leona

There, I've said it. Said the name of the person I've been for the last twelve years.

'Am I going mad, do you think?'

Lisa shakes her head. 'No, I don't think that. Coping with a difficult situation isn't a form of insanity.'

'But the way I've talked about myself... about Ria.' Even now, I can't bring myself to say the words that will turn us into that same person.

Getting up, Lisa walks to the bookshelf on the wall. She takes out a thick hardback with a shiny cover, and a slimmer paperback. She shows them to me and then, putting them back, drags her fingers along the spines of others.

'Dissociation is covered in all of these manuals, Leona. It's a common problem for someone changing their identity as there is often no emotional connection to their new name. How was the name chosen?'

I tell her how Colin thought that by using a version of Leo's name, it would be easier for me to remember. I liked it because it made me feel closer to her. She was, after all, the only friend I had. During the darkest times, she'd never forgotten me and, if it wasn't for her, I would probably not be here now. Leo wasn't her real name. It was Marie.

I miss her. The fun we shared, in those early years when we were students, and the mane of blonde hair that gave her her nickname. I wonder what she's doing now.

My cheeks are wet with tears I haven't realised I've shed and Lisa reaches forward and takes my hand. I don't know whether her code of conduct allows her to, but the gesture is warm, caring, and I'm grateful to Colin for the telephone number he gave me all those years ago. *It's for if you want to talk to a counsellor, Ria. Sometimes people on the scheme find it hard to adjust. Just call and they'll do their best to fit you in.* I thought I'd be able to manage without it, but I was wrong. Lisa is young, new to this job probably, but I like her.

'You've done really well, Leona,' she says now. 'It can't have been easy for you to relive it all, but it proves how strong you are. But…'

'What?' I snap.

'The manuals I showed you describe how dissociation techniques are used when trying to come to terms with a traumatic situation, but I'd like to know why *you* think you've separated yourself from Ria? Convinced yourself she's so far in your past that she wasn't ever really you at all?'

Without warning, the past rears up, catching me unawares. The lies I've told; the things I've done that only Gareth knows about. Someone once said that our memories define us. I wonder if they are right.

I decide to stick to a half truth. 'I thought that if I removed myself from my former self, the past wouldn't be able to hurt me.' I pinch my eyes, between finger and thumb, to try to push back the pictures that continue to form. How could I have been so wrong?

'That's understandable. Is there anything else you'd like to talk about, Leona, before we close this session? We've spoken about a lot today, and perhaps you need a break?'

There's so much I could say, but the words that come out of my mouth are not the ones either of us have been expecting.

'I'm pregnant.'

CHAPTER THIRTY-FIVE
Leona

A week's gone by and I still haven't told Scott about the pregnancy. He'd be so happy – so caught up in plans for the future. I imagine him wrapping his big arms around me. Hear the tenderness in his voice as he tells me he will love our baby. Cherish it. With just these few words, we will be turned into the proper family he's always wanted us to be. Him, me and Beth… and a tiny bundle to bind us all together. In her turn, Beth will grin at me and then at the man she's adored from the moment she met him. The only father she's ever really known.

But the more I think about it, the more I realise I can't go through with it. How can it be fair to let Scott believe that everything will be all right when he doesn't even know that our life together, up until now, has been a lie? That the Leona he thinks he knows is just a phantom created by others. No more substantial than a character in a novel.

That's not all, though. How can I bring another child into the world after everything that's happened? After everything I've done? Not just what I did to Gareth, or the fact that I allowed a monster to father my child… but the other terrible secret I've never told.

As if in answer, a flutter, like the tiny wings of a moth, makes my hand stray to my stomach. I remember the feeling so well – even though it's many years since I've been pregnant. Soon I will be showing, and I know I will have to make a decision before that happens.

The brooch I am creating in my studio is a love knot: the fine silver strands twisting together like the entwined fingers of two lovers. While I was making it, I had been thinking of Scott. Thinking how devastated I would be if ever our own fingers were to separate – how quickly I would fall apart.

I know that this baby that is growing inside me, although created out of love, will change everything. The fear I feel is immeasurable.

It's warm today and the workroom is stuffy despite the fanlights I've opened. Wanting a cool drink, I go back into the house. I've just poured myself some elderflower cordial, when the doorbell rings. Putting my glass on the counter, I go and open the door. I had expected it to be the postman, or someone collecting an order, but it's not. The person who stands on the doorstep, beside the muddy walking boots, is someone I haven't seen for a long time. Someone I hoped would never need to see me again.

'Leona. How are you?' Colin smiles at me, but his eyes are serious. He looks much the same as when I last saw him, but a little greyer, and his eyes have a few more lines around them. In the early days, I had seen him a lot, but as time moved on and I became more self-sufficient, the contact became less frequent until it dwindled to the occasional welfare check. I still had the mobile phone he'd given me, and an emergency contact number, but I'd never had to use it.

'Colin.' It takes a moment to get over the shock of seeing him. 'What are you doing here?'

'I need to talk to you.'

'What about?'

He looks across to the cottage next door. 'Not on the doorstep, Leona. Can I come in?'

'Of course.'

I step aside and, as he walks past me, I see him taking in the little sitting room with its stone walls and the things I have accumulated over the last few years: the cushions, the ornaments, the pictures fighting for space on the walls. It makes me wonder whether he ever saw the inside of my house in South Kensington. And, if he did, whether he is comparing its clinical tastefulness with this little house and its hotchpotch of things that I've collected to help me leave that all behind.

Before shutting the door, I step outside to make sure that nobody has seen him. Luckily, the holidaymakers, who are renting the other cottages in the row, are either inside or have gone out for the day. I can tell by the lack of cars in the shared parking spaces by the road.

'You're lucky Scott's not here.' What would we have told him if he had been? What lies would we have concocted together?

'It wasn't luck.' Despite the morning being warm, he's wearing a jacket. Taking it off, he lays it over the back of the settee. The action is so familiar that, for a moment, I am transported back to the hotel room with its view of the roundabout and the retail park.

'It wasn't?'

'No. I waited until he left and then waited some more to make sure that he didn't come back again. That he hadn't just popped out to get a loaf of bread or something. Scott looks nice, Leona.'

I don't answer him, fearing that if we speak of Scott, he might become tainted by my past. I don't tell Colin how he wants to marry me. How he'd like us to have a child of our own.

Colin sits down on one of the chairs by the fireplace, but I remain standing, my hands on my hips. The last time I'd had communication with him was when he'd phoned me a couple of months ago to say that Gareth had applied to the parole board for a hearing. He'd thought it unlikely that the petition would be successful but, just in case, he'd wanted me to write a statement on my views on his release, which would be taken into account at the hearing.

'What is it you want, Colin? Has something happened? Have you heard something about Gareth?' I try to think of all the things it could be and none of them are things I want to hear.

'In a way, yes. I thought you should know that Gareth's parole hearing is going to be in two days' time.'

Although I know this has been coming, the thought fills me with dread. I'm about to ask more, but Colin is leaning forward, his fingers laced together and his expression serious.

'It's not just that. There's something else I thought you should know. We like to keep an eye on the families of those under our protection and someone popped round to see your father. It's your mother I've come to talk to you about.'

'What about her?' The thought of my mother brings me close to tears. I see her dancing blue eyes, her bottle-blonde hair, so similar in colour to mine now, and hear her laugh. It's been twelve years since I've seen her and every day I miss her more.

I sink down next to him, my legs weak. Willing him not to say the words I'm dreading. 'She's not dead. Please don't tell me that.'

'No, she's not dead, Leona.' He takes my hand. Something that he's never done before. 'But it's not good. Your mother has what we now know is a form of Alzheimer's. It's progressed quite rapidly and…' He breaks off and I sense it's because he's trying to think of the best way to tell me.

'How long has she had it?'

'Your father said he first noticed things weren't right a year or so ago. Your mother started to become more forgetful. Leaving her keys in the washing machine and forgetting people's names. Things like that.'

'But everyone does that. It doesn't mean…'

'She also got lost – only a few roads from her house. Roads she should know like the back of her hand. She went to hospital, Leona. The diagnosis was conclusive.'

I feel the tears begin to fall, hot on my cheeks. 'But what if they've made a mistake?'

'They haven't. I'm sorry.' He drops my hand and clears his throat. 'She's had tests.'

Colin looks away. I see his attention taken by the collection of photographs on the stairs. Although he tries to hide it, his face signals his disapproval: photos are discouraged in case, by chance, someone should recognise an individual from their previous life. A life they were never supposed to have. When Beth asks why we have no photos of her as a baby, or a young child, I tell her that they were all lost in a fire which swept through our home while we were out one day. It's a story I've used many times to explain why we have moved, why we have nothing from our past. I say I moved away to escape the memories. In a way, it's true.

'Don't worry. There are no photos of my parents, just ones I've taken since we've moved here – Scott and Beth mostly. That's all right, isn't it?'

'It would be better if you didn't have them. Even recent ones. If someone gets a tip-off and comes looking…' He stops, obviously not wanting to frighten me. 'Not that they are going to. It's just a precaution we like everyone to take.'

I don't like him talking like this. I've always felt safe here in my little miner's cottage, surrounded by the protective arms of the Cumbrian peaks. I change the subject.

'My dad? What about *him*?'

Colin shifts in his chair. He looks uncomfortable. 'Your father managed to begin with, but recently he's been struggling. At times, your mum can become agitated, unsure of where she is and what's going on, and it's hard for him to deal with. It's been decided that it would be better if she went somewhere where she can be properly cared for. Your dad has done his best, but there is only so much he can do.'

'You mean they are going to put her in a home?'

'It's already happened, I'm afraid.'

The thought is shocking. Unthinkable. 'She's only sixty-five, for Christ's sake. I need to see her.' I stand up, looking around wildly – trying to think of what I need to take and what I can say to Scott and Beth. As far as they know, my parents were killed in a car accident when I was young and I was brought up by an elderly aunt from whom I'm now estranged.

Colin puts out a hand as if to try to stop me. 'You can't see her, Leona. You know that. I only told you because I thought you should know.'

I can't believe what I'm hearing. 'She's my mum, Colin.'

He looks at me and I know what he's going to say. 'Since you went into Witness Protection, you've been offered the chance to visit your parents in a neutral place, but you've always refused.'

I close my eyes and draw in a breath. 'You know why that was, Colin. You said yourself that the meetings would have an element of risk, even though your officers would have carefully arranged everything and would be watching. For myself, I don't care, but I could never play Russian roulette with Beth's safety. Now it's different. In one month… two months… Mum might not even recognise me. I have to go now, before it's too late.'

Colin frowns. 'I could try to organise something. See if it's possible for your mother to be taken somewhere else for you to meet her. But you have to see that, as things stand, the whole business will be unsettling for her and the arrangements will take time.'

'I need to see her *now*.'

Colin stands and turns me to look at him. 'It's not possible.' I hear the intake of breath that signals he has more to say. 'I hate saying this, but if you go to London, or try to contact your parents in any way without proper consultation, we will be forced to move you again.'

I stare at him, wide-eyed, knowing from his tone that he means it. 'I can't move. My life is here in Church Langdon with Scott.'

Releasing my shoulders, he picks up his coat from the back of the settee. 'Then you will understand why it has to be like this. It was all clear in the contract when you signed it.'

'But she's ill, Colin.'

'It's how it is, Leona. You knew that from the start.' His words are firm, but I see the sympathy in his eyes. If he could make it any different, he would – but of course he can't.

I feel the flutter again. My mum would have felt my tiny movements in the same way. She would have placed a hand to her stomach and smiled, never dreaming that she would give birth to a baby who would one day desert her. One who, at twenty-five, she would never see again.

How different it would have been if I hadn't met Gareth. If I hadn't done the things I did. I would be there for her now, and for my dad. But, of course, if I could go back in time and change things, I wouldn't now have Beth... or Scott. They are the two good things to have come out of all this.

Colin tells me he will keep in touch and then he leaves. I stand at the window and watch his car drive away and, when I'm sure he's gone, I climb the stairs. It doesn't take me long to push aside the bags and shoes on the wardrobe floor and raise the loose floorboard. Lifting out the envelope, I lift the flap and take out the photographs. From the glossy paper, Ria's vivid blue eyes look back at me accusingly. The second photograph is one of my mother and father. Dad sits on his motorbike and, beside him, my mum stands proudly, me in her arms. The final photograph I can barely look at. The baby is swaddled in a blue cellular blanket, bright eyes staring from the folds.

Sinking my head into my hands, I cry as if my heart might break. I'm mourning for my parents and the little life that barely began. But, most of all, I am mourning for Ria.

Putting the pictures back, I hold the envelope to my chest.

I know what I must do.

CHAPTER THIRTY-SIX
Beth

'I still can't believe you're going to London.'

A week had gone by since the bathroom incident, and things had gone back to normal, enabling Beth to believe she might possibly have imagined the sobbing she'd heard. But now there was this. Since the night before, when her mum had told her, she'd been trying to process the information. Her mum having an overnight stay anywhere was as unlikely as Beth passing her science exam. What had prompted this change of heart?

'It's only for a couple of days.' Her mum glanced in the mirror and ran her fingers through her hair. 'I'm just lucky someone dropped out of the jewellery-making workshop. I've wanted to go on it for ages.'

'You never said.'

She didn't comment, just picked up her keys and phone from the table and put them in her shoulder bag. 'I know it's short notice, but I'm sure you and your dad can manage without me.'

Beth watched as her mum checked the zip on her weekend case. 'Of course we can. It's just that…'

She stopped, not knowing how to put it into words. What she wanted to say was that she knew her mum hated travelling, that a shopping trip to Ambleside or Windermere was as far as she ever went, but if she said these things, she'd just sound stupid — as though she didn't want her to go. Although the truth was, she didn't. It would be the first time in her life they'd been apart and she didn't like the thought of it.

'What does Dad think?'

Her mum's back was to her and she couldn't see her expression.

'He thinks it's great. He's driving me to the station.'

As if on cue, the front door opened and her dad stood smiling on the doorstep. He'd driven the car round. 'Ready?'

'Yes.' She kissed Beth's cheek, then pulled up the handle of her case, wheeling it towards the door. 'Be good now. Get some revision done.'

Beth chewed the inside of her cheek. She so desperately wanted to tell her mum about David, about how her heart ached at the thought of his leaving, but it was too late for that. She'd never understand, and besides, her mum had that distracted look that she hated.

The car drove away and, feeling aimless, Beth went into the kitchen and stared out of the window. The backyard and the lower slopes of the fell, beyond her mum's workshop, were in shadow, as they were for most of the day. The top, though, was bathed in sunshine, the sheep that dotted it looking like white buttons on a green quilt. It was the perfect day for walking. The perfect day for drawing – not sitting in her room surrounded by textbooks and past exam questions she hadn't a hope of completing. Maybe if she went out for a bit, she would feel better for it. It might even wake up her sluggish brain cells.

Going to the little lobby by the front door, she shoved aside the coats, but her rucksack was nowhere to be seen. Damn. She must have left it in David's camper. Not to worry, her old one was around somewhere; she'd have to see if she could find it.

Having a vague memory of her mum having used it, she took the stairs two at a time and pushed open the door to her parents' bedroom. She stood in the middle of the room, hands on her hips, and tried to think where her mum might have put it.

Kneeling beside the bed, she lifted the overhanging duvet and slid open the divan drawers. There was nothing there. Just a load of winter clothes. She rocked back on her heels, noticing that one of the wardrobe doors was open a little, the red leather strap of a handbag spilling out from its dark interior. Maybe the rucksack was with her mum's old bags. Opening one of the doors, Beth looked inside. Her mum's clothes hung from the rail, a jumble of colours and shapes. Below them, on the wardrobe floor, was an assortment of items: old jogging bottoms, scarves and bags.

Beth began to rummage. 'Jesus Christ. This is worse than a jumble sale.'

At first, she couldn't find what she was looking for, but then, right at the bottom, she caught sight of the rucksack. She pulled at the nylon straps, trying to free it from the mound of other items, but it wouldn't budge. Pushing everything aside, she looked to see what was holding it and saw that one of the plastic clips of the waist strap had got caught between two of the floor boards.

Easing one to the side, Beth noticed that, unlike the others, this board wasn't fixed down and the holes, where the nails should have been, were empty. A picture came to her. Her mum was sitting on the floor, her dad's T-shirt in her hand and the wardrobe door standing open behind her. Its contents had been pushed to one side and her mum had looked flustered. Beth hadn't paid too much attention to what had been going on then, but now, she wondered what it was her mum had been doing.

Even though she knew there was no one else in the house, Beth glanced at the door to make sure she wasn't being watched. Then, lifting the loose board, she reached forward and felt around with her hand until she met with something. It felt like a large envelope. Closing her fingers around it, she pulled it out.

The envelope was large, brown... ordinary-looking. Beth sat cross-legged and stared at it. There was nothing written on the front and, from the weight of it, it obviously contained several items. Reaching an arm back into the wardrobe, she felt around to see if there was anything else hidden there, but there wasn't.

Beth's palms had become sweaty and she wiped them on her jeans. There was something about her find that bothered her. For her mum to go to the trouble of hiding it, the envelope must contain something important. Something she didn't want either Beth or her dad to see. It should have been exciting, but it wasn't. Wasn't there a saying, *what is seen can never be unseen*?

Maybe she should just put it back. Pretend she hadn't found it. But she knew that if she did that, she would always wonder and one day, days or weeks from now, she would go to the hiding place again and look inside.

Inhaling deeply, she lifted the flap of the envelope and tipped the contents out onto the floor. At first, it looked boring – just another envelope, narrower than the first, and a few old photographs. But, when she picked up the top one and studied it, she felt her skin grow cold.

Her immediate thought was that it was a photograph of herself: the dark hair and the high cheekbones were the same. When she looked closer, though, she realised it wasn't. This woman was older, her eyes a bright blue – nothing like Beth's slate grey. She looked familiar yet odd at the same time, like an identikit picture the police had cobbled together in a hurry. One you know is wrong.

There was a resemblance to her mum as well. Only *her* hair was blonde. Could this be a relative Beth had never met or even heard of? An echo of a memory stirred. Dark hair falling across her face and the touch of warm lips on her cheek. A moon and stars rotating above her head. *Sleep tight, darling*.

She shivered, uncertain whether she wanted to look at any more. In the end, curiosity overcame her and she looked at the next photograph. The same woman was standing with an older couple, a baby in her arms. She was looking down at the child as though it was the most precious thing she had seen. The final photo was of a different baby wrapped in a blue blanket. Putting the photographs to one side, Beth picked up the narrow envelope. *Birth Certificate* was written on the front.

Before she could chicken out, she tipped the folded page into her lap and opened it. The baby was a girl. *Lily.* She spoke the name aloud. It was pretty, the two syllables forming in a way that was familiar to her. She looked at the date of birth. *August 3rd 2001.* This child was close in age to her – born four months earlier. Her father was someone called Gareth Curtess and her mother's name was Ria. Who were these people?

She was just going to slip the certificate back into the envelope, when she saw that there was another in there. The mystery was deepening. Drawing it out, Beth smoothed the page with the flat of her hand and read the name. This time it was a boy, *Samuel Brian.*

Reaching into her back pocket, Beth took out her phone. Holding it above each of the photographs, she captured them on the screen. She did the same for the birth certificates. When she'd finished, she slid everything into the envelope and put it back in its hiding place, replacing the wooden floorboard and moving the bags and scarves to cover it once more.

She desperately wanted to talk to David. To find out what he thought of all this. Should she speak to her dad about it when he got home? Something told her she shouldn't. She would wait until her mum got back and confront her. She'd make her tell her the truth and then maybe she'd understand why she'd been acting so strangely these last few months.

Picking up the rucksack, Beth went back to her room and pushed her drawing book, some pencils and a waterproof into it. There was no point in dwelling on it now. She'd see if David wanted to go with her to the cairn. It would help her to take her mind off it.

But, as she let herself out of the door, she couldn't get the picture of the young woman with the dark hair out of her head. She'd known this woman – she knew she had – but when and where, she couldn't say.

CHAPTER THIRTY-SEVEN
Leona

It's early morning, three days after Colin came to see me, and a fine drizzle of rain is in the air. I'm pleased, as my umbrella serves as a barrier between me and the rest of the world. Last night, I slept little – the cheap hotel I checked into reminded me of the one Beth and I stayed in all those years ago. Eventually, I gave up and switched on the bedside lamp, turning over in my head the things I needed to say to my mum. Knowing it could be the last time I saw her. Knowing I had to let her know I hadn't just abandoned her. But, try as I might, nothing would come.

My phone vibrates in my pocket and I take it out. It's a message from Scott: *'Hope you're enjoying yourself. We're all good here.'* I stare at it, undecided as to whether I should answer him or not. If I do, it will be just another lie, but if I don't, would it make things any better? Swallowing my guilt, I write the reply as quickly as possible. I'm enjoying the course and will tell him more when I get home. As I press send, an awful thought crosses my mind. What if Scott doesn't believe me? What if he thinks…? But even as I'm questioning myself, I know it isn't likely. Scott has always trusted me, just like I've always trusted him.

Remembering how I'd spent the previous afternoon ringing all the care homes within fifteen miles of my father's home until I'd found the right one, I check the map on my phone and see that it's not far now. The road, with Mum's care home in, should be the next one on the left. As I turn the corner, the butterflies that have been in my stomach since I left Church Langdon resume their frantic wing-beat and I'm afraid I might be sick. Taking a deep breath, I continue walking. Counting the paving slabs. Trying not to think about what I might find when I get there.

And then I see it. A Victorian red-bricked building on the corner of the road. *Avonleigh House* is printed on a board just inside the low wall that encloses the home and the small car park to the side. As I get nearer, my pace quickens. There's no reason for anyone to know I'm here, but my heart is jumping in my chest regardless. The gate's open and, with a quick look up and down the road, I walk up the gravel drive to the front door, keeping my head down.

I press the bell and wait. Eventually, a voice comes over the intercom and I tell her that I'm here to see Pamela Jackson. There's a loud buzz and the door clicks open to show a reception area with chairs along the sides of the room. Putting down my umbrella and giving it a shake, I step inside. A receptionist is sitting behind a glass-panelled desk and I go up to her, waiting for her to finish on the telephone, trying to ignore the sweet pine smell of disinfectant that lingers in the air. There's no one else in the waiting area and I'm relieved. The fewer people who see me, the better.

The receptionist finishes her call. She writes something on a notepad, then looks up. As her eyes take in my make-up-less face, my fair hair scraped back into a ponytail and my plain T-shirt, I feel my scalp prickle. Although I know it's ridiculous, I can't help thinking that, by some sixth sense, she knows what I've done. That here, in front of her, is a woman who abandoned her mother.

'Yes?'

'I'm here to visit Pamela Jackson,' I repeat.

'And you are?'

I hesitate. 'I'm Nicky... her niece. I rang yesterday.'

'They'll be bringing her down for her lunch in half an hour or so. Can it wait until then?'

I glance at the clock on the wall. 'Lunch? But it's only eleven.'

The woman shrugs. 'Some of them get agitated if they don't get their food. We try and get them all to come down to the dining room, but we get some refusers.' She leans forward. 'It's easier to leave those ones.'

'These are people you're talking about.'

Although I haven't said it loudly, the woman is staring at me and I realise, straight away, my mistake. I need to be more careful. This woman stands between me and my mum and, besides, I can't afford to make a scene.

With great effort, I smile. 'I'm sorry. I understand how difficult it must be for you here. If you can just tell me where my aunt is, I'll see her before she comes down. I don't intend to stay long.'

She takes her glasses from where they rest on her grey head and settles them on her nose. 'No. Nobody ever does. It's number seventeen. Second floor. The lift's over there if you want it, or you can take the stairs. Oh, and make sure you sign the visitors' book before you go up.'

I look over to the table she's indicating, where a book lies open, a pen in a holder next to it. Going over, I see that today's date has been written at the top of the page. There's only one name under it and my heart clenches as I realise it's my dad's. His writing is large and clumsy, bringing back memories of birthday cards and Christmas present labels from my childhood. To survive, these last years, I've had to shut out all memories of my parents, but, as I see his signature, my dad's dear face comes back to me as clearly as if he was in the room. His dark wiry hair, his large nose and the twinkle in his eyes that tells me he loves me. I work it out: he will be nearing seventy now. It's hard to believe.

A turn of the page shows me that Dad's been coming in every day since Mum was admitted. Sometimes twice or three times. He promised to love her in sickness and in health and, it's clear, he's kept that promise.

And then I see another name. One that surprises me more. *Marie Jacobs.*

Leo! The thought that my best friend has found it in her heart to visit my mum makes me want to weep. For twelve years, I've not seen her. Known nothing about her life. Did she and Adam get married? Did they adopt, like they said they wanted to? So many things cut from my life. So many things I've missed since I've been Leona.

Leo has visited the last two Sundays, in the evening. It's Sunday today. Might she come again? Taking a notebook from my handbag, I tear out a page and, with a quick glance at the receptionist, scrawl a message. No address, no telephone number – nothing that can give me away. Just that I miss her. I fold it and write Leo's name on the front, then shove it in my pocket before turning to the visitors' book and pretending to sign it. After I've done this, I take the lift to the second floor.

When the metal doors slide open, the first thing I see is a drugs trolley parked up against the wall. I'm in a corridor with a series of doors on either side. Most of them are open, the nearest one allowing me a glimpse of a narrow room with a bed at one end – a small table and red leather tub chair at the other. An elderly woman is sitting on the bed in her nightdress, her white legs spindle-thin. Above her, on the wall, is a noticeboard covered in photographs. Some are black and white, one showing a young woman in a full skirt, another a man in army uniform. Others are more recent: a baby in a bouncer and a school photograph of two boys, one gap-toothed.

As I watch, a young dark-haired nurse places a cardboard cup containing tablets into the woman's hand. 'There you are, Jane. Swallow these down for me.'

She hands the woman a plastic tumbler of water and I can't take my eyes from it, remembering the feel of a pill on my tongue; the exaggerated swallow as the water washes it down to do its job.

I hear a baby cry and, although I know it's only my imagination playing tricks, I feel again the love but also the craving for sleep. The oblivion that can only be found in a foil blister.

As the nurse takes the cup from the woman and turns back, she sees me and her eyebrows rise in surprise.

'Are you lost?' Her voice is kind, reminding me of one of my teachers in primary school.

I drag my eyes away from the woman's hand as she tosses the tablets into her mouth. 'I've come to see my aunt. She's in room seventeen.'

The girl smiles. 'That will be Pam. She's a sweetheart. I'll show you where she is, if you like.'

At her reassuring words, I feel the weight that has been on my shoulders since I heard of Mum's diagnosis lift a little. 'That's kind of you. Thanks.'

'You're welcome. What did you say your name was?'

'I didn't.' My throat thickens and I swallow. I need to pull myself together. It isn't as if I'm a stranger to changing names. 'It's Nicky.'

With a pat of the woman's hand, the girl gets up from the edge of the bed and comes out into the corridor.

'I'll be back in a minute to take you to lunch, Jane,' she calls back. 'Shepherd's pie today. Your favourite.' She winks at me and locks the drugs trolley. 'She says everything's her favourite. Maybe it was once, who knows.'

I follow her along the corridor to a door at the end, noticing the pictures on the walls as we pass by. They are all of flowers. Bright. Garish. Do the residents of Avonleigh House even notice them? I hope so.

The dark-haired girl knocks on the door. When there's no answer, she knocks again, then opens it, pushing her head around the door. 'Pamela. There's someone to see you. Your niece, Nicky.' She steps aside to let me in. 'Lovely surprise, eh?'

I step forward but go no further than the doorway, scared that I might break down in front of the girl who is now collecting cups from the bedside table. Mum stands at the window, looking out onto the road. She's thinner than when I last saw her, her hair still dyed blonde but a different shade to before. More brassy. The clothes she's wearing are not ones I recognise, but why would I, when the last time I saw her was twelve years ago?

'I'll leave you to it.'

I wait until the girl has closed the door behind her, then cross the room. Mum doesn't look at me. Her face is passive, the warmth and the life missing from it. Reaching out, I take her hand, tears pooling in my eyes. Her fingers feel frail, the bones fine beneath the skin, and I feel as though I might drown in my guilt.

'Mum? It's me, Ria.'

Slowly, my mother turns her head. 'Ria?'

'Yes, Mum. Your daughter.'

With a small shake of the head, she turns back to the window. 'I haven't got a daughter.'

The words are a dagger to my heart. 'You have, Mum. I'm here, standing right next to you.'

'Go away.' Her voice is flat. 'I said I haven't got a daughter.'

A wave of sorrow sweeps over me, leaving me breathless. 'Please don't say that, Mum.'

But it's as if she's moved on to another place inside her head. 'Where's Brian? Tell him he's going to be late if he's going to take me to the dance.'

I lead her gently to the bed and sit down next to her. Unzipping my bag, I take out one of the photographs I keep hidden in my wardrobe and which I'd tucked into the side pocket the evening Colin came to see me. Thankful I'd anticipated that Mum might not recognise a daughter who looks so different. A young woman with hair as blonde as Beth's once was.

Not knowing how I'll bear it if she still doesn't know me, I place the photograph in her hands. 'Do you recognise this person, Mum?'

When she doesn't answer, I think my world is going to fall apart, and then I notice she isn't wearing her reading glasses. Holding her hand in mine, I move the photo closer to her. She looks at it and I watch her face, desperate for any sign that will tell me she knows who it is who stares out at her. There is none. Instead, she turns to the door. 'Is it lunch, yet? Is Brian coming?'

I won't let her be distracted. 'The girl in the photograph. It's Ria, Mum.' She must know her. She has to. 'Look again. Please say you remember.'

Outside the window a lorry rumbles by, the glass rattling slightly as it passes. Mum looks up and it's as if she's seeing me for the first time. She takes her hand away from mine, letting the photograph fall onto the bedspread.

'Ria, you say? I once had a daughter called Ria.' Raising her hands, she places one each side of my face. Her eyes rove across it. 'Where did she go?'

'She didn't go anywhere, Mum. She lives far away in the Lake District, but she thinks of you every day and she loves you even when she isn't with you.'

Reaching into my bag again, I take out a little blue box with *Leona Designs* written on the top in silver. I open it and lift the silver heart necklace from its cushioned pad. 'I made this for you, Mum. Ria made this for you.'

As I lift her hair and fasten it around her neck, tears spill down my face and I feel Mum wipe them away with her thumbs.

'Don't cry, love. We'll find her for you. The Lake District, you say? My Brian will know where to look. He used to holiday there when he was a boy. We'll ask him when he gets here, shall we?'

As she speaks, a shiver of uncertainty runs through me. Have I said too much? But then I look at my mum and see that the veil of confusion has fallen over her eyes again. By tomorrow, this conversation will be as if it never happened.

Not wanting to distress her, I turn away, gulping back the sobs – relieved when there's a knock at the door. The young nurse pokes her head round, a smile on her face.

'Lunch is ready, Pam.'

When she sees my tear-stained face, her smile drops and her brows pull together. 'Are you all right, Nicky?'

Getting a tissue from my pocket, I dab at my eyes. 'Yes, I'm fine. Really. Please don't worry.'

'If you're sure.' She doesn't look convinced. 'You can come downstairs to the dining room with us if you like. I'm sure we can rustle up some lunch for you too.'

I dearly want to – would do anything to spend more time with Mum – but I know I can't. Coming here today was dangerous for all of us and I daren't think what Colin would say if he found out.

'I'm sorry, but I have to go now.'

The young nurse smiles. 'You must come again. Our residents do so love having visitors, especially family. Some have no one at all. Hard to believe, isn't it?'

I turn away. 'Yes, it is.'

'Well, it's been nice meeting you. Maybe I'll be on shift next time you come.'

'Maybe.' But I know she won't be. No one will – for this is the one and only time I will be visiting. The last time I'll ever see Mum. The thought is crippling. Reaching out to her, I fold her into my arms, pressing my cheek to hers.

'It doesn't matter who I am, Mum,' I whisper in her ear, my tears wetting the soft hair at her temple, 'as long as you know that I love you. That I've always loved you.'

It's almost impossible to tear myself away, but I know I have to. The young nurse is closing the window; her back is to me.

Taking the note to Leo from my pocket, I place it on the bedside table, then, with a kiss on Mum's cheek, I walk out of the room, closing the door behind me. Without looking back, I make for the lift and, once I'm there, jab at the button on the wall as though it might make it arrive faster. Scared that if I turn, I'll see Mum walking down the corridor with shuffling steps, leaning on the young nurse's arm for support. I'm desperate to be out of here. Out of London and back home with Scott and Beth.

Stepping onto the street, my anxiety rises. What if someone knows I've been here? What if Gareth has found someone to watch the nursing home? With a jolt, I remember that yesterday was Gareth's parole hearing; I'd been so worried about my mum, I'd pushed this knowledge away. But now his face looms menacingly in the forefront of my mind and I can't get rid of it. Wanting to get away from the place as quickly as possible, I start to run. I'll go back to the hotel to pick up my things, then to the nearest tube. My train from Euston is at one thirty and I don't want to miss it.

I don't notice the blue Fiesta that's parked in the street between two others – it's so ordinary, why would I? It's only as I walk past and the driver's door flies open that I turn towards it. A hand grabs my arm, pulling me off balance. I'm so startled, I have no time to react.

'Get in.'

As the fingers tighten on my wrist, my mind goes into overdrive. Wild with panic, I try to wrench my arm away, but he's stronger than me. I kick out, the toe of my shoe making contact with his shin.

'Fuck!'

Letting go of my arm, the man reaches down to rub at his leg and it's only then I realise who it is. I'm weak with relief. 'Colin. Oh, God, I'm sorry.'

His face is serious. 'Shut up and get in the car, Leona. Anyone could have seen you.'

'I don't want to. Leave me alone. No one knows I'm here.' I look down the road. It's a residential street, but there aren't many people around.

'You can't know that for sure.'

Taking hold of my arm again, he walks me round to the passenger side of the car and, placing a hand on my head, pushes me in. It brings back memories of that night. The blue flashing lights of the police car as Gareth is bundled in. The gentle pressure of the paramedic's fingers as they move my head to see the damage my husband has done to my face and neck. Lily's eyes as Abbie leads her next door to a house where violence is something that's only ever seen on television.

I hate Colin for doing this to me. For making me remember.

'How did you know I was here?'

'I needed to get in contact with you again and found you weren't in Church Langdon. After I saw you the other day and told you about your mother, some instinct made me guess you wouldn't leave it there and it just took a phone call to the care home to realise that my instincts had been correct. When they said your mother's niece was visiting today, it wasn't difficult to put two and two together.' He thumps his fist on the steering wheel, making me jump. 'What the hell did you think you were doing?'

I've never heard him angry before. A part of me wants to curl up into a ball. Disappear.

'I'm sorry.' My voice is a whisper. 'I just wanted to see her. One last time.'

Colin looks at me and his expression changes. He knows what he's done. The effect his outburst has had on me. 'No, it's me who should be sorry, Leona. Of course, you wanted to see her.'

He looks away, his knuckles whitening as he grips the steering wheel, and I see the effort it takes to keep his voice level. 'Did you notice anyone hanging around? Try to remember. It's important.'

He's scaring me now and I glance back at the red-bricked building. 'No… No, I didn't.'

Starting the engine, Colin manoeuvres the car from its parking space and pulls out onto the road. He stares straight in front of him. 'I'll take you to wherever you're staying to get your things, then I'll drive you back home.'

I look at him. 'But I've got a ticket for the train.'

'I don't care.' He's not angry now, just sad. When he speaks, it's almost to himself. 'Christ. How could you be so stupid?'

Tears start in my eyes. 'I didn't think. I just missed my mum.'

'I understand that – of course I do. I'm not a cold-hearted bastard. But for twelve years we've kept you safe, Leona. You and Beth. It could all be undone…' He clicks his fingers. 'Just like that.'

'But it was all so long ago. Do you think Gareth will ever forgive me?'

Colin glances at me, puzzled. 'You make it sound as though it was *you* who did something wrong. Self-defence, when you fear for your life, is not a crime, Leona. Your statement helped to put a violent man behind bars and he's paid the price. It's what the judge and jury thought and it's what you must believe too. There's nothing for Gareth to forgive, but even if there was, there's not much chance he would. He's a psychopath, Leona. Forgiveness requires a conscience in both forgiver and the forgiven. I wouldn't be surprised if he's spent his time banged up scheming how to—'

He stops, mortification written across his face, and tries to change the subject, but the damage has been done.

A chill runs down my spine. 'You don't think I'm safe, do you.' It's a statement rather than a question.

We're onto a busier road now, filled with buses and taxis. It won't be long before we get to my hotel. He's quiet at first and I wonder if he's going to say anything, but when, eventually, he does, the words are the ones I've been dreading.

'I've never felt you were truly safe, Leona.'

CHAPTER THIRTY-EIGHT

Beth

'I thought you were busy today?'

Beth leant back against the cairn, feeling the warmth of the stone soak through her T-shirt. The afternoon light was golden, bathing everything in an apricot glow. 'I was, but then I changed my mind.'

David pulled a face. 'I see. Second place, am I? Oh, well. I suppose I'd better get used to it.'

Beth sighed and stretched out her legs in front of her, feeling the prickle of the scrubby grass on the back of her calves. What did he care? By the end of the month he'd be gone.

'It's like a sponge,' she said, half closing her eyes and letting the colours merge.

'What is?'

'The landscape. It's so drenched in sunshine, it looks like it's soaked it up.'

'It does… and so does your skin.' David ran a fingertip over her shoulder, where a crop of freckles bloomed, then kissed it, his lips warm against her flesh. 'You're right, though. We've had good weather so far. Let's hope it lasts. Mind you, I'm not sure about those clouds that are gathering over the pikes. It might not be so nice later this afternoon.'

Beth followed his gaze. 'Dad didn't mention anything about rain being forecast. He's out this way too, today.'

'Well, that's the Lake District for you – sunny one minute, pissing down the next. So, you're not worried our paths will cross then?'

'No. He said he was taking the party along Kennets Crag towards New Langdon Ghyll. It's a circular walk and, by the time they come back this way, I'll be back home with my feet up.'

'If you say so.' He nodded to her bag. 'Not sketching today?'

Beth leant back against him, trying to commit the feel of his body to memory. 'Sometimes I just like to listen and watch. The things I see often stay with me and I might sketch them out later.'

'Blimey. Who needs a camera when they've got you?'

As he spoke, a woodpecker began its rhythmic tapping in the woodland that clothed the lower slopes. Faint but unmistakeable.

'Do you think he's knocking on heaven's door?' David lifted a strand of her dark hair and twisted it around his finger.

'I don't think so. Anyway, I thought you didn't believe in heaven... or God.'

'I don't, but I like the song.'

Not wanting to admit she'd never heard of it, Beth tipped back her head and looked at the sky. 'If I lie here long enough, I'm hoping I might see one of the falcons.'

David laughed. 'I've said it before and I'll say it again... you're more than a little obsessed! Those birds you draw – you capture their strength and independence in a way I've only seen before in a photograph. Whatever medium you use, the essence of the bird is always there. I don't know how you do it.'

The unexpected praise made her warm inside. 'Thank you. But what about you? Did you always want to be a photographer?'

David stretched over to his rucksack. 'No, of course not. When I was six, I wanted to be a fireman and by the time I reached the grand old age of eight, it was an astronaut. What about you?'

Beth shook her head. 'I never wanted to be an astronaut.'

He poked her in the ribs. 'Smart arse. You know what I mean.' Unzipping his bag, he took out his camera. 'I've been interested in photography since I was a boy. I thought it might be the same with you and your drawing.'

'I suppose so. Art is the only thing I've ever been good at. I can't imagine doing anything else. I just wish I didn't have to go to school to learn how to do it.'

'School?' David looked at her, his head on one side.

'College,' she said quickly. 'I've said it for so many years, it's hard to break the habit.'

She bit the inside of her lip. She'd almost given it away and if he knew she was only fifteen, he'd ditch her like a shot. Why wouldn't he? It was easier not to think about what he'd say if he found out, because her life, with David in it, was a better one by far.

'And you. Where do you think you got your talent for photography?'

David put down his camera. 'That's easy. It was from my father.'

'Your father?' She remembered what he'd told her that night at the campsite. He'd never mentioned his father since.

'Yes. Though he isn't worthy of that name. Buying me my first camera was the only decent thing he ever did.'

'Was he really that bad?'

David nodded. 'Worse. One night, he pushed me too far. He'd forgotten that I wasn't a little boy any more... that I was seventeen and almost as big as him. He came home drunk from the pub and started giving my mum a hard time.'

'What did you do?'

'It doesn't matter. Let's just say, he never laid a finger on her again. Not while I was living there, anyway.'

He was silent for a moment, his forehead creased. Beth put her hand on his arm. 'What is it, David?'

'I can't tell you. If I do, it will change the way you look at me. The way you feel about me.'

'It won't. I promise you. You can tell me anything.'

He looked out at the pikes, their crags rugged against the blue. 'After what had happened with my dad, I went off the rails for a bit and ended up in the nick – just for a short while. I look back on that time now and think, *what an idiot*. So many opportunities lost…'

'What do you mean?'

'Nothing,' he said quickly. 'Just that it nearly broke my mum's heart.'

Beth looked away, trying to process her thoughts. She waited for disgust and unease to wash over her, but it didn't. Instead, she felt only sadness for the boy who'd had to put up with so much.

'Was it awful? Being in prison, I mean.' She'd seen on TV the dreadful things that could happen to a young boy in there.

David nodded. 'Pretty much. I was eighteen by then – only missed juvie by a couple of months. Adult prison was terrifying. My saving grace, the only thing that kept me sane while I was there, was that I was taken under the wing of one of the guys who was serving a much longer sentence. Said I reminded him of himself at that age. He had quite a lot of clout in there and, because of that, nobody bothered me.'

'What happened to your dad?' Beth ran her fingers down the soft hairs of David's arm.

'By the time I came out, everything had changed. Dad was ill and it looked like he wouldn't get better. He was in no state to take anything out on Mum, not physically anyway, and when he eventually went into hospital, he wanted me to go and see him. It might be that he wanted my forgiveness, but I doubt it.'

'Did you go?'

'No.' David stood up and lifted his camera strap over his neck. 'I never did.'

'I have a secret too.' Beth hadn't meant to say it, but what harm could it do?

'A secret?'

'Well, more like a discovery. Mum's been acting weirdly recently. She has these episodes… anxiety attacks. But it's not just that… There's something else too.' She reached into her pocket for her phone and went onto her photos. When she found what she was looking for, she handed it to David.

'What's this?'

'They're birth certificates.'

David zoomed in on the picture. 'I can see that, but why are you showing them to me?'

'I found them hidden under the floorboards in Mum's fitted wardrobe. I don't know whose they are or why she's hidden them. There were photos too.' She swiped back to where they were and showed him.

'Is that you?'

'I thought that at first, but it's not.'

'There's definitely a resemblance – and who are these people? Your grandparents?'

'I don't know. I've never seen my grandparents. They died in a car accident when my mum was young.'

David handed her back the phone. 'I'm not sure what to say. You're right, it is strange. One thing I do know is secrets are never a good thing in a family.'

Holding out his hand to her, he pulled her up, then pointed skywards. While they'd been talking, the clouds they'd seen earlier had moved away from the peaks and had taken over most of the blue. It was surprising how quickly it had happened. The rolling fells, which had recently been a vivid green, were now ocean dark. As the clouds moved, an occasional glint of sunshine brought the landscape back to life before drowning it in shadows once more.

'This is perfect.' David walked to the other side of the cairn and stood in contemplation, his hands in his pockets.

'What is?'

'The sky... this cairn... you.' He came back to her and turned her face a fraction. 'I'd like to photograph you, if you'd let me. Here by the cairn with the moody sky behind you. The light is just right and the breeze... the way it's moving your hair... I couldn't have planned it if I tried.'

'Isn't it too dark now that the sun's gone in?' Shadows were creeping across the slopes on the other side of the valley, deepening the inky clefts between the hills.

David shook his head. 'It's the quality of light that's important, not the quantity. When there's full sun, it's like being in a room with just a bare bulb. Everything is evenly lit. When the sun comes out from behind the cloud, it's like turning on a spotlight. It increases the contrast and the shadow, making it better for photographs.'

Beth looked down at her denim shorts and strappy top. Her walking boots. 'But what about these?'

'What about them? I don't want a series of photographs with someone dressed like they're about to go on the catwalk. What you're wearing is perfect – working with the landscape, not fighting against it.'

'But I don't know how to stand. What to do.'

'Don't worry about that. I'll tell you.' He pointed to a slab of slate that jutted out from the cairn. 'I'd like you to sit on this and look out across the valley. That's all.'

Using the great slabs of rock as steps, Beth climbed the pile of slate until she was kneeling on the one David had shown her. Gingerly, she manoeuvred herself until she was facing out into the valley. She leant back. 'Like this?'

'Not quite. Bend one knee up and rest your chin on it. No, don't smile. I want you to look thoughtful.'

Beth did as she was told, trying not to look at him as he moved around her, his camera raised to his face.

'Ever heard of the rule of thirds?'

She looked up. 'No. What's that?'

David clicked away. 'Imagine breaking the image down into thirds, horizontally and vertically. If you place points of interest in the intersections, the photograph becomes more balanced. It's the same with drawing. I'm surprised your A-level tutor hasn't mentioned it.'

'Maybe she has. I've probably just forgotten.'

David put down his camera. 'Well, whether she's told you or not, I've noticed, in the pictures that you've shown me, that you do it anyway. You must just have a natural eye for the balance of the picture.'

Beth thought of the drawing she'd done of the eagle. The one that her teacher wanted to enter into the competition. The bird was at the side of the page, looking out at the viewer, the crags reflected in its yellow eyes. The rest of the page was just a pale wash of blue, the edges feathering into nothing. She hadn't been taught – it had just felt right to do it that way.

'I think I'm done.' There was a click as he replaced the lens cap. 'It's going to rain soon… I can feel it in the air. We'd better go before it starts.'

With a glance at the darkening sky, Beth shuffled across the slate slab and began to climb back down, taking his offered hand and jumping the last part. David caught her and grinned. 'I've got some fabulous shots there. Wouldn't be surprised if one of the biggies decided to take them.'

'The biggies?'

'Yeh… *BBC Countryfile* or *The Countryman*. You wouldn't mind, would you?'

'No. It's just that I can't imagine anyone being interested in a photograph with me in it.'

'It's not just you.' David spread his arms wide. 'It's all this too… But mostly you.'

Touching the ends of her hair, he leant in to kiss her, but Beth had frozen.

'Shit!'

David took a step back. 'What is it, Beth? You look like you've seen a ghost.'

Her eyes weren't on him. They were on the figure walking towards them. A figure that, at any other time, she'd have been delighted to see.

'It's my dad.'

'Now the shit hits the fan.' David held his camera to his chest like a shield. 'He doesn't look too happy.'

Grabbing David's arm, Beth pulled him into the shadow of the cairn. Placing his arms around her waist, she buried her head in his neck. With any luck, her dad wouldn't recognise her.

She could hear the crunch of her dad's feet on the stony path, the tap of his walking poles. The footsteps stopped. She held her breath.

'Sorry... sorry.' She could hear the embarrassment in her dad's voice. 'I didn't realise anyone was up here, otherwise I would have...'

David's arms tightened. 'No harm done, mate.'

It seemed they were going to be lucky. Her dad's boots were already moving away. But then they stopped. She knew what was happening. He'd seen her rucksack.

'Beth?'

She turned to him, her face burning. 'What are you doing here, Dad?'

'Unless you've forgotten, Beth, walking on the fells is my job. More to the point, what are *you* doing here? And who is this?'

Beth saw it all through her dad's eyes. The stubbled sandy beard, the long hair pulled back into a ponytail and the camera. It didn't look good.

'David's a friend.'

Her dad raised his eyebrows. 'A friend?'

'Yes. We met one day up at the cairn. He's a photographer.'

'I see.' He looked at David, his eyes narrowed. 'And what is it you take photos of, exactly?'

'Landscapes mostly. For some of the big magazines – *The Countryman, Coast, Country Living*. That sort of thing. I've just been taking some of Beth as it happens… The light's been perfect.'

Beth felt her heart sink. Why did he have to say that? It would only make things worse.

Her dad stared at them. She'd seen that look before when he was wondering what would be the best thing to do. Finally, he rubbed his hand down his chin. 'Well, we'll leave you to your photographs. Come on, Beth. Your mum will be back from the course soon and I'm sure she'll want to tell you all about it.'

Taking Beth's arm, he started to walk back along the path, but Beth pulled her arm away.

'Can't I just say goodbye, Dad?'

Her dad nodded. 'That's a very good idea, Beth. As you won't be seeing him again.'

CHAPTER THIRTY-NINE
Leona

Colin pulls the car into a lay-by. We are on the outskirts of Church Langdon and it won't take me long to walk the rest of the way. I've been asleep for some of the journey, but during the time I've been awake, Colin's words have been going round and round in my head. A part of me is hoping that if I ignore them, they will somehow go away, but now we're back, I know I can't avoid them any longer.

'You can't seriously expect me to just pack up our things and leave tonight.'

Colin stares straight ahead. His face set. 'You know the score, Leona. You always have. If you do anything to endanger yourself, or Beth, we have to move you again.'

'But Church Langdon is our home and I can't uproot Beth. It's her GCSEs soon and she's already so... so...' It's difficult to put into words my worry for my daughter. I give up, trying another tack. 'And what about Scott? What do you expect me to say to him?'

Colin frowns. This is hard for him as well, I know. Over the years, especially in the early days when I saw him more, we've formed a friendship of sorts. 'We'd come up with another plan.' He chooses his words carefully. 'Another story.'

I shudder, knowing what this will mean and, when I hear Colin clear his throat, I realise he knows it too. Witness Protection made me leave everyone I loved behind, once before. What would stop them doing it again?

'I can't. It's impossible.'

Colin turns to me, his eyes imploring. 'Don't do this to me, Leona. You know that if you don't let Witness Protection move you again, they'll take you off the programme.'

'Maybe I don't need it any more.'

'There's something I haven't told you yet – the reason I tried to get in touch with you.' He draws himself up and, for the first time, I see in him the uniformed police officer he once was. 'I'm sorry to tell you Gareth's parole hearing was successful. He's going to be released on licence on his parole eligibility date in a couple of weeks' time.'

'It can't be true!'

My head begins to spin and the car feels suddenly very small. Running my hand along the door, I jab at the window button until it lowers. I lean my head out and drag the fresh air into my lungs.

'Are you all right?'

I pinch the bridge of my nose. 'Why didn't you tell me earlier?'

'I would have but I saw how upset you were about your mum.' His voice is flat. 'I'd been hoping that parole would be refused, but, sadly, that hasn't happened.'

'But he's dangerous. He nearly killed me and I was given witness protection. Doesn't that mean anything?'

Colin shakes his head. 'Your views in your statement were taken into account, but they've decided to go ahead with the release anyway. Since he's been in prison, Gareth's taken part in a number of treatment programmes and that's been viewed positively.'

Icy fingers creep up my spine. I've seen this side of Gareth before. Manipulating situations to suit his own ends.

'It's an act, Colin. He won't have changed. I know him too well.' My voice is choked with emotion. 'You must know it's true.'

The resignation in his face says it all. 'It's out of my hands and that's the reason why, if you came off the programme, we couldn't ignore the possibility he might try to make contact again.'

'But surely he wouldn't be allowed to. Wouldn't there be a no contact order or something?'

'Yes. He wouldn't be released without strict conditions to his licence. He wouldn't be able to make contact with you or go anywhere near your home, and the prison governor will probably argue that a tag will be needed to enforce the exclusion area. As well as that, he'd have to report to a probation officer every day. Breaking any of these rules would mean he'd be banged straight up again.'

His words are a lifeline. 'Then there's no need for me to move.'

Colin sighed. 'Witness protection is for life. There's a good reason for it. Men like Gareth are unpredictable. We've been through it all before, Leona. You know all this.'

'I hate it. It's like I've stopped owning my life, Colin. I have no control over what happens to me. I just want my life back.'

'It won't be much of a life if you're forever looking over your shoulder.'

I raise my chin defiantly. Putting on a show of confidence I don't feel. 'I'll take my chances.'

'Then you give me no choice. I'll make the phone call and this will probably be the last time we meet.' He leans across and hugs me and, as he does, a car drives past. It looks like Scott's. My heart stops, but then I tell myself not to be so stupid. He's not due home until much later.

As I get out of the car, Colin watches me, his concern evident in his frown. I'm just walking away when he lowers the window and calls out to me.

'Goodbye, Leona… and good luck.'

*

When I get back, Scott is already home. It's been raining and there's a small puddle of water where his waterproof has dripped onto the lobby floor. His walking boots are on the mat next to Beth's and both pairs are caked in mud.

'Scott?'

He appears from the kitchen, a bottle of beer in his hand. He looks tired. His broad shoulders are hunched.

He tries a smile. 'Good time?'

'Yes, but it's nice to be home.' There's something in his manner that isn't right. There have been none of his bad jokes and the laughter has gone out of his eyes.

'What is it, Scott? Has something happened?'

He glances up the stairs. 'You could say that.'

'Do you want to tell me about it?' I try to push down the thoughts that are fighting for space in my head. 'What's happened? Is it Beth?' My brain trawls through all the options; none of them are good.

He sinks down onto the settee. 'She's been seeing this guy. Quite a bit older. Looked about mid-twenties. Beth says he's just a friend – but I'm not so sure. They've met up a few times, apparently.'

I'm stunned. My heart racing. 'But when? She's either at school or here revising.'

'She didn't want to tell me, but I got it out of her. Apparently, she's been bunking off school. Going off with him in his camper van to God knows where.'

My head's spinning. 'How do you know all this?'

'I caught them together by the cairn after I'd taken the party I was leading back. We'd had to cut the walk short as someone wasn't feeling well.'

He screws up his eyes as if to rid himself of the picture. 'He'd been taking photos of her.'

'Oh, God.' My stomach clenches. 'Tell me it's not what I'm thinking.'

'No, no. Nothing like that. They were pictures of her sitting on the cairn with Lake Windermere in the distance behind her. The guy says he's a professional photographer… works freelance for the magazines: *The Countryman, Coast, Country Living*. But who knows if that's true.'

'I want her to stop seeing him.' My voice comes out too loudly and I glance at the ceiling, hoping Beth hasn't heard me.

'Oh, there's no need to worry about that, I've already told her they're not to meet again.' He looks at me. 'Maybe I should contact the police. Just in case. She's only fifteen, for heaven's sake.'

My mouth goes dry. I can't let him phone the police. The witness protection officers I dealt with work separately from those working on criminal investigations. It's the only way to make sure that we are completely anonymous. The local police know nothing about my past. If they get involved, there will be questions about Beth… about me. Ones I might not be able to answer.

'Let's not be hasty, Scott,' I say. 'He's not done anything wrong. It looks like you've caught it before it can turn into anything, and you've told Beth not to see him again. Let's leave it at that.'

'I'm surprised you're reacting so calmly, Leona. You're usually the one who likes to keep Beth wrapped in cotton wool.' Scott lowers his eyes to the floor, the hurt written across his face. 'I'm wondering if you have your own reasons for not wanting to make a fuss about an unsuitable friendship.'

I'm going to ask what he means, but his face has told me everything I need to know.

'You drove past me, didn't you?' I feel sick.

His face is a picture of misery. 'Yes.'

I know what he's thinking. I should have been at a jewellery-making course but, instead, I'm sitting in the car with a man he's never seen before. If the tables were turned, I'd jump to the same conclusion.

'It's not what you think.'

Scott puts his head in his hands and groans. 'For Christ's sake, Leona. Give me some credit.'

I think of all the things I could tell him: that the person he saw me with was a taxi driver who dropped me off on the outskirts of town for no reason; that he was someone I met at the station who offered me a lift; that he was on my jewellery-making course and drove me all the way back from London because, guess what, he just happened to live here too.

But Scott's no fool. With gut-wrenching certainty, I know I have only one option – to go along with what he's already thinking. That I've been having an affair.

Taking his arm, I lead him to the settee. 'Sit down, Scott. I need to tell you something. Something important.'

The door at the bottom of the stairs is open. Whatever happens, Beth must not hear what I'm going to say. I close it, then join Scott on the settee, our knees touching.

He's sitting looking at me, waiting for me to say something. To break his heart. My own heart is pounding. Taking a deep breath, I hold his hands in mine and try to form the words. But I can't. I just can't do it. Instead, I tell him the truth.

'The man you saw me with is Colin. My witness protection officer.'

Scott's head shoots up. 'Please don't joke about this.'

'It's not a joke, Scott. My name isn't Leona. It's Ria.'

'What do you mean, it's Ria?'

I didn't know I was going to tell him. Not this way, but, now I've started, there's nothing for it but to continue.

'And Beth's name is Lily.'

Scott frowns, trying to follow my thread. 'I don't understand. I don't understand any of it.'

I forge ahead, unable to stop. 'And she's sixteen, not fifteen.'

His mouth goes slack and I see something akin to fear cross his face. He pulls his hands away. 'Christ, Leona. Just tell me what's going on.'

And so I tell him everything: Gareth... The court case... Witness Protection... how I came to be in the Lake District when he first met me. Then I explain how Witness Protection suggested I change Beth's date of birth by a few months so that she would be in a year lower at school. A precaution, they'd said, in case he tried to find her.

Scott listens, his big head in his hands and, when I tell him about the night my husband tried to kill me, I hear him groan. It's an animal noise that comes from deep within him.

We sit in silence, then, eventually, he lifts his head. 'So where were you this weekend? What were you doing?'

'I went to see my mother.'

'I thought both your parents were dead.' Realisation dawns. 'Of course, it was just another lie. Part of the story.'

I try not to hear the bitterness in his voice.

'Mum's got Alzheimer's,' I continue. 'I haven't seen her in twelve years and I wanted to see her one last time before she didn't know me any more.'

I bow my head and relief surges through me. For twelve years, I've kept my secret. It will be so much easier now that Scott can share it with me.

'So now you know why the police can't be involved. Say something, Scott. Anything.'

Slowly, Scott raises his head and I'm shocked to see tears on his cheeks. It's the first time I've seen him cry. 'Beth must never know.'

'Of course not. Now you know, everything will be so much better.' I'm talking quickly. Scared of his expression.

His face tightens. 'I didn't know we had a problem.'

'We haven't, of course we haven't, but now that everything's in the open, we can start to live a proper life. One without secrets.'

'It's a bit late for that, don't you think?' His voice has a coldness to it I've never heard before. 'And here's something for you to think about. I never had any secrets, Leona. It was only you who did.'

He gets up and walks to the coat rack in the lobby. Takes his jacket from the hook.

The blood chills in my veins. 'What are you doing, Scott?'

He looks at me as though he doesn't know me. 'I'm going out. I need some air.'

I'm standing now, my hands helpless at my sides. 'But don't you want to talk about it?'

'There's nothing to talk about. The Leona I fell in love with would never have lied to me this way. Kept something so important from me.'

I grab his arm. 'But it's still me, Scott. I'm still the same person.'

'No,' he says, tears dripping into his beard. 'You're not.'

CHAPTER FORTY

Beth

'What's going on, Mum?'

Beth took the last step into the living room and stood with her hands in the pockets of her jeans, waiting for the onslaught. She'd been dreading the moment she'd have to come down and face the music, but now she was here, she realised something had happened in her absence. Her dad was nowhere to be seen and her mum's eyes were red and swollen.

Instead of answering her question, her mum turned to the window and looked out.

'He's told you, hasn't he? About me and David.'

She had no idea what her dad had told her mum – she and her dad had come home in silence and, once through the door, she'd run straight upstairs and into her room.

Her mum turned to look at her, dragging her hair back from her face with her fingers. She looked distracted. 'David?'

'Yes, David. That's his name, Mum… The guy I've been seeing.'

When her mum said nothing, Beth threw herself onto the settee. 'Well, aren't you going to say something? Tell me he's too old for me? Go on! If *you* don't, I'm sure there'll be others queuing up to do the honours.'

'For Christ's sake, Lily. Not everything is about you!'

Beth's head shot up. 'What did you call me?'

'Nothing.' Her mum took a step back. 'It was nothing.'

Beth had never seen her mum like this – her eyes so haunted. It scared her.

'It wasn't nothing, Mum. You called me Lily.' She searched her face, trying desperately to figure out what was going on in her head. 'Who is Lily?'

Her mum had gone pale. 'Nobody. Forget I said it.'

But Beth couldn't forget it. She knew that name. It was the one on the birth certificate upstairs. The room was beginning to swim and she closed her eyes. She felt herself being pulled back into the grip of memory. Spider-legged fringes on the shade of a light on the wall. A big double bed. Her mum's cheek against hers. *Sleep tight, Lily-Beth. Sleep tight, darling.*

She felt numb with shock. 'It's me, isn't it, Mum? Lily is me.'

'I'm sorry.' Her mum was beside her now, but it was as if all the strength had gone out of her body. She slumped onto the settee, holding one of the cushions against her chest as though it were a shield. 'I didn't want you to find out like this.'

'What do you mean? I find out I have two names and you say there might be a better time for me to discover it? And the other birth certificate? Whose is that?'

Her mum looked shocked. 'How do you know about that?'

'I'm not an idiot, Mum. If it was me, I'd have found a better hiding place than the wardrobe.'

'You had no right…'

'And *you* had no right to keep this from me. Are you going to tell me who the other certificate belongs to, or am I going to have to ask Dad?'

Her mum's face fell. 'It belonged to your brother. His name was Samuel.'

Beth's anger was hot and red. 'Christ! I have a brother and you never thought to tell me!'

'*Had* a brother, Beth. He died when he was just a few weeks old.' Her mum swallowed. 'It was a cot death.'

Another memory loosened. A pale moon and stars rotating above her head. A baby's cry. Beth's anger collapsed, folding in upon itself. 'How old was I, Mum… when he died?'

'You were just four.'

Too young to remember properly.

'But why the different name, Mum? Why call me Beth when my name's Lily?'

Uncertainty crossed her mum's face. It was clear she was struggling to find an answer.

'Your father – your real father, that is – he did things that he shouldn't have. He made it very difficult for us to live with him.'

Beth had never given this shadowy figure from the past much thought. For almost as far back as she could remember, Scott had been her dad and she'd never needed to know more.

'What things?' The question hung between them and, for the first time, Beth felt the beginnings of fear. 'Tell me, Mum. What was it he did?'

'It doesn't matter. All you need to know, Beth, is that they were bad enough that I needed to move us as far away from him as possible. I changed your name for your own safety. For several months, I called you Lily-Beth to help you get used to your new name, and by the time I dropped the Lily part of it, you didn't think anything of it.'

'And Dad… Scott. Does he know any of this?'

Her mum's head hung down as if defeated. 'Some – not everything. It's what we were talking about when you came down. He's been worried about me – the way I've been these last few weeks. The panic attacks. I couldn't keep it from him any longer.'

Beth felt fury bubble up inside her. 'So you thought you'd tell him and not your own daughter?'

'It wasn't like that.'

'Then what was it like? No, don't bother to tell me. I don't even want to know. Where is Dad?'

'He's gone out for a bit to clear his head. It's been a shock for him too.' Her mum's voice sounded strained. Pulling a tissue from her pocket, she blew her nose.

Beth looked around her. The room, the settee with its array of coloured cushions, the window with the green fells captured within its frame, looked alien – as though she'd never seen them before. First, her dad had found out about her and David, and now this. Scott had been the only father she'd known. He'd brought her up as his own and she loved him more than anything. He was a down-to-earth man, saying things as they were. What would he have made of these new revelations?

She couldn't speak. If she did, she knew she would cry. She'd already lost David, but what if her dad didn't come back? What if she'd lost him too?

CHAPTER FORTY-ONE
Leona

'Thank you so much for agreeing to speak to me, Lisa.' I fight to keep the desperation out of my voice. 'I didn't think you'd be able to, now I've told you I'm no longer on the programme.'

Going over to the door, I close it, although there's no way Beth is going to hear what I'm saying as the thud, thud of music is coming through the ceiling from her bedroom.

'I'm happy to speak to you as a private client, either in person or over the phone, Leona.' I haven't spoken to Lisa for nearly three weeks and her voice is like a balm. I press my mobile to my ear in the vain hope that it might calm me. 'But the decision you've made to leave Witness Protection is a big one. I just hope it's the right one for all of you.'

I try to hold my voice steady, but I know it's in danger of breaking. 'I told Scott about Gareth. He didn't take it well and has been staying with his mum for the last few weeks – to get some head space, is how he put it, but I'm scared he might leave me altogether.' The words come out in a rush, the final sentence ending in a sob.

'I'm very sorry, Leona.' There's sympathy in her voice. 'That must be terribly hard. Is that what you wanted to talk to me about today?'

'I don't know. I don't know anything any more.' Since he left, I've been in limbo, unable to do even the simplest of tasks.

'Does he know about the baby?'

I shake my head although she can't see. 'There doesn't seem any point now.'

'It might make a difference. I think you need to tell him.'

'I just don't know how I can now.' Thinking of Scott brings tears to my eyes.

'And Beth? It won't be long before she guesses. You won't be able to hide your pregnancy forever.'

'I know, but I just feel so bad for her. She'd started to seem so much happier.'

'Why is that, do you think?' Lisa asks.

I think of the invitation pinned to the noticeboard beside my workbench. *Year 11 Art Exhibition* printed on it. It's tomorrow evening. In the envelope there had also been a note from Mrs Snowdon, checking I'd be there, as she had an exciting surprise for me.

'She's been doing better at school recently and she's got some of her artwork on display, which she's excited about. I know how much her art means to her. I just wish she knew how much *she* means to *me*.' In truth, my daughter is the only thing keeping me going at the moment.

'Then it's important you show her. Go and see her exhibition, then you can tell her how brilliant you think she is.'

I sigh. 'She might not want me to. It's not just Scott who knows about my lies. I called Beth "Lily" by mistake and had to tell her the truth. So now they both know. God, it's such a mess.'

'Does she know everything?'

'Not the whole truth – just that her name was once Lily and that we'd moved to the Lake District because of something her father – her real father, that is – had done.'

Lisa's voice remains calm. 'She had to know sometime.'

Suddenly, I'm overwhelmed by tears. Big, ugly tears that trickle down my chin. It's hard to catch my breath between the sobs. 'I've ruined her life as it is, without adding a baby to the equation.'

'It's going to be all right, Leona. Just let it all out. You've had a difficult time of it recently.'

'I... I... thought I wanted to get rid of it. The baby.' My shoulders heave. 'But, I don't think I can. I can't do it.'

'Tell me what it is you're afraid of, Leona. Is it because of the cot death? Are you afraid it might happen again?'

Wrapping my arms around my body, I rock back and forth. Remembering. Hating myself. 'It's not just that. It's something else.'

'I think it might help you to talk about what happened. It's not good to bottle things up. I realise why you haven't been able to tell Scott, but with me it's different. I know your story... your background.'

'Yes.' I wipe away the tears with the heel of my hand. I want to tell someone. If I don't, I'm scared I'll go mad.

'Would you like to make an appointment to see me tomorrow?'

'No, the phone is fine.' If I don't tell her straight away, I might chicken out.

'I'll let Ria tell you.'

CHAPTER FORTY-TWO
Ria

It was a difficult birth. Samuel had arrived into the world red-faced and screaming and, after he'd fought the breast for two days, Ria had given up and given him a bottle. As she looked at his tiny, screwed-up face and wide eyes, she tried to find the feelings she'd had for Lily in the early days. That overwhelming love that would make her give her life for this tiny child.

When she couldn't find those feelings, guilt made her do the very best she could for him. It wasn't Samuel's fault that she felt this way, and he would never get any affection from his father, for Gareth had made it clear from the start that he didn't want another crying baby in the house. Not that Lily had cried much. She'd always been a quiet child.

Every day was the same. Each morning, Ria would drag herself out of bed and into some sort of routine. She'd taught Lily to stay in her room until she came to get her, so as not to wake her father, then together they'd tiptoe to the kitchen. Lily would sit at the marble island with a bowl of cereal and Ria would lie Samuel in the carrycot she kept downstairs so that she could make Gareth his breakfast. It was important to have it ready for him once he'd had his shower and stopped at the hall mirror to check his hair. She didn't want to give him any excuses to get angry. Not when the health visitor could call round at any time.

Some days were better than others. There were times when Gareth had gone to work, and she was sitting on the floor playing with Lily or pushing the pram through the private gardens outside their flat, that she'd forget what it was she was afraid of. Forget the way her heart would stop when she heard his key in the door at the end of the day.

These were the good days. The days when she told herself she was getting anxious about nothing. Gareth was a good husband. He provided for his family. If he was angry at times, it was because she should have been more mindful of his needs: made sure Lily's toys had been picked up before he got home, or that the baby wasn't crying. Gareth, Gareth, Gareth. One excuse after another. Never his fault.

She never saw Leo now and, when her parents rang, she made excuses not to speak to them for long, knowing that it would put Gareth into a bad mood if he found out. They were trying to turn her against him, he'd say. They were old-fashioned and didn't understand the way their marriage worked.

He was right – they didn't. No one did.

And, always, there was the overwhelming tiredness. The bone-aching exhaustion that made her head ache and her eyes feel as though they had been sanded. Samuel woke two or three times every night, his face screwed-up and red, his cry making her rush to pick him up. Petrified he'd wake Gareth.

She'd take him to the kitchen for his bottle, praying he wouldn't fight it as he usually did. Unlike Lily, who had settled happily to her feed, it would sometimes take an hour to get a few millilitres of milk inside him. She'd change him and then pace the kitchen floor with him over her shoulder, scared that her husband had been disturbed. When at last Samuel fell into a fitful sleep, she'd return him to his crib and lie on top of the covers of her bed, ears pricked for the slightest sound that would tell her he had woken again.

As the weeks went on, she found it harder and harder to function. Her tiredness was a burden she carried with her whatever she was doing and, when she looked in the mirror, she was shocked by the dark circles under her eyes. The health visitor had stopped coming and she knew she should go to the doctor, but even the thought of taking the tube to her nearest surgery made her feel like weeping.

Then, one evening, Gareth came home and threw a packet of tablets into her lap.

Picking up the box, she looked at it. 'What are these?'

'Zopiclone. They'll help you sleep.'

'Where did you get them?' Ria turned the box over in her hand. 'Don't you need a prescription?'

Gareth went over to the sideboard and poured himself a drink. 'What does it matter where I got them? They're in your hand, aren't they?' He put the stopper back on the decanter. 'Ungrateful bitch.'

Ria flinched. She was glad that Lily was already in bed. 'I'm sorry. Of course, I'm grateful. It was kind of you to think of me, but I can't, Gareth. I have to be awake for Samuel.'

'Not if you take a low dose. You'll get to sleep, but then you'll wake up if the brat's screaming.'

'Don't call him that. He's your son.'

'That's what *you* say. You're such a slag, it could be any number of people's bastard. Not that it makes any fucking difference to me.'

In his carrycot on the floor, Samuel began to cry.

'Fuck this. I'm going out.'

'But you've only just got home.'

Without answering her, Gareth left the room, slamming the door behind him.

Ria's body ached with weariness, but there was no one else to pick the baby up. She went over to the carrycot and lifted him out. Since Samuel had been born, Gareth had barely acknowledged him. Surely, he didn't really believe that he wasn't the father?

*

Ria lay in bed watching the green digits of the clock flash the minutes away. Samuel's last feed had been two and a half hours ago and, as usual, he'd been fractious. Since then she'd been awake, listening to his little sounds and praying he would give her longer this time. She knew it was unlikely, though. He'd wake for another feed in half an hour as he always did, and the thought made her want to cry. All she wanted was some rest, a break from the endless repetition of feeding, changing, and pacing with a baby who wouldn't settle. If she didn't fall asleep soon, it would be time to get up and do it all again. She couldn't face it. She just couldn't.

On the bedside table, was the packet of sleeping tablets, a glass of water next to them. Would it hurt to take just one?

Picking up the box, she opened it and read the leaflet. As Gareth had said, it was a low dosage – just 3.5 milligrams. It would take around an hour to work. If she took one now, Samuel would be fed and changed before they took effect and then she would get three hours' blissful sleep until the next feed.

She looked at Gareth's side of the bed. It was empty. When he got home from wherever he'd been, she knew he would fall onto the bed in the spare room in his clothes and nothing would wake him. There was nothing to stop her feeding the baby here for once.

Pushing back the covers, she went over to the crib and lifted it, with its stand, to the side of the bed. Samuel didn't stir. He was fast asleep on his back, his arms bent as if in surrender. Ria looked at his little face, wishing she could feel something for him. But it was sorrow, not affection that tugged at her. Sorrow for the child she had no feelings for. A child born not out of love, but out of submission.

She went to the kitchen for his bottle of milk and placed it on the bedside table. When she'd done that, she picked up the packet of sleeping tablets. Hesitating only a moment, she pushed one of the white pills out of its foil bubble and swallowed it down with some of the water. Immediately, the tension she'd been feeling eased. Samuel would wake soon, but this time she wanted him to. As soon as he had fed, she could sleep. She lay back on the pillow and waited.

Samuel was crying, but it was as if his cries were coming from far away. With difficulty, Ria forced her heavy eyelids open. Her head was muzzy, her mouth dry. With a great effort, she reached across to the bedside table and switched on the lamp. She looked at the clock. How could that be? Without realising it, she'd slept for an hour and a half.

Samuel's cry was getting louder. She knew she should be doing something, but the fog in her head wouldn't clear. Through half-closed lids, she saw the bottle of milk. That was it. The baby needed a feed. With shaking hands, she lifted him from the crib and rested him on a pillow across her lap. Taking the lid off the bottle, she touched it to his lips and was surprised when he took the teat into his mouth straight away.

Ria leant back against the padded headboard, feeling Samuel's soft weight in her arms. She listened to the suck of his tiny mouth and felt the down of his cheek as she stroked it with her finger – something she'd never done before. She felt warm… relaxed, even… and, for the first time, when he had finished every last drop in the bottle, she felt sad. She'd miss the clutch of his tiny hand on her finger when she put him back in his crib. The sweet smell of his head.

But, even through her drowsiness, she knew she must put him back. It was as if her mother's instinct had kicked in. Lifting him from the pillow, she held him to her, kissing his tiny cheek.

'Good night, little one. Sleep tight.'

CHAPTER FORTY-THREE

Leona

A wave of sorrow sweeps over me, leaving me gasping, and my heart clenches with the familiar pain. 'I didn't know how much I loved him until that night. Can you understand that?'

'Of course I can,' Lisa says. She thinks she understands, knows what happened, but she doesn't. No one does, except for Gareth, but by the time I've finished my story, Lisa will know too.

'When I woke up again, there was a strange metallic taste in my mouth. It was nearly morning. I remember how the light crept under the curtain.' I sink down onto the settee, struggling to find the words. 'Samuel was beside me in the bed and I knew straight away he was dead.'

Lisa sounds surprised. 'That's not what you told the paramedics.'

'I couldn't. Gareth wouldn't let me. He'd heard my scream and came straight away. I let him take charge... He's good at that. He picked the baby up and put him in the crib. He said that if anyone knew the truth – that I'd taken a sleeping tablet and fallen asleep with Samuel beside me – they would call me an unfit mother. They'd take Lily away from me. I was distraught. I didn't know what to do, so I went along with it. When the ambulance came, we told them we'd found him dead in his crib.'

I cover my face with my hands, knowing that, on the other end of the phone, Lisa's face will be mirroring the disgust she must be feeling at what I've just told her. I'm surprised, then, when her voice holds nothing but sympathy.

'Even if he was in your bed, Leona, the cause of death would likely still have been Sudden Infant Death Syndrome.'

I shake my head. 'No, it was me… I caused his death. Gareth said so. I was careless. I must have rolled onto him. Stopped him breathing.' My body begins to shake as my grief brims over. 'If it wasn't for me, he'd be here still. Beth would have a brother.'

'Oh, Leona…' Lisa's clear, professional voice has slipped into something softer. 'You've kept this to yourself all these years. That must have been so hard. The anxiety you've experienced since your pregnancy is perfectly understandable. You need to remember that, although it can be frightening, anxiety is not a weakness. It takes strength to fight it every day.'

Her kindness floors me. 'Lisa… I'm terrified that if I have this baby, I might kill it too.'

'It was a terrible thing to happen, Leona, but you didn't kill Samuel. You must believe it.'

But I'm not listening to her. I'm hearing Gareth's words the first time I tried to leave him.

Set foot outside this house and I'll tell everyone what you did. I'll make sure I have sole custody of Lily… and I'll make damn certain that you never get to see her again.

CHAPTER FORTY-FOUR

Leona

I push open the doors that lead into the school's large hall. At the end of yesterday's phone call, Lisa advised me to keep everything as normal as possible and this is what I'm trying to do. The hall is filled with parents and students, and as Beth and I walk amongst them, a thought that hits me is like a physical pain: this will be the first school event I've been to without Scott.

I turn to Beth, trying to make my voice as neutral as possible. 'Will your dad be here?' I'd heard her on the phone to him last night, in her room.

I see her flinch at the word *dad*, then she shrugs. 'No. But Granny Fay is coming. It's fine.'

How I hate this new Beth. The one who's trying to make out she's not hurting. The one who will shrink away if I try to comfort her. But I know I'm just as bad. Even though it breaks my heart that Scott wants to avoid me, I'm trying not to let it show.

'Yes, of course. Anyway, Mrs Snowdon says she has a surprise for me. I'm looking forward to finding out what it is.'

My voice is too bright. Too artificial. Knowing that we should be talking about the things that I told her, not carrying on as if nothing has happened.

'Like surprises are always nice?' Beth turns away and I realise what I've said. 'Nice' would not be the way to describe the surprises I've sprung on my daughter recently.

The students' artwork has been pinned to large boards that have been positioned around the edge of the hall in front of the wall bars. Each piece of work has the student's name printed above it, along with the title and a short description. Fay is standing next to one of the boards, talking to Beth's art teacher. I give her a wave and I'm so relieved when she waves back that I have to resist the urge to run over to her and ask if she's seen Scott, ask how he is. If he's missing me.

Mrs Snowdon says something to Fay, then comes across to us. 'Lovely to see you, Mrs Travis. Beth's been so excited to show you her work.'

I glance at Beth, but she looks away. If it's true she's been excited, she doesn't want me to see it.

'I've been looking forward to it too,' I say. 'Do you want to show me which ones are yours, Beth?'

Fay has joined us. She gives my hand a squeeze. 'Are you all right?'

I want to tell her that my heart is breaking, but instead I give a nod, then follow Beth across the hall to where a board has been set up away from the others. Several people are clustered around it.

'Why is this one on its own?'

It's Mrs Snowdon who answers. She stops short of the display board, her hand on my arm. 'Before you look at Beth's work, I just want you to know how proud we are of her at Lady Edburton. Your daughter is a very talented artist.'

I smile. 'I know.'

'The surprise,' she continues, 'is that the series of three pictures you'll see displayed here, have all been entered into a national competition. The Baxter Prize – you may have heard of it. I'm thrilled to tell you that your daughter's work has been shortlisted, but she wouldn't let me tell you before. She wanted it to be a surprise.'

'Goodness! How wonderful.' I can hardly believe it. If anything will boost Beth's confidence, this will.

'The competition is run by a national newspaper and is for young artists between fourteen and eighteen years of age. Each year there's a theme – this year it's *Freedom*. Come and have a look.'

Beth's cheeks are flushed pink. Coming round behind me, she puts her hands over my eyes and leads me to the board. When we reach it, she stands back. Gone is the blank face; it's been replaced with a look of anticipation and I see now how nervous she's been.

'These are my pictures, Mum.'

There are three – two smaller ones with one larger one in the middle. As I stare at them, they start to swim before my eyes and my skin begins to prickle.

Beth is looking at me, trying to read my expression. 'What do you think?'

I press my cheeks with my hands, fighting to remain in control. This is not Beth's fault. It's just a coincidence. It has to be.

From its display board, an eagle is looking back at me with its yellow gaze, a tiny mountain crag reflected in each of its pupils. Dragging my eyes away, I look at the other pictures. In one, a feather floats weightless to the bottom of the paper. Looking, for all the world, as if a breath of wind could blow it away at any moment. In the final picture, the paper is empty except for a bird of prey in the left-hand corner, a braided leash trailing from its leg. It hovers, body curled, talons outstretched, above a crow.

I'm not seeing a painting, though. I'm seeing the talons of an eagle wrapped around Gareth's forearm. The tattoo that I'd once loved. The tattoo my eyes had fixed on as his hands had tried to squeeze the life out of me.

Beth pulls the sleeves of her hooded top over her hands. Something she does when she's nervous. 'So, what do you think?'

Despite the indifference in her voice, I know she's desperate for me to like them. To tell her that I'm proud of what she's done. But I can't. For the truth is, the pictures fill me with horror I can't hide.

'Mum? What is it?'

I press my hands to my mouth, too frightened to speak. Scared of giving myself away. I want to get out of this hall, away from the birds with their eyes that never leave their prey. The talons that grasp.

Mrs Snowdon hasn't seen any of this. She's speaking to Fay and a man with a camera around his neck. Smiling, she turns to me.

'Mrs Travis. This is Nick King from the *Cumbrian Herald*. He'd like to take a few photos of your daughter next to her paintings, if you haven't any objections.'

The man nods to me. 'If I could have a few words from Beth, too, that would be great. Just the inspiration for her artwork and her ambitions for the future. It won't take long. It should be in next week's edition and I can make sure you get a copy.'

It takes a while for the man's words to sink in, but when they do, my reaction is instant. Taking Beth by the arm, I pull her away. 'No,' I say. 'No photos, and she won't be giving an interview.'

Fay is at Beth's side. She puts her arm around her. 'What are you talking about, Leona? Don't be ridiculous.'

People are staring at me, but I don't care. Pulling Beth away, I push through the parents in the hall, dragging her behind me. She tries to shake off my hand, but my grip on her arm is too strong.

'Mum, stop it! What the hell has got into you?'

I don't answer her. Just pull her along the corridor, through the double doors and out into the car park – all the while desperately trying to ignore the tears that are running down her face. We stumble along the driveway to where I've left the car.

'It's for your own good, Beth,' I say, opening the car door. 'You won't understand it now, but you have to believe me.'

I'm not surprised when she gets into the back, instead of next to me. She presses herself into the corner of the car as far away from me as she can.

Outside the window, the darkening fells are heavy and judgemental. I want to believe that Beth will forgive me, but I know, in my heart, that this time I may have created a rift between myself and my daughter that might never be mended.

CHAPTER FORTY-FIVE
Beth

Beth slammed the bedroom door closed and locked it. She would never forgive her mum for this. Never.

Tears of humiliation coursed down her cheeks, but she did nothing to wipe them away. By tomorrow, the whole of the school would know about how her mum had gone mad. Had been rude to the photographer and dragged her out of the exhibition like a child.

It was like the mum she'd known was turning into someone else. A stranger. Lying on her bed, she pressed her thumbs into her eyes, creating a pattern of stars beneath her eyelids. Whoever this person was, she hated her.

She turned onto her side, scrunching up her pillow and burying her head in it. If only David was here to talk to... or her dad. Except Scott *wasn't* her dad. Her dad was someone else. Someone she didn't remember. She knew his name, though. It was Gareth. Gareth Curtess. A man who'd done something so bad that her mum had moved them both away and changed their names.

Slowly, she sat up, pushing her damp hair away from her face. It was clear her mum wasn't going to tell her anything more. The only way she was going to find out who he was... who *she* was... was to do it herself. Taking out her phone, she entered his name into the search engine, surprised at how nervous she felt. The results came up instantly and, as she read them, Beth felt her world fall away.

Gareth Curtess tried for attempted murder of wife…

Former broker jailed for twelve years after attempted murder…

Wife gives evidence against husband who tried to kill her…

Then there were the pictures of him taken at the time of the trial. You could see from the photographs that the suit he was wearing was expensive, his face clean-shaven, his hair artfully gelled. As Beth swiped through the photographs, she saw that what was noticeable in all of them was his arrogant expression – his pale eyes staring back at the camera with defiance. She knew that if she got up and looked at her own face in the mirror, the reflection looking back at her would have those same slate-grey eyes.

Beth put her phone face down on the bed beside her. She didn't want to look at it. Didn't want to read the articles. Her father had tried to kill her mum, and that was all she needed to know. His genes were her genes. She was the daughter of an attempted murderer.

Reaching under her bed, she pulled out her rucksack, stuffing it with anything she could lay her hands on: T-shirts, jeans, underwear. She hesitated a moment, then reached for the stuffed horse with the black woollen mane and pushed it into the bag with everything else.

She didn't know where she was going, but she didn't care. All she knew was she had to get away – away from this cottage. Away from a life that was nothing but a lie.

CHAPTER FORTY-SIX
Leona

I open my eyes. There's a crick in my neck and ridges on my cheek from where the rolled edge of the cushion has pressed into my flesh. Sunlight filters through the curtains and I realise it's morning. I must have fallen asleep on the settee when I came home.

Memories of the previous evening come flooding back and I groan. What a mess I've made of things. Glancing at the ceiling, I wonder if Beth is awake. I must talk to her. Explain everything. If I don't, I might lose her forever.

Going into the kitchen, I make two cups of tea and take them up the stairs. When I get to Beth's door, I listen. There's no sound. She must still be asleep. I tap gently and then a little harder and, when there's still no answer, try the handle. I'm surprised when the door swings open: recently, she's taken to locking it.

Straight away, I see that the room is empty. Leaning my hand on the doorjamb for support, I try and marshal my racing thoughts. She must have gone out for an early morning walk. Maybe she's gone to stay with Fay. Yes, that will be it. Scott's there – it's the obvious place for her to go. Especially after last night.

Pulling out my phone, I see there's a missed call, but I don't stop to find out who it's from. Instead, I call Beth's number. *The mobile you have called is currently unavailable.* I stare at it. Has she switched it off, or is she somewhere with no signal?

I message Scott. The words blurring. *'Is Beth with you?'* As I wait for his reply, our previous conversations come up on the screen, making my eyes fill with tears. It's the usual stuff, shared jokes and casual endearments:

> *'Love you, wife.'*
> *'Don't miss me too much, you big bear.'*
> *'Back soon beautiful, got fish and chips.'*

When I get no reply, I phone him.

'Leona?' He sounds tired, as though he's just woken.

'Is she there, Scott? Is Beth with you?'

I hear him yawn. 'What do you mean is she with me? Of course she's not – she came home with you last night. Fay saw you leave.'

My heart beats faster. 'She must be there, Scott. Please go and look. She's probably asleep on the settee.'

There's the sound of feet on the stairs, then his voice again. 'No, she's not here. Anyway, how would she get to Ambleside from Church Langdon in the middle of the night? She'd hardly have walked?'

I hear my voice breaking. 'If she's not with you, I don't know where she is.'

Scott sounds wide-awake now. 'Don't worry. There's bound to be a simple explanation. I'll get some clothes on and come over.'

'Will you? Oh, Scott, thank you. I'm worried sick.'

Fifteen minutes later, Scott lets himself in. I'm at the door waiting for him, and when he sees the state I'm in, he pulls me into his arms.

I bury my head in his fleece. 'Where is she, Scott? Where's she gone?'

I feel his big hand on the back of my head and feel his lips against my hair. 'We'll find her. She can't have gone far.'

I pull away. 'I'm sorry. I'm sorry for everything. The lies...
The hurt...'

He takes my hands in his. 'I'm sorry too. I never really gave
you a chance to explain. While I've been at Mum's, I've done a lot
of thinking. It must have been bloody awful for you. The trial...
everything that happened before. I'd kill the bastard if I ever got
my hands on him.'

Fear grips me. 'Do you think that's where she's gone? To find him?'

'Does she know?' He sounds shocked.

'The only thing I've told her is that he did something bad.
Something that gave me no choice but to leave London. I didn't
tell her his name. But she found her birth certificate. I don't know
how she knew about it – I'd kept it hidden in the wardrobe.'

'Witness Protection let you keep it?'

I shake my head. 'No. They wanted me to give them all my
personal documents. Most I handed over... my driving licence...
my marriage certificate... even my own birth certificate, but I lied
and said I couldn't find Beth's or Samuel's. It was stupid, I know,
and I don't know why I did it. Maybe I thought that there might
come a time when Beth would need to know the truth.' I clutch
at Scott's arm. 'What if she read Gareth's name on it? What if she's
gone to find him?'

Scott frowns. 'I thought he was in prison.'

My stomach gives a fearful twist at the two words I need to tell
him. Words that will change everything. 'He's out.'

Scott's mouth drops. 'Out?'

'Yes. He got parole.'

'Jesus Christ.' He goes to the window and looks out. Pulls back
the net curtain. 'What if he came here?'

'He won't.' I rationalise, logic taking over. 'He's tagged and
there are strict conditions to his licence. Beth might have gone
there, though.' And then worry sweeps over me again. 'Do you
think we should tell the police?'

Scott runs a hand down his face. 'They'll only say to wait. Teenagers go missing all the time. Honestly, I'm sure there's nothing to worry about. She knows the fells and has, in all likelihood, gone off sketching. She's only been gone a few hours and will probably be back before you know it with her tail between her legs. You know what she's like.'

But I don't know. I don't know anything any more. 'Are you sure?'

'Of course I'm sure. She's a teenager and we're not supposed to know what's going on in her head.'

I relax a little. 'I expect you're right, but Beth was angry with me. The exhibition... I couldn't let the press photograph her in case someone from our past saw it – recognised her. Colin told me that we shouldn't do anything to bring attention to ourselves. That it's even more important now that I'm no longer on the scheme.'

'You left?' He turns to face me, his hands stuffed into the pockets of his walking trousers. 'Christ, Leona, why did you do that?'

'It was when I went to see Mum in the care home. When Colin found out, he said they'd have to move us again.' I indicate the room with my hand. 'From here. From the Lakes. A clean start, where nobody would know us. Away from everything and everybody we know.'

Scott leans his forehead against the window pane and I know he's trying to take it all in. Outside the window, the morning sun is painting the fells with a palette of vivid greens. The beauty is lost on us, though.

'You never told me that. If you'd left, you would have had to leave me too.' He says it to the landscape. The fells he walks every day. The place where he was born.

'Yes, I would and that's why I couldn't do it. I could never have left you and I didn't want you to spend the rest of your life feeling responsible for my decision.'

'You'd give up yours and Beth's safety for me?' His voice is incredulous.

'I'm sick of it all, Scott. Moving is like switching between two worlds. One where people know everything and the other where they know nothing about you at all. With each move, feeling as if someone's behind you, packing away your life. Can you imagine what it's like to have to change the subject every time someone asks you about the past, to not be able to share anything honestly or get close to anyone?'

'You got close to *me*.'

'And that's why I can't do it all again. I fell in love with you, Scott, and that's the way it is.'

He comes over to me and pulls me to him. 'I want you to tell me everything about your life before. If we're to make a proper go of things as a family, there can be no more secrets between us.'

No secrets. If only he knew how many there still were. 'I *will* tell you, but before we start, there's something you should know.'

'That I'm a big fat idiot for leaving you when you needed me most?'

Moving away, I take his hand and place it on my stomach. 'No… that you're going to be a father.'

He looks down at his hand. 'My God! Do you mean it? A baby… really?'

'Yes, a baby. But there's something else I need to tell you.' A lump forms in my throat. I don't know how to begin.

'Go on, Leona.'

My hand moves over his and my eyes close. No more secrets. No more lies. Not when we are going to be bringing another life into the world. 'After Beth, I had another child. It was a boy and we called him Samuel. He died because… because I fell asleep with him in my bed just after I'd fed him.'

Scott says nothing, just looks at me.

'I couldn't sleep. Every day Gareth would threaten me, or worse. I never knew what he would be like from one day to the next. I was anxious all the time… exhausted. I took a sleeping tablet. I shouldn't have, but I did. It was only a very low dose, but it was enough to make me fall asleep for longer than I should. The doctors said it was a cot death, but I'll never know for sure if it was something I did. Maybe they wouldn't have said that if they'd known he'd died in our bed and that we'd put his little body back in his crib after.'

Scott puts his hands either side of my face. 'You did nothing wrong. How did you survive living with that bastard?'

I turn my head away. 'I survived by shutting down. Packing up my feelings and burying them deep inside me. I learnt not to cry. Not to show emotion. I used to be happy-go-lucky, but in the years I was with him, I changed into what he wanted me to be. Until all the bits that were me had disappeared. It was only by becoming Leona that, little by little, I started to find myself again.'

Scott's face is wet with tears. 'I'm so sorry.'

I press a hand to his cheek. 'Don't be. It was you who allowed the girl I was to come out of hiding. You made me feel safe. Loved. It will be a while yet, but, one day, I know I'll emerge from the cocoon I've been in for the last twelve years a stronger person. Maybe even a better person.'

He strokes my hair. 'You're perfect to me.'

'When I tell you about the night Gareth was arrested, you might not feel the same way, Scott. You wanted the truth and I'll give it to you… Then what you do with it will be up to you.'

'I don't understand?'

'You will.'

Knives of doubt cut through my fragile confidence, but I know I have to go on, even though I'm scared Scott might leave me again when he knows what I did. Terrible things that I've hidden even from Lisa. But I've pulled on that first thread of truth and now I must allow the rest to unravel.

CHAPTER FORTY-SEVEN
Ria

The force of Gareth's hand knocked her to the floor. His eyes were cold, his lips a thin line as he stood over her.

'Leave me and I will make sure she knows your dirty little secret.'

Her fear was overwhelming. Paralysing. He would kill her. She knew it. With blood hammering at her temples, she pushed herself away from him across the floor, but he was quicker. Grabbing her by the throat, he forced her to stand. He was too big. Too near. She could feel the press of his fingers on her neck. See the talons of the eagle moving as his forearm tensed.

Gareth's face was as hard as if it had been stamped on a coin. Though it was close to hers, she could barely recognise him, anger making his smooth features ugly. She was shocked to see the hatred in his eyes, and it was then that she realised he had probably never loved her. Not really.

He pressed harder, his eyes never leaving hers. Ria pulled at his hands, but he was too strong. She was struggling to breathe. The room was blurring.

'Daddy?' Lily's childish voice was forcing its way through her fading consciousness.

She felt Gareth's fingers release from her throat and she slumped down onto the floor, her hand to her neck. Lily was standing in the kitchen doorway, her stuffed horse clutched to her chest, her face creased from sleep.

'I want Mummy.'

Ria's body ached all over. Her face was bloodied and bruised. She held out her hand to Lily. 'Mummy slipped in the kitchen, darling. There's nothing to worry about. Go back to bed and I'll come in and kiss you good night in a minute.'

Lily's face crumpled. 'Come *now*.'

'You heard what your mother said. Get the fuck back to bed!'

Gareth's voice echoed in the empty space of the kitchen and Lily turned on her heels and ran across the hallway to her bedroom.

Ria could hear her daughter crying, but she was too afraid to get up and go to her. Between her and the door was her husband. Red-faced. Beads of sweat trickling down his temples. His anger hung in the room, sucking the life from it.

With effort, using the barstool to help her, she pulled herself up. 'Let me go to her, Gareth.'

'Shut up.'

Blood was running down her chin from her cut lip and she could feel her eye already beginning to swell. She desperately wanted to comfort her daughter, but she was scared to anger him more. 'Please. She'll be frightened.'

'Stay where you are.' His eyes were heavy and he reached out to the breakfast bar for support. Picking up the solicitor's card, he ripped it into pieces. 'Try a stunt like that again and the world will know you killed your baby. No court in the land will give you access to our daughter when they hear what really happened.'

Ria's body felt light, as if it might float away. 'Please, Gareth. I've lost one child already.'

Even though it had been months ago, her heart still ached with the loss of him.

Pulling the barstool away from the island, Gareth hauled himself onto it. He looked at her through bloodshot eyes. 'Don't think this is over.' Folding his arms on the marble worktop, he slumped forward onto them.

Ria waited. Not daring to move. It wasn't long before she saw his broad back, in its tailored shirt, rise and fall in a regular rhythm. He'd nearly killed her, yet he was able to sleep. How could this be the man she'd married? Without taking her eyes off him, she edged her way around the kitchen units, panic growing again. Urgent. Insistent. His words were going round and round in her head. *Don't think this is over.* She touched her fingertips to her swollen throat. There was no doubt in her mind that next time he'd finish the job. She'd seen it in his eyes. She was trapped with nowhere to run. No place to go.

She thought of Lily, curled up in her bed with her horse pressed up against her cheek. If anything happened to her, what would become of her daughter? She had to stop him before it was too late.

The pasta jar sat on the island next to the pepper mill and the cappuccino maker. It was solid. Heavy. Its thick, green glass reflecting the light from the spotlights that were trained onto the worktop. There was no choice. As if in a trance, she crossed the room and picked the jar up, bringing it down as hard as she could onto the side of Gareth's head. The sound was sickening and immediately Ria was aware of the enormity of what she'd done. She dropped the jar and watched it roll across the limed oak floorboards, scattering pasta – its green glass slick with her husband's blood.

He slipped sideways and, as if by instinct, Ria stepped forward to break his fall as he slumped to the floor. She stood there looking at him, shaking uncontrollably. Blood was trickling down his head, staining the floorboards and, as she watched, mesmerised, she saw his fingers move. He was alive. Her relief was quickly swamped by panic.

Quickly, she pulled out her phone and pressed the buttons. 'Come quick,' she sobbed when the call was answered. 'My name is Ria Curtess… and my husband has just tried to kill me.'

CHAPTER FORTY-EIGHT
Leona

It hadn't been self-defence as I'd told Lisa – or as I'd told the police when they'd arrived at the house and seen Gareth lying on the kitchen floor, his face covered in blood. Not really. I could have walked away, taken Lily and run out of the flat. But I hadn't. For I knew, in my heart, he'd come after me.

Scott sinks his head into his hands. 'Christ almighty. Did you want to kill him?'

'I don't know what I wanted… Just that it would stop. I'd lived in fear for so long, it was the only thing I could think of to do. I knew that Gareth had no control over his temper and that next time I might not be so lucky. I did it to protect Beth as well as me.'

He looks at me. 'And they bought your story of self-defence?'

'The police had seen the marks on my neck where he'd tried to strangle me. I'd also shown them the threatening messages he'd left on my phone. They interviewed both Leo and my parents… my neighbours too. Leo told them I'd been planning to leave and that she knew about the abuse. I wasn't the first apparently – Gareth was already on their radar. Other girlfriends had made complaints in the past, but had withdrawn their statements at the last minute.' I raise the back of my hand to my cheek. 'He could be very persuasive.'

Scott bends forward, his hands on his thighs, breathing deeply as though trying to take control of his emotions. I know that he will leave me – this time for good. Nobody would stay after hearing the story I've just told.

'Scott? Please tell me what you're thinking.' I hold my breath, waiting for his reply.

His eyes are on my stomach. 'If that had been me,' he says, 'I'd have done the same thing. You were protecting your child.'

When I feel his fingers knit with mine, I'm giddy with relief. 'Do you mean that?'

'Have you ever known me to lie?'

I shake my head. I never have. 'I love you.'

'I love you too. We'll get through this together, Leona, I promise.' Pushing back his sleeve, he looks at his watch. 'But we need to decide what to do about Beth. I don't like the idea of Gareth being out of the nick, even with a tag. Maybe we should phone around. You get in contact with the school and I'll try her friends. I'll do it outside… I need some air.'

He goes outside, his phone pressed to his ear, and I stand alone in the middle of our little living room and think of my daughter who, all the time I've been talking about the past, could be anywhere. Lost. Alone. Angry with me and her life. And no wonder – I've been so busy trying to protect her, I've forgotten how to be a normal mother.

Riddled with guilt, I pick up my phone to try her number again, but as I do, it rings, making me jump.

I answer it without looking at who it is. 'Beth?'

There's a clearing of a throat on the other end. 'It's not Beth. It's Colin. I tried you earlier, but you didn't answer my call. I need to talk to you.'

'I'm sorry, Colin, but…'

There's an edge to his voice. 'I know I'm not officially supposed to be doing this now you're no longer on the Witness Protection Scheme, but there's something I thought you should know.'

'What, Colin? What is it?' Outside the window, a cloud passes over the window, a cloud passes over the sun and the fells lose their colour. I hold the phone tighter, knowing that whatever it is he's going to say will not be good.

'It's Gareth. He didn't turn up to his appointment with his parole officer. No one's seen him and his tag was found in a bin near the flat he's been living in.'

'When? When did this happen?'

He sounds embarrassed. 'Two days ago.'

I grow cold. 'Oh, my God, Colin. Where is he?'

'We're not sure, but his disappearance is being treated as a priority. It's only a matter of time before we find him. I don't want you to worry, though. He doesn't know where you are. I'll be contacting the local force just in case and I'm already on my way. I'll be with you as soon as I can.'

Tears come silently and without warning. 'Beth's disappeared,' I whisper. 'I don't know where she is.'

I think I hear an intake of breath. 'When did you last see her?'

'Last night. We had an argument.'

Colin's voice changes. He's calm. Efficient. A man used to dealing with a crisis. 'I want you to listen carefully, Leona, and do what I say. First, go up to Beth's room and make a note of what's missing: phone, money, clothes. Anything that will give us an idea as to where she's gone. Is her coat there? Did she take a rucksack or a sleeping bag? Get Scott to phone anyone who knows her, but most importantly, I want you to stay put until I get there, do you understand?'

'I can't just do nothing. I have to go and find her.'

'I mean it, Leona. I want you to wait.'

'All right.'

He ends the call and I let my hand fall to my side. Through the window, I can see Scott. He's standing on the wide grassed area shared by all the cottages, his mobile to his ear. As he ends the call, one of the holidaymakers from a couple of doors down comes up the path with a bag of shopping. Scott speaks to her and she shakes her head. A few minutes later, he comes back in.

'I've phoned all of Beth's friends whose numbers I've got, but no one's seen her. They said that…' He stops, seeing my tear-stained face. 'What's wrong?'

'I spoke to Colin. Gareth's broken parole and gone missing. He says there's no way he could know where we are, and wants me to stay at the house, but I'm scared, Scott.'

Scott's voice is strained. 'If Colin said there's no way he can find you, you have to believe him. The only way he'd know you were here is if you'd told someone.' He stops and takes my shoulders, his dark eyes looking into mine. 'You haven't told anyone, have you?'

A memory stirs. My mother's hair soft against my cheek as I whisper to her.

'Only my mum. I didn't think it mattered because she doesn't even know what day it is.'

'Oh, Christ.'

I'm on the verge of tears and he sees. Drawing himself up, he forces a smile. 'I'm sure there's nothing to worry about.'

'Do you really think so?'

He answers my question with another. 'Did you tell Colin about Beth?'

'Yes, he says we should make a list of everything she's taken with her. It might give a clue as to where she's gone. I'll look now.'

Running up the stairs, I fling open her wardrobe and pull out all her drawers. Then I get down on my knees and look under her bed. Her sleeping bag is missing and her rucksack and sketchbook. It's as I'm going back out that I notice that the torch, which she always keeps beside the bed in case there's a power cut, has gone too.

I go back down and tell Scott what I've found. He's sitting on the settee, his fingers steepled under his chin.

'I think the fact she's taken her sketchbook is a good thing,' he says. 'Maybe she went out early to draw.'

'But the sleeping bag?'

'You're right. Looks like she was sleeping out last night. Thank God, the nights haven't been too cold. Christ, Leona. Where could she have gone?' He stands and paces the room. 'We have to think… What were her favourite places?'

My mind is a blank. There are so many walks we've done. So many fells climbed. She hasn't been out with me as much, recently, and of course I realise now it's because there was someone else whose company she wanted more.

I grab Scott's arm. 'What if she went to meet that photographer guy, David? What if she's with *him*?'

'If we had his number, we could phone him?' He looks out the window at the distant tents on the higher slopes of Blackstone Farm. 'Beth told me he was camping in an old VW over there, but I haven't seen the van since that day I saw them together on the fells. I'd presumed he'd got bored and moved on… But you never know. He might just have moved to a different campsite.'

I force my mind to think. 'Maybe we could try phoning one of the magazines he works for. They might have a contact number for him.'

'Good idea. I'll go to the pub and get Pete to round up a few of the guys to form a search party. We'll get some kit together and be ready as soon as you call with any information.'

Scott goes to the front door and opens it. Reaching back in, he unhooks his waterproof jacket from the peg. 'Looks like I might be needing this. It's not looking too good out there.'

Taking out my phone, I google one of the magazines, then click on the contact number for their London office. A receptionist answers and I tell her why I'm ringing. There's the click of her fingers on the keyboard, then she comes back on and tells me she'll call me back. It's the same with the next one I try.

Disappointed, I ring Scott. He answers straight away and I tell him what happened.

'Never mind. You can let me know when they ring back. There are quite a few of us here and some of the holidaymakers want to help out too.' In the background, I can hear voices, the scraping of chairs on a slate floor. 'We'll find her, Leona, don't worry. The question is, where to start looking first. If only we knew her favourite places.'

I shake my head, although he can't see. 'She never told me anything. All I know is she used to like to go out and sketch the birds. She's sketchbooks full of them. Shall I get one? It might give us a clue. Hold on a minute.'

I run upstairs and come back with an armful of her books. Tucking the phone under my chin, I flick through them. In amongst the horrible birds of prey are some sketches of places I recognise.

'She's drawn the tarn by the Three Shires, the packhorse bridge and the cairn on top of the fell behind our house. I don't know this place, though.' It's a photograph she's stuck in. Wondering if it's one of David's, I describe to Scott the pool of dark green water, the pillars rising out of it to form a vaulted cavern.

'I know where that is,' he says. 'It's called Temple Quarry. It's disused now but the sheer sides are popular with climbers. At the bottom is a cave with what looks like a lake but is actually the flooded workings. You can get to it two ways – from the lower road via a series of miners' tunnels or from the quarry top.'

The place looks eerie. 'But why would Beth go there?'

'Kestrels nest in the cliff face and, at the top, there's a slate bench overlooking the water far below. It's probably where she sat to draw the birds. I expect that was the attraction.'

'Do you think that might be where she's gone?'

'I don't know, but if she's drawn it in her book, it's as good a place as any to look. She could have slept there or there's also an old slate-miners' bothy close by. That's a possibility too.'

'Can you reach the top of the quarry by car?'

'Yes. The path from there is overgrown but manageable.'

'I'll take my car and meet you there.' I'm eager to be going.

'No, don't do that. Someone needs to be at home in case Beth comes back and, anyway, Colin will be on his way. I'll get some of the others to drive to the places you've mentioned and I'll go to Temple Quarry myself. Ring me as soon as you hear back from the magazines. I doubt the phone reception will be up to much, but we can always hope.'

He rings off and I try to think of something to do to pass the time, but can't settle to anything. The thick flint walls that once made me feel safe, now feel like they're closing in on me. I go to the window, wondering if there is anyone out there watching me. Watching the house. Colin says I'm safe, but right now I don't feel it.

I wish Mum was here to tell me everything's going to be okay... wish I could tell her all that's happened. But the mother I saw at the nursing home isn't the one I used to know. I remember the narrow bed, the window looking out onto the street, the bedside table with its water jug. Then, I remember the folded note I placed there for Leo to find – my whispered words in my mother's ear. What if I wasn't the only person to visit my mother that day? What if they read my note? Spoke to my mum? How could I have been so stupid?

A message flashes onto the screen of my phone. It's from Scott. *'Have split up into pairs to search. Am on my way to the quarry now.'*

I'm full of nervous energy. Pacing the room like a caged animal. I'm just reminding myself to breathe, when the phone rings.

'Hello, Mrs Travis. I said I'd ring back with information about the man you were asking me about.'

'Yes. If you could just give me his phone number, I'd be very grateful.'

The girl's voice is apologetic. In the background, I can hear the sounds that indicate a busy office. 'I'm afraid we haven't got a number, but there's something you should know.'

She starts to tell me and, as she does, I go cold.

CHAPTER FORTY-NINE
Beth

The sketchbook lay open on Beth's lap, the blank white pages taunting her. She'd hoped that sketching the birds that circled above her would help to clear her head, but it had been the opposite. She would never forget the humiliation of being dragged out of the school hall, or the cold eyes of her father staring out at her from the newspaper article.

Closing the book, she placed it next to her on the slate bench, then stood up and walked to the edge of the quarry. Below her was the flooded workings where David had taken his photographs and, beyond that, the cavern where she'd left her sleeping bag. That day with David seemed a million years ago now. A time when she had been happy. Had thought she knew who she was.

Beth yawned. Last night, she'd hardly slept. The cave had been cold, lonely too, and, as she'd tried to get comfortable in her sleeping bag, the slate floor hard beneath her, she'd been petrified that her torch might give out. At least it had been a clear night. She'd been glad of the company of the bright moon and the stars that twinkled in the dark circle above the slate walls, but, even so, when at last the sky began to lighten, sending orange fingers across the sky, she'd been relieved.

Thank goodness the woman who'd offered her a lift had believed her story that she was meeting friends for a barbeque in the cave.

If she hadn't, she'd be back at home with a mother who didn't care that she had no friends. No normal life.

Stepping back from the quarry edge, Beth looked up at the sky. Heavy clouds were gathering and it didn't look as though it would be long before it started to rain. She'd given no thought to what she was going to do next, but now, as the wind began to pick up, making the skin of her bare forearms stand up in goose bumps, she knew she couldn't stay there forever.

'Beth?'

At first, she thought she was hearing things, just a trick of the wind as it blew across the bleak quarry top. But when she turned and felt her heart give a leap of joy, she knew that the figure who stood before her was not one she'd conjured up from her imagination.

David held his long hair back from his face with one hand. In his other hand was his camera. 'What are you doing here?'

Feeling flustered, Beth pointed to her sketchbook. 'Drawing.'

'Alone? How did you get here?'

'It's none of your business.'

She heard him sigh. 'Don't be like that, Beth.'

'How do you expect me to be? You disappeared from my life without a second thought.'

David frowned. 'It wasn't like that.'

'How was it then?'

Lifting his camera strap over his head, he clipped the lens cap into place. 'I saw how it must look… Okay?'

'How what must look?'

'You wouldn't understand.'

'Try me.'

He took a step towards her. 'You think I don't care about you, but I do. That's why I made you think I'd left.'

'Where did you go then? I haven't seen your van at any of the local campsites.'

A smile played at the corner of David's mouth. 'You've been looking, then?'

Beth said nothing – too tired to deny it. Anyway, it didn't matter. Nothing mattered any more.

'I parked at a site on the other side of Windermere. I still had some shots I needed to take, but after knowing how your dad felt, I thought it better to base myself somewhere else. From what you've told me, he's a decent guy and I didn't want any trouble between the two of you. But seeing you again makes me doubt the wisdom of what I did. It was a cowardly thing to do.'

As he spoke, drops of rain had started to dot the path around them, soaking into the dry earth. Cooling Beth's skin and speckling the slate bench. She looked down at her T-shirt. 'I left my rucksack, with my waterproof, in the cavern. My sleeping bag's there too.'

'You slept in the quarry?'

'Maybe.'

He put his head on one side. 'Want to tell me about it?'

'Maybe later.'

'Fair enough. Anyway, you can share my waterproof.' He untied it from around his waist. 'Always prepared, me. I never trust forecasts. We'd better find some shelter.'

'The cavern?'

'No. The rain will have made the path down too slippery. There's a miners' bothy not far from here. We'll go there.'

Above them, the clouds had joined to form a dark blanket. David held the waterproof above their heads and, together, they ran down the path as quickly as they could without slipping. There was a rumble of thunder in the distance.

The rain was harder now. Running down Beth's neck. Plastering her hair to her face. As she ran, she could feel her shorts sticking to her legs. 'We're going to get soaked.'

'Just a bit further.'

The bothy was nestled into the hillside, almost invisible against the boulder-strewn slopes. Its roof was just an overhanging slate slab with a wall built around it, a small opening leading into the dark space inside. Ducking their heads, they stumbled in.

Beth looked around. The place was little more than a cave, the stone walls cold and damp. At one end was a makeshift bunk, made from planks of wood and, on the ground, someone had left a couple of crushed beer cans and an empty biscuit packet. Beth touched her walking boot to one of the cans, watching it roll.

'Who's been here, do you think?'

'Kids, probably,' David said, wiping the rain from his face with his sleeve. 'Walkers would have the sense to clear up after themselves.'

He stood with his hands either side of the opening, shoulders hunched, looking out. The rain was coming down hard now, blurring the scenery and bouncing off the moss-covered threshold. 'Don't think we'll be going anywhere for a while.'

'What shall we do?'

'Wait until it eases, I suppose, then make a run for it. You should go home and let your mum know you're okay.'

'I don't want to. She's not bothered about me. She's mucked up her own life and now she wants to muck up mine.'

'I'm sure that's not true. Come here, you're shivering.' He reached for her hand and pulled her to him. The heat from his body warming her. Beth leant her body into his and David kissed the top of her head. 'Please tell me what you're so upset about. You never know, I might be able to help.'

The thought of telling him everything was like slipping into a warm bath. She longed to do so, but if she did, would he still like her? Who could possibly like a girl whose mother was losing the plot and whose father was a psycho? But there was no one else to tell and if she kept the terrible thing she'd found out to herself any longer, she'd go mad too.

She took a breath. 'My name isn't Beth, it's Lily.'

And so she told him everything. About how she and her mum had come to be in the Lake District… About her real father… About how her mum had lost her mind at the exhibition.

'So that photo you showed me was your mum.' David's voice seemed to come from far away. 'How she used to look?'

Beth nodded into his jumper, her tears dampening the wool. Outside, the rain had got harder still. Drumming against the stone walls of the bothy as though it wanted to get in.

'That's some story. No wonder you've been unhappy.' David smoothed back her hair, then pressed his forehead to hers. 'I can't bear to see you like this.'

'The thing that's making me the most unhappy is you leaving. I love you, David.'

She froze. The words had come out of nowhere and could not be unsaid. The weight of them hung in the cold space of the bothy, taunting her. Her head was still against David's, his hands resting on her shoulders, and she thought she felt him tense. Minutes passed, but he said nothing. What was he thinking? Why didn't he speak?

At last, David raised his head and when he did, his voice was husky with emotion. 'I feel the same.'

'You do?'

'Christ, I don't want to…'

Nothing mattered now. Nothing could hurt her. There was something she knew that changed everything. Beth pressed her lips to his and, after a second, felt him respond. Immediately, she could tell the kiss was different to the ones they'd shared on the fellside, or in the camper van. Before, there had been a slight reserve on his part – a pulling away when things got too heated. Now his mouth was hot on hers, his lips moving, and she could feel her own body responding.

Turning her head, she whispered in his ear. 'I want you to make love to me.'

David's reaction was not what she'd expected. Letting go of her, he sat back, his fingers raking his hair. 'I can't.'

'Why not?' She stopped, embarrassed.

'It's just…' He buried his head in his hands. 'Oh, fuck.'

'You have feelings for me, but you don't find me physically attractive, is that it?' Her voice was loud in the empty space. Desperate. She should have known. He wouldn't be the first to think this way.

'Christ! Listen to yourself.' There was frustration in his voice. 'How can you say that? Don't you know how hard it is to say no to you? You can't imagine how fucking much I want to give in to this.'

She could sense David's indecision. The fight that was going on inside him. She couldn't bear it. With a hand either side of his face, she pulled his head down to hers and kissed him again, lips parted, her tongue seeking out his.

He gave a low moan and then his hands were under her T-shirt, his fingertips a brand against her skin. She wanted more. Shifting away, she crossed her arms and lifted her top over her head. He watched her, his face flushed. Slowly, he lowered his mouth to her collar bone, tracing the delicate ridge of bone with his lips. Tipping her head back, Beth closed her eyes. He loved her and nothing else mattered.

CHAPTER FIFTY

Leona

'We've never had anyone by the name of David King working for us. A guy with that name applied for a contract job a year or so ago, but we didn't take him on.'

I grip the phone, my knuckles turning white. 'Can you tell me why?'

'I'm afraid I can't do that.'

I remember then what Scott told me. 'He said he was a freelancer. Can you check again?'

She sounds as if she's trying to keep her patience. 'I've checked and there haven't been any freelancers with that name either. Not in the last few years anyway.'

'There must be some mistake.'

'There's no mistake, Mrs Travis.'

The phone hangs limply in my hand and I try to digest what she's just told me. Why has David been lying?

Picking up my keys and my coat, I run out to the car. I'll message Colin later.

When I reach the scrubby area of moorland that serves as a car park at the top of Temple Quarry, I see that the only vehicle parked there is a green VW camper van. Could it be David's? Scott's Land Rover isn't here, he must have parked it on the road by the lower entrance, and I wonder what to do. Taking out my phone, I press his number. He answers straight away, but I can hardly hear him.

'Where are you?' I ask.

I can barely make out what he's saying. Something about the bothy. His voice comes and goes. I manage to tell him where I am, but he's not happy.

'Jesus, Leona. I told you to stay at the cottage. What about Colin? The police?'

'I left Colin a message. Told him where I'd be.'

I tell him about the phone call I'd had with the magazine.

'Please tell me you're kidding me?'

My voice is strained. 'Why would I joke at a time like this, Scott?'

'I'm sorry it's just – Christ! Do you think she's with him?'

'I don't know. It's possible.' The thought fills me with dread. 'I thought I'd check the top of the quarry first and then, if she's not there, take the path down to the cavern itself. I need to find her. Reassure her that we're not angry with her. It was me who made her run away in the first place.'

'Don't do that. The path will be dangerous after all this rain.' I hear him speak to someone. Hear him repeating what I've just said.

'Who's that you're talking to?'

Scott's voice fades in and out. 'Some guy… helping… tell him where…'

The phone cuts out and I shake it in frustration. Putting my phone back in my pocket, I walk away from the car. Since leaving home, the wind has picked up and the sky is now the colour of washed slate. I can see from the ground that it must have rained hard here and, from the way the dark clouds are pulling down towards the fells, it's clear it will again. It's lonely here. Bleak.

An uneasiness takes hold as I realise how alone I am. How exposed. For twelve years, I've avoided places like this, a price I've had to pay for twelve years living with a target on my back, but now I have no choice.

Zipping up my jacket, I see the sign, *Temple Quarry* etched onto the old wooden post. It leads into a narrow belt of deciduous woodland. It's more sheltered in the trees; the only sound is the sighing of the wind in the higher branches and the sharp crack of twigs beneath my boots. There's a rumble of thunder somewhere to the east and I walk faster. The wood seems darker now, the branches of the trees more tangled. Would Beth really have come this way at night and, if she did, how did she get here? It's beginning to seem more and more unlikely.

With every step, my anxiety builds. A darkness pressing in on me. I replay Lisa's words in my head. A mantra to calm me. *Anxiety is not a weakness. It takes strength to fight it every day.* But only someone superhuman would be able to fight the demons that are with me as I carry on alone through the trees. It's only the thought of Beth's face that keeps me going.

As I walk, I get the unsettling feeling that I'm not alone. That someone's watching me. But I can't think like that. I can't give in to my fear. A branch snaps and there's a cry. I turn towards the sound, my body freezing. It's followed by a rustle and the leaves around me shiver. Panic brings life back to my limbs and I run, stumbling blindly along the path, for what seems like an eternity. At last, I break through the trees at the edge of the wood, not bothering to look back as I already know what's hunting me.

A jay flies from the green canopy, its screaming call echoing in the silence. It's only then that I stop running, hands on knees, trying to catch my breath as I watch the blue flash of the bird's wing as it flies away. I've let my imagination get the better of me. I'll be no help to anyone if I carry on like this.

I'm standing in an open space at the edge of a vast quarry, machinery left rusting amongst the heaps of unwanted slate. A few more steps and I'd plunge into an abyss so deep it takes my breath away. At the bottom is a pool – almost black between the slate walls that girdle it. I stand back to stop my head from swimming. A little way from the drop is a makeshift bench of slate. I touch my hand to it, feeling the wet stone – sure that this is where Beth comes to sit.

The slate is cold beneath my hand, the silence heavy, as it always is before a storm. I peer down again into the cavernous void. Here and there around the pool are dark recesses in the rock face. Tunnels where the miners once worked. Is this where Beth slept last night?

There's a loud clap of thunder and the heavens open. In minutes, I'm soaked. The nearest shelter is in the woods I hated so much. With a sinking heart, I run back to them.

CHAPTER FIFTY-ONE
Beth

The hard planks were digging into her back, the blankets they'd found in a bag under the bunk rough against her skin. Beth didn't care, though. Nothing could spoil her happiness. Turning her head, she kissed David's chest, running a hand over the smooth skin of his throat, tracing with her finger where his tan faded to milky white.

He turned to face her, his hand moving to her temple. As she felt his fingers draw through her hair, she smiled. She'd heard that the first time was often a disappointment, but it hadn't been for her. At first, she'd been nervous, scared of doing the wrong thing, but David had been patient. Guiding her. Leading the way when she wasn't sure what to do. She'd been surprised at how gentle he'd been. How loving.

'Are you all right?' David propped himself on his elbow and looked at her.

'Of course I am.'

He looked relieved. 'I just wanted to be sure.'

'What we did… It isn't something I'm going to regret, I promise.'

David kissed her hair. 'Me neither, but I think we should go soon. The rain has stopped and who knows who'll be passing this way.'

'In a minute. I just want to lie here and remember.' It was true. She wanted to remember every detail. Every touch.

'Just a little while longer then.' He lay back down and closed his eyes.

Beth smiled and curled herself around him, resting her head against his chest. Feeling his heart beating. Soon, she felt his breathing become slow and regular, the hand that had been caressing her bare skin, slipping from her shoulder. If only they could stay like this forever.

But it was not to be. From somewhere outside, she could hear voices. Not close, but close enough to make her slip from the blanket that covered them, pull on her shorts and top and go to the door. Opening it a crack, she listened, the stone floor cold on her bare feet. The voices were coming from the direction of the quarry and she recognised one of them straight away. It was her dad. Calling her name over and over. Whatever happened, he mustn't find her in here with David, or all hell would break loose. If she went to him now and told him she was okay, he wouldn't need to go to the bothy.

Her walking boots were on the floor beside the bed. Quickly, she pulled them on and laced them up. Being careful not to wake David, she ducked under the slate overhang and slipped outside. Without looking back, she disappeared into the rain.

CHAPTER FIFTY-TWO
Leona

My phone rings. Beyond the trees, a veil of rain sweeps across the bare ground on the quarry top and I'm relieved to see it's Scott who's calling. I jab at the button to answer it, then listen to what he's telling me, my heart racing.

'Have you found her? It's chucking it down. I can hardly see my hand in front of my face.'

'We've been to the cavern and her rucksack and sleeping bag are there. It looks like it's where she spent last night. I looked and there's no sign of her sketchbook. If she's gone to the quarry top to draw, we'll soon find her.'

'I've just been there. I couldn't see her.'

'Try not to worry. I'll be with you soon and Eddie should already be up there. I sent him to find you to say we'd discovered her things, but I guess you haven't seen him.'

'He wouldn't have seen me as I've been sheltering in the trees. Anyway... who *is* Eddie?'

'He's one of the guys who's been helping me with the search. He was at the pub when I got there earlier, talking to some of the locals. Been staying at the campsite on his way up north apparently, and when I asked for some volunteers, he was very happy to help.'

'Eddie?' There's something unsettling about the name. 'Listen, Scott. What does he look like?'

'Is it really important what he looks like? The longer we're on the phone, the less chance there is of finding her.'

'Just humour me. I need to know.'

There's a pause and I imagine him wondering how to describe him. 'He's average height, broad shoulders… What do you want me to say?'

'His eyes, Scott. What colour are his eyes?'

'I don't know, grey? Anyway, I'm nearly there now. I can see the sign to the quarry.'

I can't breathe. 'Scott, listen to me…'

But the reception has gone again.

I can't think properly. Memories come rushing back. My carefree laugh, my fingertip touching the freckled skin of Gareth's wrist, tracing the feathered lines of his tattoo, our naked bodies reflected back at us from the mirrored wardrobe doors. The echo of my voice as I make a joke: *Eddie… I'll call you Eddie. Like Eddie the Eagle.*

The storm has closed in. A huge spike of lightning whip-cracks the peak on the other side of the valley. Rain beats down. Guessing Beth might have taken the rocky path that leads down to the cavern to find shelter, I push through the trees until I'm back out on the quarry top. My fear is all-consuming. I must find Beth before *he* does.

The wind has picked up, disorienting me. I take the wrong path and have to retrace my steps. It's hard to see in the driving rain. I'm about to give up when I see a sign, half-hidden by the undergrowth, its message chilling me further.

DANGER!
Steep unfenced rock faces and deep water
Strictly NO abseiling, climbing or diving

The wind has pushed back my hood, allowing needles of rain to drive into my face, but I don't care. My only thought is to find my daughter. I force my way through the brambles that snag at my clothes, not caring when a thorn rakes the skin of my hand. As I stumble along the slippery slate path, the dark, gaping throat of the quarry is my constant companion. I push away the hair that's plastering my face and force back a wave of nausea at the sight of the quarry sides that fall away to my side. One slip and I would be over.

There are voices ahead. One of them is Scott's. I see a shape. Two shapes. Is it Beth who's with him? The rain is heavy now and I can barely see. As I draw nearer, I realise it's not her. It's another man. I have no plan. No thought of what I will do when I reach them.

'Scott!'

He turns. His face almost obscured by the hood of his waterproof. 'Look at you, Leona. You're soaked. You should have waited.'

But I'm not paying attention to what he's saying. The man I saw with him is no longer there.

'Where is he?'

Scott frowns, the rain dripping from his hood. He looks around. 'Who? Eddie? He's…'

The arm around my neck forces me backwards. I clutch at the sleeve that covers it, desperate to relieve its pressure on my throat.

Scott lurches forward, but when he sees I'm being pulled towards the quarry edge, he stops.

Gareth's breath is hot on my cheek. 'Thought it might be a bit of fun to call myself Eddie. It was our little joke, wasn't it, Ria – in the days before you became a lying little bitch. Eddie the Eagle… Bet you didn't know I'd fly this far.'

Scott holds out his hand, realisation dawning. 'Let's talk, Gareth.'

'Talk! She put me away for twelve years. You don't think I'm leaving without finishing the job I should have finished that night?'

The wind has blown up again. It's debilitating – unexpected gusts rocking us. And still the merciless rain lashes down.

'Was it David who told you? Is that how you found out where we were?'

'I don't know what you're on about. You managed to lay the trail all by yourself, lovely lady. Such a sweet note you left for your old friend, and such a pretty necklace. Didn't take much digging to find out who was behind Leona Designs… not once I knew you were in the Lake District. Never underestimate the elderly, Ria. It's amazing who they'll blab to when they're lonely. Your mother was pretty sparky when I had someone visit her. Couldn't wait to tell him your little secret.'

As I picture my poor mother, Gareth increases the pressure of his arm and pinpricks of light punctuate the sky. I'm struggling to breathe, my neck aching from the angle he holds me at.

'Don't hurt her.' Scott steps forward again, pushing against the wind. His voice desperate. 'Think of what it would do to Beth… Lily. Take me instead.'

It's like Gareth is not listening. 'She thought she was so clever when the courts believed her little story, but she's not. I'm the one who's always been in control.'

'How's that?' Scott's playing for time. I can tell by the way he looks beyond us up the path. He's hoping Colin might come… the police.

Gareth's arm releases a little, allowing me to draw in some air. His face is against mine and I can tell, by the movement of the muscles in his cheek, that his mouth is twisted into a smile. 'I bet she didn't tell you about the baby.'

'Samuel? Yes, she did. I know all about it. How she fell asleep with him in her bed. It's not a secret any more.'

He laughs. The sound bouncing off the walls of the quarry. 'That's not what happened. It was me who put him there in the first place. When I got home late that night, the brat was in his cot. I thought he was asleep, but he wasn't. He was dead. Cot death… Just like they'd said. I picked him up and put him in the bed next to her. Made her believe she'd killed him. It was my little joke.'

A cry escapes my lips and he laughs harder. 'I knew it was something I could always use against you.'

Gareth has always known my weaknesses. He's the eagle and I'm the prey. Even in prison, he'd have been planning the opportunity to catch me.

Scott's face is thunderous. 'You're a monster.'

The rain is relentless, beating down on the slate path, making it shiny. I clutch at Gareth's sleeve, exposing the talons of the eagle that wrap around his wrist as he drags me back with him towards the edge. It will take just one more step for us to be over.

CHAPTER FIFTY-THREE
Beth

Beth broke into a run. She could hear raised voices. An anguished shout. A woman's cry that broke off as suddenly as it had started. On the path in front of her, there were three people frozen into a tableau. She stopped. Seeing it as if from some half-remembered dream. Only it wasn't a dream. It was a nightmare.

Her mum was there, a man's arm around her throat. As Beth watched, terrified, she saw her mum grapple at his sleeve as she tried to free herself, drawing it back to expose the eagle tattoo on his wrist.

Memories pulled at her.

She was no longer sixteen, but a four-year-old child standing in the doorway of a kitchen. Watching. Not understanding. Her mother was there, her face white against her dark hair, a man's hands around her throat. The same hands that were pressing round her neck now.

She watched the talons of the eagle on the man's wrist flex as he tightened his hold. Her bird of prey pictures… Her obsession. Now she understood what it was all about.

Her mum's frightened eyes were fixed on her as they had been all those years ago, but this time her stepdad was there too, his body poised but powerless. He knew, as Beth did, that it wouldn't take much for the slate at the edge of the quarry to shift beneath their feet. The path was narrow. Vertiginous. One false move and they could both plunge to their deaths.

Beth didn't know whether it was the four-year-old or her grown-up self who shouted it, but the words burst from her as they had twelve years ago.

'Daddy!'

CHAPTER FIFTY-FOUR

Leona

Gareth turns, distracted, and stares. Beth is standing a little way from us, her hand reaching out to him, her eyes pleading. Does he recognise her? Does he know she is the daughter he used to love? As his grey eyes lock with hers, I feel the change of pressure in his arm. He's curious. Wondering, probably, how this new development might be used to his advantage.

It's my only chance. Moving my head, I bite down as hard as I can on his forearm. The metallic taste of blood fills my mouth.

Gareth yells, releasing his arm. Scott runs forward but I'm quicker, pushing Gareth away from me. He stumbles, his feet slipping on the rain-slicked slate, his cry ringing out as a piece of the quarry edge breaks away. It happens as if in slow motion – one minute he's there, and the next he isn't.

Scott and I stare at each other in horror.

I am only a few centimetres from the edge and when I look down, I see him. He hasn't fallen far, but is lying on a small ledge where scrubby trees have grown. The place where he has landed is steep, covered in scree. He's on his side, looking up at me with frightened eyes. The loose shale is edging him ever closer to the final drop.

Above our heads, a helicopter circles. The police will be with us soon and our nightmare will be over. But will it? I know that, for as long as Gareth is living, he will be the predator and I the prey.

Beth runs to me and throws herself into my arms, and I hold her tightly, rocking her as I used to when she was a child.

Scott steps to the edge and looks over. In his rucksack, there is the rope he always carries in case any of his group get into trouble. There's no reason why he would have taken it out. If he threw it over the edge, it would reach Gareth easily. He looks back at me and I see the struggle in his eyes. I don't move. This can't be my decision.

Slowly, he takes a step away from the edge. Then another.

He comes to us then, taking us in his arms, his face hidden by his hood. I press my head against his shoulder, not wanting to hear the scream. The sound of a body hitting the water that I know will come. Scott pulls us closer.

It's how we're standing when Colin finds us, two uniformed officers bringing up the rear. Colin stares at my red and swollen neck.

'God, Leona, are you all right? And you... Beth? Scott?'

'We're fine.' Scott jerks his thumb at the quarry edge. 'But that bastard isn't. He slipped. There was nothing we could do.'

I'm about to speak when Beth looks up. Her eyes slip over to Scott's rucksack. 'No, there wasn't, was there, Mum?'

She's challenging me not to say anything. Like Scott, she's made her choice.

I shake my head. 'There wasn't.'

Colin goes to the quarry edge and looks over. When he comes back, his eyes lock with mine. For a moment he says nothing, then turns to the uniformed officers behind him.

'No one could survive a fall like that. This area is treacherous – it should be closed off. We must just be thankful there weren't more casualties. Let's go back and get you into some dry clothes.'

Battling the wind and the rain, we make our slow and careful way back up the slippery path to where the vehicles are waiting. As the flashing lights of the panda car come into view through the trees, Colin turns back to me.

'It's finally over,' he says.

Maybe I imagine it, but I think I see the ghost of a smile on his lips.

CHAPTER FIFTY-FIVE
Leona

Graham Hargreaves holds open the shop door. 'Afternoon, Leona. Cold today.'

I get into the warm, smiling at the electric heater he has next to the till, and let Graham close the door behind me, shutting out the bitter February wind.

'Is it in yet?'

Graham smiles. For three days now I've been into the shop asking whether the edition of *Cumbrian Living* I've ordered has arrived. Going behind the counter, he takes a magazine from below and slaps it on the counter. 'This what you're after?'

I fall on it, swiping through the pages until I see what I'm looking for. The title is 'Country Haunts' and the photographs are in black and white, credited with David's name. It turns out he was a photographer after all – had gone to college after he'd left prison and got his qualifications. He'd thought it would be easy to get a commission, but somehow word had got around about his past and it hadn't happened. He'd made up the story about working for the magazines to impress Beth.

But he's certainly talented and has proved that perseverance pays off – for here is my beautiful daughter, her long limbs white against the dark slate of the cairn. The wind blowing her hair and the clouds heavy with rain. Her face is pale, her expression enigmatic – so different from the carefree girl whose art exhibition

I have just come back from. It was put on by the school to celebrate her winning the Baxter Prize.

The picture in the local paper showed her with the eagle picture as a backdrop – me and Scott by her side. The name above the picture says Lily-Beth Newman. When Scott and I got married, there was no doubt in her mind that she wanted to share his name too. He was, after all, as much of a dad as she could ever wish for.

She's happier at school now too. Carina has moved to sixth form college and, with her gone, Beth has found herself some proper friends. We count David as one too. She sees him whenever he's in the area and we've decided to let their relationship play out as it will. After all, she is sixteen and sensible enough to make the right decisions and, despite their difference in age, we can see how he brings a light to her eyes that hasn't been there before.

'How are you all getting on?' Graham pats my hand. People know, of course. After Gareth's death, it would have been impossible to keep our story quiet, but, with the exception of a very few, people have been kind. Supportive. We could have moved, but decided not to. We like it here. It's our home.

'We're all just fine, Graham. But thank you for asking.'

A muffled cry makes us both look down. George is awake. I bend to the pushchair and take him out, holding him to my chest. He has Scott's dark hair and my blue eyes; an unusual combination, Fay says, but striking. His middle name is Samuel – Scott's idea, and I love him for that.

Since Gareth's death, I've had no more anxiety attacks, but last week I saw Lisa again – just to show off my baby. I remember the way she kissed the top of his head and smiled at me. *You'll make a wonderful mother*, she said. *You've proved that already with Beth.*

In a few days' time, Leo will be coming to stay. We're not having a church christening, just a naming ceremony with a party afterwards, and Scott and I have asked Leo to be George's 'special adult', a role I know she'll take very seriously. Our reunion was emotional, but full of laughter too, as I always knew it would be, if that day ever came. She'll be bringing my dad with her and I've asked David to take lots of photographs of us all to show my mum when he gets back.

Putting George back in the pushchair, I wheel him to the back of the shop.

'Need any help to find anything?' Graham calls after me.

'No, thank you. I'm just after some frozen peas.'

I go to the freezer compartment and stop with my hand on the sliding door. Ria is looking back at me, but this time there is no fear in her eyes.

You see, I whisper to my reflection, *I never really left you behind.*

A LETTER FROM WENDY

Writing a novel is one of the hardest things I've ever done. It's also one of the most rewarding. Without readers, though, an author would be nothing – so I'd like to say a huge thank you for choosing to read my debut *What She Saw*.

If you did enjoy it, and want to keep up-to-date with all my latest releases, just sign up at the following link. Your email address will never be shared and you can unsubscribe at any time.

www.bookouture.com/wendy-clarke

Writing a story set in my favourite part of the country, The Lake District, has given me immense pleasure and it would be lovely to think I've inspired you to visit this stunning area if you haven't already. If you do, you're in for a treat! Leona's miner's cottage is based on one my husband and I have stayed in many times. It's in a village very much like Church Langdon. I wonder if anyone can recognise it.

I hope you loved *What She Saw* and if you did, I would be very grateful if you could write a review. I'd love to hear what you think, and it makes such a difference helping new readers to discover one of my books for the first time.

I love hearing from my readers – you can get in touch on my Facebook page, through Twitter, Goodreads, Instagram or my website.

Thanks,
Wendy x

 @WendyClarke99

 WendyClarkeAuthor

 wendyclarke99

www.wendyclarke.uk

ACKNOWLEDGEMENTS

Every writer wants to find someone who loves their book as much as they do and I found this person in my editor, Jennifer Hunt. Jennifer believed in me, and my debut novel, from the word go and for that I will always be grateful. Her editorial comments have only made this novel better. Thanks also to Kim and Noelle, who work so hard at marketing and publishing, and the rest of the Bookouture team for their support. I know how lucky I am to be part of this great family!

No writer can travel this journey alone and so my next thank you goes to my amazing writing buddy, Tracy Fells, who has been with me through thick and thin. Without her support and encouragement over coffee and teacakes, I don't think this could have happened. Thanks also to my RNA writing chums, whose ears I bend every month over coffee.

Also on my list of thanks is Jennifer Young who critiqued my novel as part of the RNA New Writers' Scheme. She told me this story would one day be published and I'm delighted that she was right.

Not all my friends are from the writing world, of course, and I'd like to thank 'The Friday Girls', Carol, Barbara, Jill, Linda and Helen, who keep me sane when I've had enough of writing. I've tried not to bore you with too much talk of edits and deadlines and hope I've succeeded!

Thanks also to Graham Bartlett for answering my endless questions about police procedure (any mistakes are entirely my own) and Simon Whaley for helping me with the photography scenes.

This book couldn't have been written without the support of my family: my children, Laura and Eve, my step-children and their partners and especially my mum who has cheered me on from the sidelines since the day I started writing.

Finally, the biggest thank you must go to my husband, Ian, for his endless patience when my computer stops working, for helping me with sticky plot problems, for loving the Lake District as much as I do and for being my number one supporter. You're a star!

Printed in Great Britain
by Amazon

43054631R00187